Golfing, Gardens, & Ghosts

Mary Seifert

Books by Mary Seifert

Maverick, Movies, & Murder
Rescue, Rogues, & Renegade
Tinsel, Trials, & Traitors
Santa, Snowflakes, & Strychinine
Fishing, Festivities, & Fatalities
Diamonds, Diesel, & Doom
Creeps, Cache, & Corpses
Pranks, Payback & Poison
Juleps, Jockeys & Justice
Airplanes, Atlanta & an Assassin
Golfing, Gardens & Ghosts

Visit Mary's website and get a free recipe collection!
Scan the QR code

Golfing, Gardens, & Ghosts

Katie & Maverick Cozy Mysteries, Book 11

Mary Seifert

Secret Staircase Books

Golfing, Gardens, & Ghosts
Published by Secret Staircase Books, an imprint of
Columbine Publishing Group, LLC
PO Box 416, Angel Fire, NM 87710

Book layout and design by Secret Staircase Books
Cover images © BooksRme, Jmpaget, Elena Melnikova

First trade paperback edition: January, 2026
First e-book edition: January, 2026

* * *

Publisher's Cataloging-in-Publication Data

Seifert, Mary
Golfing, Gardens, & Ghosts / by Mary Seifert.
p. cm.
ISBN 978-1649142344 (paperback)
ISBN 978-1649142351 (e-book)

1. Katie Wilk (Fictitious character). 2. Minnesota—Fiction. 3.
Amateur sleuths—Fiction. 4. Women sleuths—Fiction. 5. Dogs in
fiction. I. Title

Katie & Maverick Cozy Mystery Series : Book 11.
Siefert, Mary, Katie & Maverick cozy mysteries.

BISAC : FICTION / Mystery & Detective.
813/.54

"It took me seventeen years to get three thousand hits in baseball. It took one afternoon on the golf course."
Hank Aaron

ONE

The suffocating weight on my chest made me gasp. "Down, dog," I wheezed, sliding Maverick's forepaws to the floor. Scrambling to sit up, I took a deep breath and sniffed in surprise. "Where did you get bacon?" Maverick's warm sweet-and-smoky-scented breath dragged me the rest of the way from my first hours of recuperative rest following a jam-packed last few weeks of school.

I thought I finally had a chance to sleep in on the first morning of summer break, but my dog had other ideas. Maverick's inner alarm had sounded. I lugged myself down the stairs and out the door before the unpredictable June temperature soared again, begrudgingly accompanying him on a spirited walk as the sun broke over the horizon.

Trotting behind my dog, my thoughts meandered the chaotic path I'd taken toward my current career. What do you do with a degree in the study of codes and algorithms when you no longer had the desire to study codes and algorithms?

The field of education hadn't been on my radar initially, but last August, I moved to Columbia, Minnesota and began my first year teaching high school mathematics. Honestly, I accepted the only offer I received, so I discovered my calling by default. My first year surprised me. I enjoyed challenging my students, seeing eyes light up when a math conundrum finally revealed its solution, and supported the successful endeavors of both our science club and mock trial teams. Having worked out the kinks, I hoped my second year would be even better.

To successfully complete the variety of new tasks I'd been given throughout the year, I learned to use my time efficiently. Too efficiently, it seemed. Consequently, I'd already exhausted my summer to-do list. I didn't look forward to the protracted day ahead and its ensuing boredom. How could I relax with three long months of unproductive days filled with so much time to kill? Little did I know what a prophetic choice of words those were.

My energetic black Lab tugged me along the sidewalk, urging me to go faster, his body rippling with muscles we were both learning to control. It had taken a while, but I'd grown to adore my dog. Maverick overflowed with unconditional love, and I choked up remembering how he'd saved my life in more ways than one.

We stopped along the path, and I knelt and rustled his ears. "Thanks, Maverick."

Upon our return, the smells emanating from the kitchen made Maverick and me drool. The tags on the dog's collar rattled as he towed me, skiing behind him, through the kitchen where I discovered the source of the heavenly aromas.

Dad held aloft a metal spatula. His growing culinary repertoire outshone my meager gastronomic menu; I made one recipe I could rely on being edible, and it wasn't breakfast fare. Guilt crawled across his face. "Katie, darlin'," Dad said, sounding perplexed. "I wasn't expecting you to be up so early."

My brows shot to my hairline as I eyed the mound of crispy hash browns, a dozen fried sausage links, eight pieces of buttered toast dripping with honey, at least a pound of sizzling smoky bacon strips, and a large glass bowl containing what had to be a dozen steaming scrambled eggs smothered in melted golden cheese. I pointed at all the food, cocked my head, and raised an eyebrow. Dad's handsome face turned pink.

My dad, Harry Wilk, had lived with me for most of the school year. He was too well to stay in the care facility and too unwell for my stepmother to feel comfortable leaving him home alone while she clambered up her corporate career ladder. Their separation weighed heavily on Dad, and they still hadn't finalized their future plans.

"I always cook for a crew and haven't quite figured out how to pare down my recipes. I hope you're hungry." He wrinkled his nose. "My eggs leave something to be desired, though."

I heaped the breakfast cuisine onto a plate and nibbled at the savory fixings. The slight layer of char on the eggs under the gooey cheese barely registered. "Not bad, Dad," I said truthfully. "But I can't eat like this every morning, or I'll gain fifty pounds this summer."

"You could use another ten, though. The industrial chow you subsisted on while I was in the step-down unit left a lot to be desired. I know." He patted his stomach.

It hadn't been only the food. Worry about his prognosis after a traumatic brain injury contributed as much, if not more, to my initial weight loss, but between my landlady's exceptional cooking and Dad's consistent attempts to regain his status in the kitchen, my clothes no longer hung on my frame. I never went hungry. Nor did one drop of Dad's superlative caffeine concoction laced with brown sugar flavoring and oat milk spill as he reverently placed the vintage flowered porcelain cups of my favorite morning brew on the table. He plopped into the chair next to me and gave me a warm smile.

"Well, darlin', what are your plans for today?" He blew on his hot coffee and took a tentative sip.

"I …" The corners of my mouth turned down. Having grown up on the nerdy side, I always organized every minute of my life, parsing complex tasks into manageable morsels. Solving problems, decrypting codes, and unraveling puzzles came easily, but I'd never successfully dealt with so much unstructured time, certainly not an entire summer. I couldn't remember the last time I hadn't been able to keep busy. But today I had nothing. "I have no idea. After walking Maverick, the only item on my agenda is walking him again, but he panted through half the outing this morning. It's getting too warm earlier in the day for him to walk far."

Dad wriggled in his seat and sat up straighter, running his fingers through his salt and pepper hair. He flashed his vivid eyes at me.

"What?" I asked.

He seemed ready to burst. "I can't imagine you didn't inherit my ability to sit still and do absolutely nothing. I'm the king of procrastination."

I laughed. "This from a man who plans every minute of

his day."

"Yes, but I make certain I plan all my sitting-still time first. I might have some ideas for you."

I wiped off the sticky residue clinging to my fingertips and brushed away the toast crumbs. Tilting my chair, I stretched to nab a pen and memo pad from the counter. Poised to take note of Dad's constructive contributions, I said, "Do tell."

He leaned back in the chair and crossed his arms. "You could pick up a new hobby."

I gently placed the pen on the table, thinking I'd get better ideas from the food, and dug in. With a forkful of hashbrowns hovering in the air, I said, "Could you be a little bit more specific?" and devoured the tasty spuds.

"I could teach you to cook. Maybe. Or you could bike."

I plopped my elbow on the table and supported my cheek in my hand. "You and Ida have tried to teach me to cook. It's been practically impossible, and there's only so much biking I can do." I shook my head, yet listened for something novel.

"You could sleep in."

"Tried that." I side-eyed my pup and exhaled.

"You could learn a craft like … crocheting or knitting."

Two more words made the list. He waited for an enthusiastic response, which he didn't get, but nuggets of ideas turned over in my head as I chewed my final morsel of bacon. Our landlady, Ida Clemashevski, was a creative whiz not only at cooking, but with her passions for art, acting, music, and probably crafting as well.

"There's always fishing," he said, cautiously optimistic. "Or get a part-time job?"

I jotted a few words next to his recommendations and drew a fish.

Dad asked, "What's that?"

Having confirmed my lack of any artistic talent, my sketch disappeared under scribbles. "I'll think about taking up a hobby, but meanwhile, it seems I'll simply have to resign myself to mundane chores ..." I hopped up from the table. "Nothing exciting. Something like doing the dishes." I juggled the serving platters, plates, and silverware and deposited them in the sink, leaving the delicate cups for a second trip.

Soap foamed under the cascade of hot water, and I scrubbed slowly to eat up at least a portion of my free time. Although Dad reached for a towel, I shooed him out of the kitchen, knowing how much he valued his predictable weekday schedule: a hearty first meal of the day, a one-mile walk around the neighborhood—rain or shine, an in-depth read of the newspaper from cover to cartoons, an exercise class at the Y, and his volunteer stint at the library.

"No doubt, by week's end you'll have discovered a new and more streamlined method for doing dishes. You know I love you." He kissed my forehead and headed for the door and a day of sunshine. "But we've got to keep you occupied and out of trouble, or you'll never get rid of the crazy nickname you earned."

I called to his retreating back, "Just because I've been in the wrong places and involved in the resolution of several serious crimes, I really don't think I deserve the moniker 'Katie Wilk, the murder magnet.'"

TWO

After drying and stacking the dishes, scouring the sink, sweeping the floor, and polishing the counters, I read the clock. My shoulders drooped as I wondered how to put a positive spin on the five hours I still had until noon when my phone screen lit up, and I brightened.

"Jane," I sang cheerily. "What's going on?"

"Katie," she wailed. Not prone to emotional outbursts, Jane's stress disturbed my peace and quiet. New teachers tended to flock together, and by the end of September, Jane Mackey and I had become inseparable. The more we learned about each other, the stronger our bond of friendship became. We thrived on the energy of the students and volunteered to advise two extracurricular assignments together. She was my best friend.

I asked carefully, "What happened?"

"Drew and I planned for an October wedding during MEA break, and he's already taken the time off." She hiccupped back what sounded like a sob.

I nodded, but figured she couldn't see me, so I grunted an 'uh-huh.'

"We had most of the logistics worked out except for the reception venue." She sighed. "Most of the local spots we considered had been booked out a year or more in advance, but the manager of the new place, Promise Pavilion, assured me if we paid the entire amount up front, we could lock in the date."

Uh-oh. I could see the writing on the wall.

"But she absconded with the funds," Jane stammered. "They've shuttered the doors. We forfeited our payment, and we have no place to go. I don't want to wait, Katie. What am I going to do?"

"What did Drew say?" When Jane didn't answer, I pulled the phone away and viewed the screen to check our connection. "Jane?"

"I haven't shared the news with him yet," she sobbed.

"And your dad?"

"I told him I could do this on my own. I'm not ready to break down and ask him for help."

"We'll figure something out. Why don't you come over—" Heavy pounding on my back door interrupted our call. "Hold on, Jane."

I opened the door. She stood on the top step, tears streaming from her red-rimmed brown eyes down her cherubic cheeks. The buttons didn't match the buttonholes of her wrinkled white shirt, and I'd never seen her in shredded jeans.

"Oh, honey." I pocketed my phone and opened my arms. I wobbled when she crashed into me. She'd piled her blond waves on top of her head, and the messy ponytail grazed my chin. I blew the tickling tendrils out of my mouth and tried to keep a straight face. "Let's get this figured out."

She took a step back and looked up at me. "You'll help me?"

"What's the maid of honor for?"

"What did I ever do to deserve you?" Jane dabbed at her eyes, and I suffered another bone-crushing hug. "Now what?"

I pondered for a moment, and the necessary solution hit me like a brick. "Ida knows everybody and everything in Columbia," I said. "She'll know what to do."

Jane sniffed and straightened. "Let's get to work then," she said tremulously and marched to the door separating the apartment we rented in the rear from the rest of Ida's Queen Anne home. Jane rose to her height of almost-five-feet, and inhaling deeply, rapped. The door flew open before she completed the third brisk knock.

"It's about time, *mo stór.*" Ida adopted an Irish brogue when she played the part of Thomas Dylan's wife, Caitlin, in a community production, and her Gaelic still rang true. In answer to our dubious faces, she interpreted for us. "My dear. I heard all about Promise Pavilion."

She swallowed Jane in an embrace. The green-belted, shiny purple skirt swished above Ida's yellow sneakers as she rocked Jane back and forth. The multitude of decorative chains draped over the neon-green, ruffled peasant blouse she wore jangled musically. Her flaming red hair curled around the brown head scarf adorned with tinkling gold-colored coins and defied age determination, though I knew she'd retired from teaching art at our high school a few years ago.

"What can I do, Ida?" asked Jane, pulling away before succumbing to the smothering hug. "Do you have any brilliant solutions?"

Ida batted her emerald eyes, flashing lids covered with sky blue eye shadow. She puckered her hot-pink-colored lips in a thought-filled gesture. Her larger-than-life personality defied her size, a half inch shorter than Jane, and the rainbow rebel finally said, "No."

Jane staggered.

"Not yet anyway, but I'll think of something. Come in and tell me all about it."

Jane plopped into a chair at the kitchen table. Ida heated water for tea, and when the kettle whistled, she poured the scalding water over the tea bags she'd placed in two cups and sat. They put their heads together, and I understood the meaning of 'third wheel.'

"I'll just …" I jerked my head toward the door and slipped back into my kitchen where Maverick waited for me. He tilted his head in a 'now what?' communication.

"I might need to find something for Jane and me to do today to get her mind off the venue problem while Ida performs her magic," I said, rubbing his velvety ears. "It'll give Ida time to explore her vast connections, and as Jane's best friend, it's up to me to keep her busy."

The list I'd made from Dad's suggestions to take up free time beckoned from the tabletop, but the concept of a hobby filled me with dread. I picked up a pen and paced, waiting for inspiration, and it came in the form of a handsome face.

After meeting Pete Erickson, I'd thought romance might have a place in my future after all, and instead of solving Jane's dilemma, I jotted a few of his favorite activities —

biking, dining, hiking, and walking—but an ER doctor worked full days and some evenings as well. Those dreams vanished, leaving Jane and me big blocks of empty time. I needed something to keep Jane occupied.

Frustrated, I thumbed through yesterday's mail and happened upon the summer community activity catalog.

I dropped into the chair at my table and fanned the pages, brightly color-coded, yellow for youth, green for teens, and red for seniors, until I came across five blue pages of offerings for adults' enrichment. The list included swimming, navigating computer software, how to apply for a job, community awareness, line-dancing, yoga, and lessons in a variety of sports.

In addition, the center pages provided a calendar highlighting local festivals, summer parades, road races for running or biking, tournaments for chess, softball, golf, pickleball, and fishing, concerts and cultural events, plus deals for seasonal businesses including campgrounds, pools, and garage sales. I circled the activities occurring this week which might interest my friend.

As I tapped the pen against the page, Jane exited Ida's home looking slightly shell-shocked. I rose quickly and guided her to the table. "Can I get you anything?"

She shook her head. "Ida said not to worry. She's going to make some calls." Jane turned her luminescent brown eyes, still brimming with unshed tears, to look at me. "Meanwhile, she said we should get our dresses."

"Aren't you wearing your mother's bridal gown?"

She blinked a few times and smiled indulgently. "I am wearing her dress for the wedding, but Ida suggested I look at purchasing a party dress for the reception." Her voice cracked. "That is, if we have a reception." She inhaled and lifted her chin. "We need to shop for a dress for you too."

Panic widened my eyes. "I thought I was going to wear my blue dress." I hated shopping. I'd never been able to choose flattering clothes to fit what I felt was a weird shape and depended on friends and family to do the dirty work.

"Don't worry, I'll make sure the adventure is fun and easy." She almost laughed. "But I don't think I'm in the right frame of mind to shop yet." She closed her eyes, inhaled through her nose, held her breath, and exhaled through her mouth like the true yogi she was. She opened her eyes, looking somewhat calmer. "What do you propose we do now?"

I hurriedly glanced at the catalog in front of me and turned it for her to peruse.

As her forefinger traveled down the list, she shook her head and rolled her eyes. "Nope, not fishing or pickleball, and I already know how to do yoga." She taught beginning classes at the Y. "But …" She tapped the page appreciatively.

I leaned forward to see what caught her eye. "Golf?"

Jane forced a smile. "I have a set of clubs in my car I haven't been able to use as much as I'd like since moving to Columbia. I need a partner. It's good exercise, and look." She drummed her fingers against the calendar. "There are fundraising tournaments all summer for deserving causes. Here's one for hospice, one for the high school music department, and another for the biking club."

"Jane," I said solemnly. "I've never swung a club." Maverick laid his head on my lap, and I scratched behind his ears. I gave him permission to put his paws on my knees. He licked my cheek, and my anti-golf determination wavered, remembering how enjoyable learning new things this year had been. However, I wouldn't share the memory with Jane immediately.

"Golf is a lifelong skill and it's about time you learned. I'll bet we can scrounge up a set of clubs for you." Her smile seemed genuine, her mind no longer solely fixated on her wedding venue or lack thereof. She punched in the numbers she read from the catalog. "Hello. I'm calling to set up a time for private golf lessons." She listened for a few seconds. "The head pro has an opening in fifty-five minutes." I shook my head. She read the clock. "Fabulous. I'll be there. Yes, I'll be renting gear, at least in the beginning."

I suspected an attempt at bait and switch.

"Name? K-a-t-i-e—W." I reached for her phone to stop her, but she snickered and wriggled out of my grasp. Her eyes twinkled mischievously. "I-l-k. Yes, I'm totally a beginner. See you then. Bye," she said rapidly.

"Jane, what have you done?" I huffed.

She pocketed her phone and grinned smugly. "Hey, blue eyes, now let's get you properly attired."

"What?"

THREE

Jane and my landlady might both only stand close to five feet tall, but each presented a formidable front. Jane ignored every argument I had against learning to golf, and after I got over my initial jab of fear, I figured my lesson would give Ida time to search for an answer to Jane's quandary. Perhaps one and done?

Jane dragged me out to her forest-green Ford Edge and drove downtown to one of her favorite retail therapy establishments, Bella's Boutique. I clenched the seat belt strap over my chest, vividly recalling my first wild ride with Jane, who considered a stop sign merely a suggestion. She slammed on the brakes and parked minutes ahead of my GPS projected arrival time. I inhaled deeply, finally able to take a breath.

If I had my choice, I'd have worn a t-shirt and shorts when golfing, or I'd have gone to the local sports store and picked out comfortable athletic wear, but Jane said real sportsmen had a dress code, and she didn't trust me to be outfitted to her standards.

"I'd lend you some of my clothes, but …" She looked down and behind me with a trace of aversion. I craned my neck, wondering what mess I had on the back of my shorts, and she continued. "My clothes on your long legs might be considered rather salacious. You'd have tongues wagging for sure."

I balked at the unnecessary expense, but she assured me she could afford it. Her dad owned Sapphire Skyway, a charter airline catering to wealthy individuals who traveled frequently. He'd generously provided funds for our mock trial team's recent trip to attend the national competition in Atlanta. Although Jane seldom dipped into her reserves, her dad provided an allowance for her few indulgences, and Bella's stylish stock made his only daughter happy. I had to admit, the baby blue, stretchy pleated golf skirt, hosting deep pockets for ball storage, and the coordinating collared shirt looked cute, even on me. Bella also gave me a great price on a second turquoise set.

Among Jane's superfluous purchases (she could certainly shop fast), the hot pink number suited her well, while the advertisement for the New Age white golf shoes Jane bought insisted they were in vogue and guaranteed to improve even the finest golf swing. Personally, I'd have to do some practical research, checking their benefits, before switching out my tennis shoes and investing in a pair myself.

"Bella," Jane said. "What do you think of our local golf courses?"

The gold and silver bangles rattled on her wrist as Bella

cut the tag from Jane's skirt and then from mine. "Columbia claims a public par 3 in addition to two private courses. Do you have one in mind?" Bella asked, as she bagged the new purchases and our old clothes.

Her white sleeveless shirred chiffon shirt looked so comfortable I almost asked where she bought it before noticing it on the mannequin behind her. Instead, I asked, "What's a par 3?"

The two faces turned in unison. Bella covered her tiny smirk with an explanation. "Par 3 refers to the average number of strokes expected on each hole for the length of the course."

Jane furrowed her brow and pulled out her phone, pulling up the webpage she'd accessed for my lesson. "What about this one?"

"Oooh." Bella's hand fluttered to her smooth cheeks, and she squealed. "Shady Oaks Golf Resort and Spa is markedly ritzy. Most of the patrons pay ridiculous yearly dues to play. Many don't live in the area, but there is a landing strip on the property, so they fly in. I love when they visit Bella's Boutique. I don't mean to gossip, but …" She lowered her voice and combed her curly brown hair behind her ear, flashing a large hoop earring. "I hear membership numbers are fluctuating because of some rumored changes. Are you playing there?"

"I booked lessons for Katie."

"I'm sure not many of the members will admit to needing the services of the two pros on staff, and providing private lessons is one way for them to earn their keep." Bella's blue eyes darkened. "I've heard it isn't cheap."

My head whipped around to Jane.

"That's why I'm paying for the lessons. It's a birthday gift."

"My birthday is more than a month away."

"An early birthday gift, and I get to take advantage of the perks." Given the sneaky smile she bestowed on me, I had a feeling she'd researched her recent purchase and knew more about Shady Oaks than she let on.

A delightful bell tinkled as we made our way out the door of Bella's charming shop.

"Explain to me again why I'm taking golf lessons," I said, juggling the shopping bags from arm to arm, traipsing out to her SUV.

Jane's eyes flicked away from mine, a sure sign she was looking for a suitable answer without divulging too much information. "I love to golf, but Drew isn't around to play consistently, and I've attempted to play solo on the municipal course." The rear gate on her SUV rose gracefully, and she maneuvered the purchases around her white padded leather golf bag. "However, I've run into your friend too many times to count. Her boyfriend always asks if I want to join them." I felt my lips pucker in a question I didn't ask. "It's that guy she brought back with her from Atlanta. He's very accommodating and a scratch golfer, but it's uncomfortable and difficult to decline his insistent invitations because there are often people waiting, and I think the manager would rather have groups than solos on the course. If you and I play together, I don't think ZaZa will even come near me."

The answer reveal dumbfounded me. I stammered, "ZaZa plays golf?"

"She does now," Jane said, her blond waves bouncing. "A lot. It doesn't matter what time I get onto the course, they're always ready and waiting. ZaZa is a newbie, but her boyfriend is coaching her, and consistent play has helped her game tremendously. However, I'm sure she'd prefer me to be anywhere else."

"I'm sorry you're on her list of casual adversaries by your association with me."

"I'm not sorry. She's really not my cup of tea."

ZaZa Lavigne and I had attended the same master's degree program, studying mathematical cryptanalysis. She, too, had an abrupt career change, and among all the high schools in the United States, ZaZa had accepted a job at Columbia High School mid-year after one of my associates landed in jail. It seemed her sole purpose was to make my life miserable. She had some preconceived notions I couldn't dispel. When being civil didn't work, I avoided my nemesis at all costs.

I tuned in when Jane concluded, "If we like it, maybe we can join Shady Oaks."

"So, my golf lessons are for you. I'm good with that."

She slammed the tailgate. "Absolutely." She glanced at her wrist. "Five minutes."

Jane took off on her speedy way, zipping around Lake Monongalia, barreling along a drive replete with tall trees, under the Shady Oaks sign, along a white wooden fence, and through hairpin curves, making my toenails curl. We followed the one-way signs along the paved drive. My jaw dropped as we rounded the last bend revealing three shiny new BMWs, an old and a new Mercedes, a bright red sportscar, a couple of cute Mustangs, and a three-story cream-colored stucco clubhouse. With a backdrop of majestic trees and surrounded by a shimmering body of water, Shady Oaks looked wonderfully inviting.

Jane parked, and as she alighted from the driver's seat, four young adults circled the car and offered to assist with clubs, shoes, bags, or anything else. Jane explained our purpose and hinted at perhaps utilizing their services later.

They politely retreated.

I stepped gingerly onto the sidewalk, gazing at the pristine landscaping, sparkling windows, and arched ornamentation. Dark-colored pavers snaked around carefully manicured bushes and plush green grass. Jane opened her trunk and, with a practiced flair, hefted her clattering clubs by the cushioned strap, and slid them onto her shoulder. I followed her to the entry.

"Hi, Galen. You work here?" Galen Tonlenson, one of our successful mock trial and curious science club students from last year, stood behind a lectern flanked by large stone planters overflowing with colorful blossoms.

"Second summer now, Ms. Wilk." He adjusted the stiff collar on his uniform. "The hours are good, and the perks are cool. I golf at least five times a week." He peered at Jane and raised an eyebrow. "I thought I knew all the members. What can I help you ladies with?"

"Ms. Wilk has a lesson scheduled with Barclay Byron." Jane hooked her arm on the lectern and bowed her head in my direction. I fluttered the tips of my fingers next to my cheek in a shy acknowledgment. I was sure that if he could have done so without being noticed, he'd have rolled his eyes.

"Ms. Wilk?" He searched Jane's perky face, and I thought I could see the wheels turn in disbelief. It looked like he wanted to say, 'I'd sure like to see that.'

He ran his finger down the list in front of him and stopped. I hoped my name wasn't there. He checked his watch and picked up the phone. "Sorry, I've got to make a call."

Setting the receiver back in its cradle, he said professionally, "You are two minutes late, but Mr. Byron will still accommodate you." He screwed up his face apologetically. "Enter the main doors behind me and take the hallway to the right as far as you can go. You will end up at the pro shop and you'll find Mr. Byron. Enjoy." Although his lips formed a serious line, his eyes crinkled in delight.

"Thanks, Galen, and stay cool," I said.

Jane blew a damp tendril from her cheek. "It's going to be a warm one. Stay hydrated, and thank you, kindly, young sir." Jane curtsied, and a tiny smile cracked his business façade. She collected her clubs and dragged me through the glass doors into another world.

The humidity dropped and the comfortable temperature felt completely natural. I peeked around the large green plants bracketing the entrance at the elegant interior adornments. They surpassed the outside. I gawked at the high ceilings, crystal chandeliers, polished silver surfaces, and solid wood furniture. I stepped from the black and gold marble inlay on the floor onto a luxurious scarlet carpet and stared at the composition of some exemplary decorating.

The thick floor covering muffled my careful steps, and I noticed with a start, Jane had disappeared. After a moment of panic, her head popped out of the hallway, and she grinned. "Psst. Over here."

I rushed to catch up with her, and we promenaded through the quiet wing without a sideways glance. As we neared the end of the long hall, heated voices reached us, and Jane put out her hand to stop me.

"You can't do that," a female voice whimpered. "I have a contract."

"Had. It's gone. You have one week," came the pompous male reply. "You need to leave now. I'm expecting a client."

I shook my head. I was not going in there, but Jane had other ideas.

FOUR

From behind the closed door came the sound of a whoosh and a click, and all went quiet. Jane took that as our cue. The cumbersome bag she carried had to weigh almost as much as she did, but she slid the hefty clubs from her shoulder and stood them in the rack outside the door. She turned the knob, and before I could bolt, she trooped through the door with me in tow.

A tall man stood at the exit with his back to us, looking out the picture window over a practice putting green, tiny flags fluttering in a synchronous dance. He turned, and I was nearly taken in by the tanned, chiseled face looking smooth and plumped, the clear hazel eyes, and self-deprecating smile. His sandy-colored hair flopped onto his forehead as if of its own accord, but the closer we got, the more it appeared as if he'd used an inordinate amount of product. I guesstimated his age older than me but younger than Dad.

"You must be Katie Wilk." In two steps, he reached Jane and buried her small hand in his.

Jane snorted and withdrew her fingers. "Nope, but my friend here goes by that name."

His eyes flickered with amusement. "Katie, I'm Barclay. Pleased to meet you. You're here for our beginner's package—equipment rental and four lessons, correct?"

Before I processed the word 'four,' Jane answered for me. "Correct. And I'm here to ensure it goes well."

"Okay, supervisor."

"I'm Jane Mackey. I'm heading to the driving range." She gave me an encouraging glance. "You'll do great."

Before I could object, she marched out the door.

Byron reached for a white, stainless steel water bottle with a forest green lid. He held it up as much for me to admire as he did. The graphic on the outside featured a flag stuck on a putting green situated within the outline of the southeast corner of the contiguous United States. He slurped greedily and gazed after Jane. "Feisty little thing, isn't she?"

I'd never say it out loud, but I wouldn't want to be caught within a mile of Jane if she ever heard anyone call her a little thing—feisty maybe, if you were willing to have the wind knocked out of your sails.

Barclay Byron led me to the display of rental clubs. "Take your pick."

I grabbed a club I recognized as a putter, two smaller metal ones, and another with a larger head.

Byron shook his head and yanked the clubs from my hands. After exchanging them for others he preferred, he glowered, waiting for me to challenge his selection. When I didn't, he said, "I'll provide the balls."

Did I detect a hint of a pause, a raised eyebrow? Innuendo? What was I thinking? Was I supposed to laugh or was it my imagination? It had been much easier dealing with high school students. I always expected the worst and was often pleasantly surprised. This was uncharted territory.

"You'll need tees, and I definitely recommend a golf glove." His grip on my left hand made me uneasy as he slid his fingers over mine. I gently tried to pull away, but he held tightly as he thumbed through a display and removed a women's medium. "You have long, narrow fingers. This will work." He finally let go, and I swallowed hard. "I'll just add this to your invoice."

I continued to accumulate golf paraphernalia, including a white cap and two ball markers.

"On the course, you'll encounter continually changing light conditions, and I recommend the sunglasses designed for golfing by—"

"No, thank you." He must get a kickback, I thought uncharitably.

He fit the clubs into the dividers of a surprisingly lightweight, narrow nylon bag and chuckled. "It's time to hit the links." Then his features drew into a scowl. "Now, where did my electronic tablet go?" He slid items to the side, searching. "It must be our resident ghost. Never mind. It'll show up sooner or later."

A ghost?

He hefted a large golf bag filled with a variety of clubs. I squeezed past him, and as he held the door, he inhaled deeply. "What's the intoxicating scent you're wearing?"

Before I thought about it, the words tumbled from my lips. "Labrador retriever." The confusion on his face almost caused me to laugh.

"Rrrrright. Let me curate your tour first." We headed toward the meticulously lined-up bank of golf carts arrayed in a rainbow of colors. He fastened his bag to the one closest to the first tee box and gently slid a long club with the maroon and gold colors of the University of Minnesota from a silken sheath. He ran his fingers down the shaft and cradled the large head in his hand.

"This is an unparalleled Honma Beres 09 5S Fairway Wood, a precision club built to attain maximum distance with pinpoint accuracy, the likes of which you'll never see again." He lined up behind an imaginary ball, swung, and held his position watching the illusory orb make a satisfying flight. "Ace, of course."

"It doesn't look like any kind of wood I've ever seen."

If looks could kill, I'd be laid out on the ground.

He shook his head and said, "Carbon fiber." As he flattened the sleeve to re-cover the club, he eyed it curiously, scrutinizing markings written on the fabric. "Son of a gun." He squinted and rattled off a series of numbers. "Forty-three, thirty-three, fifty-one, thirty-two, arggh."

Numbers are therapeutic and have always drawn me like a fly to honey. Gawking over his shoulder, I noticed a curious pattern of numbers scrawled in black ink and scooted a millimeter closer to get a better look.

A moment later, I hastily leaned back as Byron furtively glanced toward the door to the shop while crumpling the cloth and stuffing it into one of the side pockets of his golf bag. He clicked keys on his phone, eyed the screen, and mumbled something sounding like, "Gotcha."

"Anything wrong?"

"Not anymore." His tone was chilling.

When his cool eyes raked over my face, I discovered I'd stepped too far into his personal space and couldn't step back fast enough. "Sorry."

"I've got to make a call. Give me one minute."

He stalked behind the corner of the building, and although he spoke softly, the call ended with a vehement, "I expect the results today."

I recoiled when he reached toward me, but he merely relieved me of my golf bag. He secured it to the rear of a two-passenger red golf cart and hopped onto a green one. "I'll meet you on the path." He gestured, and his vehicle hummed down the hill.

I slid across the seat into the driver's spot and searched for a way to get the cart moving. Byron watched and waited at the foot of the hill. I scanned the dashboard. There was no key, no button. Byron gestured for me to join him. I felt for a gearshift, running my hand over the surface and along the edge on the underside. None of my ideas to get the contraption to move made any headway. Out of the corner of my eye, I saw Byron snicker.

The cart had to travel the grounds. I circled the steering wheel, running my hands from top to bottom. In frustration, I lightly stamped my foot and nicked the pedal. My head jerked backward and forward. Voilà. I carefully depressed the foot controller and, aside from the embarrassment of wrenching my neck, soared off the knoll as if I'd done it every day. Byron didn't wait, and hopefully didn't notice my continual spurts and starts, sending me lurching ahead and jolting to a stop as I learned how to operate the four-wheeler.

We motored along the path, whizzing by hole one, identified by the flag flapping from the pin on a picturesque carpet of manicured green. Byron ignored the golfer, wearing a yellow and navy plaid sweater, frantically waving to get his attention. He raced ahead, intent on completing a tour of the front nine holes in as little time as possible, pointing out the tee boxes, fairways, greens, the rough, various bodies of water, bunkers, stakes marking penalty areas, a beverage cart, and the groundskeepers.

We came to a halt atop one of the rolling green hills overlooking the course at hole nine. "This is beautiful."

Byron tilted his head and said in a condescending tone, "Our turf has a better pedigree than most people in Columbia."

My face heated. More familiar with places like Shady Oaks, Jane knew what it would take to be accepted, and my new golf attire suddenly felt like my first line of defense.

We circled back to the beginning and pulled up behind Jane on the driving range. She nailed a ball, swinging her club with enough force to send her shot over the one hundred fifty-yard marker. I watched in awe.

She approached her bag and was so intent on switching out her clubs, Barclay Byron's voice was unexpected.

"Jane, I bring you, my pupil."

I bowed my head.

"I thought we should begin on the driving range, Katie," he said, stepping onto the grass. "Take out your driver and a tee. I'll nab a bucket of balls."

The tee wriggled free from a leather strip, but unsure which was the driver, I hoped for inspiration, a clue of some kind. Byron returned and said, "It's the club with the largest head."

He lined me up on a patchy area between two green metal markers next to Jane and began his instruction. "The set-up and the swing can make or break your game."

He droned on, and the details sounded easy enough, but I contorted with each sequential directive, twisting like a pretzel, and almost crumpled to the ground.

I ran the directions through my head again, coiled stiffly, and swung. My hand thrummed when the club connected with the ground, and my first swing took out a big chunk of grass. I replaced the divot and tamped it down as I'd seen done by the television professionals. The second time I topped the ball, causing it to roll a mere twenty-four inches from the tee, but at least it headed in the right direction, which is more than I can say for the third drive. I missed and struck the ball on the backswing; the ball rolled in reverse. The fourth swing missed entirely, and I lost my balance, landing flat on my back.

Jane's gentle voice cut through my embarrassment. "Keep your eye on the ball, Katie."

The next swing caught the small sphere and sent it sailing off to the right. On successive swings, I consistently hit the same tree a dozen times.

"We can fix your slice," my friend said.

I smiled and turned to thank her, but her dark eyes had locked on and sent imaginary daggers through Byron as he berated a young woman standing next to the beverage cart wearing a white polo shirt and jean shorts.

Her lips trembled. "I'm telling you I tried, but they weren't ready." She burst into tears and ran for the clubhouse.

FIVE

Why can't I take lessons from you?" I whined. The membership brochure I picked up crumpled in my sweaty hands as Jane's wheels rapidly devoured the pavement. "Under your astute tutelage, I consistently hit the same tree thirteen times in a row. Byron ordered me to correct my slice, but when he wandered back to the mobile drink and snack stand, you're the one who told me how."

"He owes you three more lessons. We've paid him—"

"You mean you paid him." I cocked my head and squinted.

She disregarded me. "We're paying him to help you. His instructions are decent enough. They're accurate and should do the job. You know how to listen, and you're a rule follower. When you complete your lessons and we're golfing—"

"Which of the three courses will we golf?"

"Shady Oaks. While you were busy, I bought a membership. If we play here, we won't randomly run into ZaZa." Her eyes challenged me, but I had no comeback. "And the perks of membership provide special dividends, additions to reservations, maybe even specialty items."

"This is a beautiful course."

"And when we're golfing, if you still need advice, I'll lend a hand, but you're taking to the sport quite nicely. I wouldn't want golf to get in the way of our friendship. I can get kind of …"

"Bossy?"

"No." I'm not sure she considered the word I volunteered for even a second. "Competitive."

Hanging on tight, we careened around a corner. I snuck a quick look and understood the serious set of her jaw. "Why do you think Mr. Byron yelled at the woman manning the beverage cart?" I said in a rush.

"He said she wasn't wearing the prescribed uniform. I understand his irritation, but his reaction was over the top."

If Jane hadn't paid him, I wondered how he would've reacted to my tragic excuse for a golf swing. "I have my second lesson tomorrow. Will you be there?"

"I don't think so. If I'm not there, he'll have to do his job. And Ida texted. We're touring two wedding reception venues tomorrow morning."

"I told you she'd find something." I crossed my arms and nodded my head before my hands flew in front of me and slammed against the dash to keep me steady, sitting upright, not colliding with the door.

Jane nodded. "Maybe, but Ida told me not to get my hopes up. She hasn't heard anything about either one, positive or negative."

We didn't say a word for the remainder of the rapid trip

until she pulled into my driveway. Jane parked her SUV and turned to me with an earnest look. "Do you have anything planned for this afternoon?"

I shook my head, realizing too late I should have made something up.

"I'm ready to go dress shopping. I'll pick you up at two."

Ida sat at my kitchen table, brushing Maverick. The grave look on her face took my breath away, and I rushed to kneel beside her. "What's wrong?"

"I've come up empty for a place to hold Jane's reception."

I relaxed a smidgeon. "But you have those venues to visit tomorrow."

"I have a bad feeling about them, and my feelings are seldom mistaken."

I nibbled my lip in concentration. "Ida, I just know you'll find something. After our dress shopping—"

She perked up, and her eyes lit. "You? Shopping? I'd love to see that."

"Very funny." I turned up my nose and continued, "I'll talk to her about a different date—"

"Or a different state," Ida said. "I'd go to Georgia for Jane."

"We all would, but she calls Columbia home now."

Ida locked her hands on her knees. Dispirited, she hauled her body from the chair. "We might as well eat. I'm trying out a new pasta salad recipe. It's in your fridge."

"Let me get it. What would you like to drink?"

She slumped back into the chair. "I made a pitcher of Arnold Palmers to go with it. I'll have one of those."

"Arnold Palmers?"

Dad's cheery voice coming from the doorway added to the mix. "Named for one of the finest golfers of all time. I loved watching him in his final Masters Tournament." The cap he tossed ringed a hook by the door. He planted a kiss on my cheek and rubbed his hands in anticipation. "What's for lunch?"

"If I remember correctly, you watched a lot of golf." I dished pasta salad onto three plates and an embarrassing epiphany dawned on me. "Was taking care of me the reason you didn't continue playing?"

Dad's enigmatic smile said it all, and I gave him a one-armed hug as I delivered his lunch. Dad met the demands of being a single parent with equanimity. He'd never let on that my needs and desires must've often supplanted his own.

"Maybe I'll take it up again. What do you think?"

"Hmm," I nodded and hummed as I tasted the heavenly salad—a perfect blend of fresh veggies, olives, small pieces of pepperoni, tiny chunks of mozzarella, Italian spices, olive oil, balsamic vinegar, and rotini topped with freshly grated Parmesan cheese. Ida used her own blend of fragrant leaves for the tea, and she'd squeezed the citrus fruit to make her lemonade for the perfect liquid homage to golf.

When he'd cleaned his plate, Dad patted his stomach and asked, "What's for dinner?"

Ida tapped his forearm and said in a reprimanding tone, "Harry," as Jane burst through the door.

"Ready, Katie?"

I slowly cleared the dishes, working up my courage. "Let me change first, and I'll be as ready as I'll ever be."

Jane's excitement carried us downtown to a bridal shop near Bella's Boutique. "I checked out their website," she said enthusiastically, braking hard. "The owner is known for her buying trips to Paris and Milan. Many of the dresses here are one of a kind. I can't wait."

The gaudy signage tacked above the entry of the First and Last Wedding Shoppe should have been a clue, but in the throes of Jane's wedding bliss, I failed to notice the flashing hot pink neon open sign and the name of the proprietor— Tempest.

I held the door for Jane, tipping my head as she bounded past me on cloud nine, all smiles and positive energy. I followed but spun around, searching for the source of an irritating squawk and finding it in the closing door. My eyes adjusted to the dim interior, and the cracked ceiling, curling linoleum tiles, and peeling green paint became evident, but in Jane's dreamy state, she happily pranced to the counter and dinged the call bell. The excruciating wait softened the effervescence in her eyes, so I jingled the bell a second time.

"I'm coming already." The terse voice sounded from the back room. Footfalls clacked across the floor and a tall, voluptuous woman with pale skin glared at us with piercing black eyes as she combed her fingers through a helmet of short, straight glossy black hair. She adjusted her black skirt and slinky shirt, which seemed out of place among the racks of white. "What do you want?" she said through a slash of blood-red lips.

Not acknowledging the curt reception, Jane said excitedly, "I need a dress for my wedding."

"Do you have an appointment?" The woman stepped up to the narrow counter on sky-high heels, towering a foot over Jane.

I surreptitiously glanced between the rows of clothes, searching for any other customer. "Do you think you could fit us in?" I hoped I didn't sound as sardonic as I felt.

A young man came out of the back room, tucking in his shirt tails. His longish dishwater blond hair hung limp, but his smile was satisfied. "Have a good day, T," he said. He plied his lips with balm and exited the shop.

The woman heaved a sigh. "I suppose I might be able to squeeze you in, but I know we'll have to order whatever you choose. None of our samples come in your size."

Not to be deterred, Jane said, "Do you have any of the one-of-a-kind dresses advertised on your website?"

The saleswoman pursed her lips and said slowly. "It'll certainly need altering. You're hardly ideal model-sized material." I bristled. "When are the nuptials?"

"October," Jane said with such assurance, I almost forgot she didn't have a place to hold the reception yet.

"Don't you think you're cutting it awfully close?" The woman evaluated Jane top to bottom and appreciated what she saw. We lucked out as she took in Jane's trendy labels and name-brand purse and not my ratty jeans and faded Cougars t-shirt. "It'll cost you, but I'm sure we can get it done. What are you looking for?"

"I'd like a party dress. No train. Lots of glitz and glam, one that sways when I'm dancing." Jane wiggled. "And we need a dress for my maid of honor." She directed her eyes to me. "She's Katie and I'm Jane."

"Tempest. Tempest Byron."

How many Byrons could there be in Columbia?

SIX

I didn't think I'd luck out on my first foray into shopping, but I love that dress. Don't you, Katie? I mean, who would have thought they'd have a designer dress I'd like in Columbia, Minnesota? Right? I'm so excited. It's finally getting real."

I didn't have to answer. Agatha Christie's words of wisdom fit the circumstances. "An appreciative listener is always stimulating." And I couldn't get a word in edgewise, anyway.

"The dress is so unusual. I just know I'll feel like royalty when it's altered."

Jane glowed, in and out of the dress. It fit her personality. The super-sized velvet clamps on the back, shoulders, and sides gave her a good approximation of what she could look like in the feathery, scintillating gown once they modified it to her size and specifications, but they had a lot of work to do. Fortunately for Tempest, Jane didn't balk at the exorbitant price quoted for the alterations.

Consumed with contentment, Jane forgot about my dress for the time being. Maybe she'd forget altogether. She cooed and clucked, driving a mere five miles an hour over the speed limit, and returned me to 3141 North Maple Street. "I'll check in with you tomorrow after your golf lesson." She took a short moment to breathe and added, "You should find out if Barclay and Tempest are related. They're an odd combination and a story in the making."

I hopped from the car and waved before she could think of anything else for me to do … like look for a bridesmaid's dress. Maverick greeted me inside the door, leash in his mouth, ready to go for a walk again. "Okay, my friend. Although it's not as hot as predicted, it's still too warm for you to be out exercising for any length of time, so we won't go far."

He dragged me a greater distance than I probably would've taken him. While we walked the two miles, I rehashed the instructions I'd gotten from Byron in preparation for my next lesson. Even if I'd never be a contender, Jane simply wanted a body with her on the course, and that I could certainly do. Couldn't I?

When we arrived home, I filled a water dish for Maverick and a large tumbler with Arnold Palmer for me—a new favorite. I sat at the table and sipped the icy brew, smoothing the crinkled Shady Oaks golf membership brochure I pulled from my pocket. It demanded attention. I pored over the eight pages, scanning the professional photos of the grounds, noting the features, and gaping at the membership costs and benefits in addition to spa treatments and available accommodations.

When I got over the sticker shock, I figured if I found

summer employment, I might be able to pay my own way to golf with Jane on occasion and help her avoid ZaZa. I returned to the page of amenities and wondered how I could have missed the most important photo in the center of the layout. A photographer tastefully blurred the edges of the lavish spread. In the foreground, the backs of ten formally attired wedding attendants lifted flutes filled with a sparkling, golden beverage to an elegant couple silhouetted by sunlight streaming through an arched window. I dialed the number at the bottom of the page.

"Shady Oaks Country Club. How may I direct your call?"

The voice was familiar. I checked the number and said tentatively, "I'd like to speak to someone about your wedding venue."

"Katie Wilk, is that you?" I had hoped it wasn't Barclay Byron's glib voice, but I was wrong. "Why didn't you say something this morning? When's the big day?"

"Hi, Mr. Byron. I'm calling for Jane."

"Remember, Barclay please. Hold while I connect you to our catering service. Let me know if you have any difficulties. And be ready for tomorrow."

Seconds later, a breathless female answered. "Reneé Forge. I hear you'd like to book the country club for a wedding. What date did you have in mind?"

"It's not for me. It's for my friend."

"Okay, but I still need a date."

Fingers crossed, I gave her Jane's name and first choice.

"Do you have an approximate number of guests?"

Reciting the nice round number Jane mentioned once upon a time, I hoped it was still in the ballpark. The woman inhaled deeply. Keys clacked, and a crash sounded through my speaker.

"Miss Forge, are you okay?"

"Sorry, I dropped my phone," she said a bit distant from the mouthpiece. A minute later, in a calmer voice she said, "The date is open."

I could barely contain my excitement. "I have to inform the bride. Can you hold that date?"

"I can give you twenty-four hours without a down payment."

"No problem. I'll talk to her as soon as we hang up."

I heard the swish of a pen, slicing across a page. "Done."

I dialed Jane. Her phone rang until voicemail picked up. "Jane. Important. Call me. It's Katie."

Five minutes later I tried again. "Jane. It's Katie. I've got some news for you."

Three minutes later, I banged on our adjoining door, thinking Ida might know how to get hold of Jane or at least be able to add the country club to her venue search. No answer there either.

Although she lived within walking distance, I raced to my car and shoved the key into the ignition, believing I'd find Jane at home, and I'd be her superstar. No one responded to my pounding except her grouchy neighbor in the next yard who hollered, "She ain't home."

I went to Drew's next, but he was a no-go as well, and he always answered unless he was working. Jane and I met him in August during teacher orientation. He'd been hired as a new communications teacher and had rounded out the three Musketeers. The students loved him, and he'd done an outstanding job, but he resigned after completing his undercover assignment, helping to root out and break up a drug pipeline in our school—his job for the Bureau of Criminal Apprehension. Not to mention being good with the kids and an officer in law enforcement, he wasn't hard on the eyes, and he could dance. Jane fell hard. Matched perfectly, they couldn't wait to tie the knot, and I'd do everything I could to help.

I tried Jane again. "Jane. Katie. Call me."

Sometimes insecure, the idea I'd somehow done irreparable damage to our relationship, instigating this avoidance niggled at the back of my mind. Then I thought perhaps my phone was out of order until it rang. Thinking it might be Jane finally returning my call, I answered tersely, "Hello."

"What's wrong, sunshine?" Pete Erickson's warm baritone sent a zing up my spine and a smile to my lips.

"I'm sorry. I've left a dozen messages for Jane, and she hasn't picked up. I thought you might be her."

"It must be important."

"It is, and I'm so excited. I think I've found a place for her and Drew to hold their wedding reception and … oops. Please don't divulge this information to Drew. I don't know if she's told him yet, but the manager at Promise Pavilion shuttered the doors, took the money, and ran."

Pete joked, "Oh, he knows. He's just waiting for her to come clean."

It took me only a moment to understand why Drew knew and hadn't spoken to an exceedingly independent Jane. I shrugged. "He'll be happy to now know they could hold their reception at the Shady Oaks Country Club."

Pete didn't say anything, and some of my euphoria escaped like air from a pinhole in a balloon. "What do you think, Pete?"

"I'm still processing having the reception at the most exclusive country club in the five-county area. I think their wedding will be one of a kind, and I can't wait. I only hope we all survive the process. Jane can be overbearing."

I laughed with him. "I haven't been able to contact Jane. Have you heard from Drew?"

"Last time we talked, he said he had work to do, but he'd be home mid-week. Are you busy tonight?"

"I'm not busy any night from now until the last week in August." My time could easily be used for more entertaining activities, and the crucial information I had for Jane took a back seat. "What do you have in mind?"

"You don't need to be members to dine at Shady Oaks. How about a little reconnaissance?"

SEVEN

As I sipped a lovely pinot noir, lost in the chocolate brown orbs and the adorable dimples across the table from me, I almost missed the tasting part of dinner. Pete directed my attention to the flavor profile of an exquisite lobster bisque, half of a wedge salad, and scallops seared to perfection, before sharing a serving of rich, caramelized crème brûlée accompanied by a lovely Sauternes. Jane would have superb choices for her wedding reception fare—if she so chose.

While Pete paid the bill, I meandered through the antiquated dining area and atrium, verifying Ida Clemashevski's signature on two of the stunning abstract pieces of art and admiring vintage portraits and landscapes adorning the walls, snapping photos to share with Jane. Among the notices tacked neatly to the bulletin board at the entry to the pro shop hallway was a help-wanted sign. I focused my phone camera on the QR code and clicked the link to investigate later.

"The stars are out in force. Would you like to take the long way home and search out some of the nocturnal highlights? There is a new moon on a cloudless night. We should be able to see a sky full of luminaries."

My heart fluttered. "Yes, kind sir, I would."

We drove a short distance away from Columbia's light pollution. Pete pointed out Ursa Major, Ursa Minor, Gemini, Leo, Libra, Draco, and Virgo. After our eyes adjusted to the inky black, a blinding ball of white streaked across a sky as dark as pitch.

"Quick, make a wish," Pete said.

I closed my eyes and made my special request. There might have been a few more meteors, but my wish came true immediately, and I was too preoccupied to notice. Two hours and a long goodnight kiss later, it was too late to contact Jane, but I sent a text.

Jane. Research Shady Oaks Golf Resort and Spa for your reception. Katie

Unable to relax, I clicked the link to the job description and connected to the Shady Oaks website. Not surprisingly, the ad touted free training and the benefits of part-time work as a beverage cart attendant.

How could filling out an application hurt?

Six hours later, my day threatened to repeat with only minimal modifications. By the end of our four-mile trek, Maverick panted and plodded through our remaining steps. The oppressive and humid heat had taken on a life of its own, and I didn't think we'd be able to take a second walk.

I devoured a slightly more minimal breakfast with Dad; he didn't prepare the sausages. After donning my new turquoise golf outfit, I wished my men well and set off for Shady Oaks.

My phone buzzed and I filled the air in my car with a hearty, "Good morning."

A stern voice said, "Katie, you do realize when you call or text me, I already know it's from you, right?"

My ears warmed. "Yes, I do, Jane. I guess when I'm excited, I tend to cover all the bases." My shoulders rose to my ears, and I grinned, glad she couldn't see my embarrassment and tease me more mercilessly than she had. "What's up?"

"We've already seen the first venue. I can't say no until we have a contract in hand, but ugh, it was dark and dingy, and they use outside biffies for a crowd of over thirty. We're on our way to number two."

"Did you listen to my message? Are you going to look at Shady Oaks? It has wonderful reviews, and Pete and I had a remarkable dinner there last night."

Jane's tone relaxed. "Thanks for asking Reneé to hold the room until we could see it. Ida and I have an appointment at eleven thirty. Would you like to join us? Your lesson should be finished by that time."

"Absolutely." Anything to break up the expected ennui of the day. "Gotta run," I said, pulling into the parking lot. I felt much more prepared as I secured my white cap with its oversized visor onto my head, hefted the golf bag onto my shoulder, and strode to the entrance.

"Good morning." Galen saluted. "It mustn't have been too awful if you're back. And you're early."

"Yes, I am," I said, quite pleased.

"Have a great lesson."

"Thank you." I pranced past him and down the hall, and just like the day before, I heard raised voices emanating from behind the closed pro-shop door.

"I told you before, I need you to come through."

"And I will, but it'll take time."

"I want a guarantee."

"And I can't give you a guarantee …"

One of the voices sounded as if it neared the door. Not wanting to get caught eavesdropping, I scurried back the way I'd come and meandered across the lobby down the opposite hall. The inscription above the first door on the left read Human Resources. It had to be a sign, and I thought it would be much more difficult to say no if you met an applicant for the job in person. My presence would either give me a hand up or a crushing defeat.

I took a deep breath and turned the knob on the door. The warmth, charm, and vintage sophistication of the rest of the building didn't make it this far. Tan plastic partitions divided the space into a half dozen identical cubicles housing royal blue mesh chairs and tricolor light fixtures atop skinny status poles, indicating when someone was on a call. A red light flashed above the single occupied desk. My golf bag slid from my shoulder and landed with a thump. The woman manning the desk in front of multiple monitors glanced up and tapped her earpiece. "May I help you?"

"My name is Katie Wilk. I filled out an application to work the beverage cart—"

"I'm so glad you stopped by. I'm Lark." The woman brushed back strands of short, wavy, gray hair. "We lost our old girl yesterday, and I haven't waded through all the paperwork yet, but your application is on top." She alluded to a short stack of printouts and handed me a copy of the job description. "Problem is, I'm in need of someone part-time right now, and if you think you'd be willing and able—"

I perused the duty list and looked up with glee after noting the hourly wage and the perks included in the employment package. "I can begin this afternoon if you can use me."

Her shoulders relaxed. "That was easy. There's still the matter of a background check, but we can move ahead, provisionally." She peeled two stapled pages from a drawer. "Could you read and sign this contract while I get you a uniform?" Her shoulders bunched up again. "That's okay, isn't it? All the employees in service wear the same blue polo and khakis, and if you don't …" She pouted apologetically. "… you can't work here."

"That's fine. It makes getting ready easier." I smiled.

"Sorry. Until last week, I've been in charge of events, but one of the new investors is shaking things up. Management just transferred me to this job. You're my second hire. Let me know how you think I can improve."

The job of a teacher never ends. "You're doing great. I think I wear a medium shirt and—"

She held up one finger and touched her earbuds with the other, saying, "Yes, sir." She frowned. "Yes, sir. I understand. I'll check lost and found, but is she certain the bracelet was in her room before she went to breakfast?" She touched her earpiece again and popped up from the desk. "I'll be right back. Meanwhile, you can familiarize yourself with answers to the most frequently asked questions. Guests repeatedly hound our employees for information about the grounds, the local area, the history, the restrooms, and the ghost."

"The ghost?"

EIGHT

Marketing. When things go missing, we blame the Ghost of Shady Oaks, but most of the items show up in lost and found." She pointed to a printed flyer and bolted to a closet at the back of the room, returning seconds later with a garment bag. "Try these. If they don't work, I'll get you another size. Can you be here at three for a short training session? I'll show you where your locker is, and you can begin the afternoon shift. It lasts until seven today."

"No problem. Anything else?"

Her eyes circled the room. "I don't think so, but we'll know soon enough. Won't we?" She bent her head to the tasks on her desk and waved dismissively.

The hands on the wall clock inched their way closer to the top of the hour, and though an early arrival wouldn't be in the offing, I didn't want to be late again.

"I guess I'll see you at three," I said quietly.

I hadn't yet heard the chime of the grandfather clock in the atrium, and I scampered to the pro shop, excited to have my day filled with activity. When I stepped inside, Byron still had two minutes, so technically, he wasn't late. I entered the eerily empty space, cocky. I had places to go and people to see.

"Where's Byron?" I whirled at the deep voice I wouldn't have associated with such a rail thin man.

"I just got here myself, but I'm scheduled for a lesson so I'm sure he'll be here soon." He couldn't have gone far. His had been one of the two voices I'd heard earlier.

The tall man paced in front of the display of clubs and repeatedly checked his watch. When Byron finally arrived, I wondered if the three-minute tardiness was payback for my less-than-punctual arrival yesterday.

The man ran his palm over his skinny tie. "I need it now, Barclay."

"Let's take our little discussion outside where we can appreciate a little privacy, Dennis. I'll be right with you, Ms. Wilk."

Dennis recoiled as Byron's hand grazed his shoulder, and he led them out the door toward the carts. Byron returned a minute later, alone, wearing a bitter smile. "Some people." He shook himself and plastered on a taut grin. "I don't see your friend, Jane. Do we need to wait for her?"

"She's not joining us today. She's finalizing her wedding plans."

"What a shame."

Did I detect a note of disappointment? "Yes, in fact, she bought a dress from First and Last Wedding Shoppe."

"Ah, Tempest."

"Is she related to you?"

"My soon-to-be-ex-wife," he said, deadpan. The tips of his ears reddened, and his eyebrows flicked in irritation. "Did you meet her assistant?" He placed air quotes around the word assistant. "Her constant companion, Clive, is the justification I needed." Byron ducked behind the counter and came up grumbling and mumbling, "It's not here."

"Is your tablet still missing?"

He glared at me as he held the tablet aloft. "No. Today I'm missing my souvenir water bottle from the 2004 Masters."

He waited as if I should be impressed. "Were you a competitor or a spectator?"

He snorted. "If I'd have golfed a Masters Tournament, I wouldn't be …" He looked out the window and his voice trailed off. "The memento will show up. Things always do. It's merely an inconvenience." He grabbed a bottle of water from a small fridge. "Let's get going, shall we?"

We stepped outside. The grounds appeared to perspire, glistening with dew, and he marched me to the practice green. After another long and involved dissertation on the physics of putting, I warmed up with two dozen successful strokes. "Not bad. It looks like you won't need as much instruction to putt." He lifted his chin. "I hear you accepted our newest posting."

Caught off guard, I swung the club and missed. Word circulated here at a blistering pace. I didn't know why I was surprised.

"It's a big deal; beverage sales are important contributors to our bottom line." He cocked his head and checked his watch. "Set your clubs in the stand and come with me." Noting my dubious expression, he added, "Not many golfers get to see the inner workings of Shady Oaks, and it might come in handy in your new position."

I faked an enthusiastic response. "Oh, boy."

We walked down a path at the back of the clubhouse. Byron opened a padlock and slid the heavy barn door along the track. We ventured into an enormous interior space with polished oak walls and a pressed cement floor.

"Nearly two dozen majestic mounts lodged in these stables until 1983, but the only horsepower we house here now belongs to these babies." He slapped the hood of a red riding lawnmower, one among a fleet of red and green machines. He brushed phantom dust from his shirt and began an expository discourse on gardening tools. "In the attached addition are the blowers, trimmers, sharpeners, extra blades, rakes, sprayers, applicators, shovels, gloves—any turf tool imaginable."

I craned my neck to look through the other doorway, and my eyes widened at the lethal mien of the shiny metal implements.

"Herbicides, pesticides, fungicides, and fertilizers are locked in the adjacent storage unit. Don't mix them with the food," he said with a dash of snark and pointed to another outbuilding. "You'll find the refrigerated beverage carts in there and cartons of supplies stacked in alphabetic order against the outer wall."

We walked out the rear of the landscape management building onto a pebbled path amid a field of waist-high grasses. Byron nodded to an out-of-place stone hut built into the side of the hill and partially hidden by the vegetation. "The old caretaker's cottage, last used about twenty-five years ago."

Byron checked over his shoulder and slipped through

an opening in a wooden fence hidden by climbing ivy. My eyebrows rose, but I followed.

A path covered with stone chips divided the garden into beautifully manicured rectangular plots of color, each measuring about ten feet by twenty feet and bordered with extremely short, sculpted shrubbery. Colors exploded, and among the myriad flowers, I recognized tulips, irises, daffodils, lavender, and inhaled the delicate perfume of lilacs at the peak of their fragrance. A plethora of identifiable greenery grew in a vegetable plot. The heady bouquet of basil, rosemary, and thyme filled the air. Burbling water cascaded into a pool where a number of large orange and white Koi roiled and splashed when Byron tossed in a handful of what I assumed was fish food. A turtle sunned itself on a boulder next to a pergola housing a wrought iron table and four chairs.

"This is gorgeous, but awfully quiet."

Standing in front of a large plant, he drew a pair of nitrile gloves and a clear plastic bag from his pocket, extracted a small set of clippers, and handed them to me. "Fresh mint for the beverages gives a little class to the presentation and you more tips. Snip a few leaves but only from this plant." He removed a skeleton key from his shirt pocket. "I'll be right back. Don't. Touch. Anything. Else."

"But …"

Byron's chin jutted toward the plant. "There," he said. He stepped to a gate on a five-foot fence at the rear and inserted the key. The fence held back a tangled mess of stems, blooms, and leaves in varied colors, sizes, and shapes. I frowned with incomprehension, and he said, "This is a private garden." He turned the key, and his eyes gleamed when the gate swung open.

He headed into the jumble of plants. Shrugging, I

snipped and inhaled the fresh scent of the bright green leaves. After securing the cuttings in the baggie, I marked time by examining the peculiar greenery. Nothing looked familiar, and the less than friendly back part of the garden gave me the willies. Learning to golf never sounded so good, and surprisingly, I couldn't wait for Barclay Byron.

I'd just about given up on Byron, but with the stealth of Maverick in hunting mode, he appeared next to me, shaking the contents of a second baggie. He seized my mint, and we moved to the exit. "Fresh is best. I've been identifying all that's in this botanical accumulation, but I've got a long way to go."

He relocked the gate behind us and marched me back the way we'd come, changing back into his golf pro persona. We'd gone full circle and stood on the putting green next to my clubs. He set out twenty more balls at varying distances from five short pins with proportionally small flags.

"Back to work. Remember what I told you. Align your ball. Read the green. Compensate accordingly."

I thought I followed his instructions, but he pressed his lips together in annoyance. "Use the proper grip," he ordered.

I ended up putting much better than driving. To Byron's surprise, more than seventy-five percent of my putts hit their mark, dropping into the hole at which I aimed.

"You do like to dominate the green," Byron said, surprised. "Good job. Let's continue working on your short game—putting today, chipping and pitching tomorrow."

In my mind, the long game required strength and accuracy, but the short game used physics to control the speed and lift of the ball, and mathematics to gauge the distance and the best angle for the ball to travel. It reminded me of playing billiards but in three dimensions, and I loved pool halls.

Byron dropped a dozen more balls on the green, and I took steady aim toward each hole. I needed much less direction to putt and thought it might be a good time to ask about Tempest. "How long has your wife owned the bridal boutique?"

"Too long," he snorted. "It's nothing but a drain on our finances, but it'll keep her busy until …" He shook his head and changed topics. "Your accuracy astonishes me. Most golfers tend to catapult their ball onto the green in one stroke and use no finesse to finish. You might yet be teachable."

"Maybe I should drive with my putter?"

He canted his head and grinned. When he reached for my hand, I brought up my wrist and read the clock face. "I've got to run. Thanks, Mr. Byron—"

"Barclay, please."

"Yes, well, I've got an appointment, and I've kept you past time. Thanks for today."

Byron sighed and waggled his eyebrows, saying, "Anytime."

I raced up the incline and ran past Dennis, who was standing next to the pro shop door. I overheard him call out, "Byron, I need a word."

NINE

The Shady Oaks representative in charge of catering apologized. They'd be unable to provide the standard dinner tasting menu on such short notice; the chef couldn't locate a few of the essential ingredients. The impromptu sampling, however, tasted almost as good as the prior evening's delectable supper, which perhaps had more to do with the company I'd kept than the actual food.

The bite-sized servings of succulent crab cakes, grilled steak, and sea bass on a plate garnished with carrot purée whetted my appetite. After digging into one-third of a crisp, fresh Caesar salad with homemade crispy ciabatta croutons, perfectly juicy roasted chicken, and creamy dressing, and another third of a strawberry spinach concoction with bacon and a berry vinaigrette, I didn't think I could eat another bite, but I still found room to help finish off a superb flourless chocolate cake. Sated, we retired to a conference room.

When our discussion ended, Jane smiled. Her eyes focused on some distant, future exhilarating vision. Ida stood gazing out the window overlooking the first hole. Head up. Chin out. Arms crossed over her ample figure. Their faces relayed satisfaction, and I took it to mean they approved of the venue. However, Jane still recited a short list of concerns. "Unless we get a lot of snow in September, the golf course will remain open to its members, and we can't make it totally private."

Ida grunted. "No biggie."

"I can deal with a non-refundable down payment, but there are fewer food choices."

Ida bristled. "But remember there *are* choices and far superior fare."

Jane nodded absentmindedly. "Our lunch *was* scrumptious. It's a little more expensive than the pavilion, but worth every penny and ..." Her eyes circled the ceiling. "Shady Oaks' illustrious past and reputation are exemplary. I trust it'll be here for the long haul. Barclay Byron has observed the day-to-day goings on and still invested—"

"Mr. Byron is part owner?"

"Two shares. It's a relatively new investment. One of the shareholders had some financial concerns, and Byron capitalized on the hardship, buying into Shady Oaks." Jane sidled next to Ida. "I really don't think I can find anything better in the time I have remaining before October. I do feel good about it. Don't you?"

Ida draped her arm over Jane's shoulder and smiled.

The elegant dining room opened onto a great floor for Drew and Jane to showcase their dance moves, kicking up their heels with the grace and flair of a modern-day Ginger

Rogers and Fred Astaire. The walls of glass looked over the manicured lawn, which, in October, would be set off by a riot of brilliant fall reds, yellows, and oranges of the deciduous trees dotting the acreage. Hundreds of receptions had already taken place on the grounds, and the photo array contained decorating tips and hints from flowers to fabric. Best of all, Ida approved of the food. We exchanged looks and nodded.

Jane turned at the timid knock on the door. "Come in."

"I have a contract for you to read through. Have you decided, Ms. Mackey?" Reneé clenched a handful of printed pages.

Jane's eyes sparkled. "Yes, thank you, Reneé. I'll give you the down payment right now." She stretched out her hand and collected the pages in exchange for her credit card. Reneé ran it through her hand-held reader. Jane signed the bill with a flourish and slipped the receipt into a thick black leather folder.

"If you'd like to see how we set up for a wedding, you're welcome to stop by for a peek at any of the dates highlighted in the contract. Just give me a call, and we'll coordinate a visit."

"Thank you. Everything was wonderful. May we give our compliments to the chef?"

"Certainly. Follow me."

We neared the kitchen and heard banging and a voice saying rather harshly. "Where is it?"

Reneé's face blanched. "Maybe now is not a good time. He has quite a mercurial disposition. I'll be sure and pass along your kind words to Chef Antoine." She escaped through a swinging door and left us gaping at each other, wondering what else had gone missing.

Jane, Ida, and I made our way through the atrium. Jane

gave me a sidelong glance and said, "I'm set, but you look ready to sprout happy flowers. What's going on?"

My shoulders rose to my earlobes, and I answered with an overkill of glee. "I got a job."

They both stopped in their tracks. "Where?"

"Right here."

Ida looked at me askance. "When?"

"A few hours a day whenever they need me."

Jane giggled. "Why?"

"The pay isn't bad, and …" I couldn't contain my enthusiasm. "I can play golf for free."

Jane sobered. "Can you play now?"

"Ah." I paused, tapping my chin and making a show of mentally scanning today's calendar—empty, but for my employment. "As long as I'm ready to begin work at three, I'm in."

"Ida can take my car home. Drew's back in town, and I'll call him for a ride. Then he can see this beautiful place for himself. He said he'd happily agree to any decision I make as long as we get married, but I'd like to confirm this suits him."

Jane retrieved her golf bag from the back of her car and tossed her jangling keys to Ida, who slid into the front seat and closed the door. The engine roared. Normally, Jane wouldn't have relinquished her wheels, but she danced in place with bright, shining eyes, waved to Ida backing out of the parking space, and squealed, "It's real, Katie. My wedding is real."

Galen chuckled when we checked in again. "You picked the perfect day to golf. According to the schedule, there's an opening in five minutes. Sign in at the pro shop and enjoy."

I hefted my bag onto my shoulder and traipsed back down the hall.

"Let's walk the course today," Jane said, surprising me.

"I'm too wound up to ride in a cart. I have to get rid of some of my butterflies."

The whir of an industrial fan filled the notable quiet in Byron's absence. His counterpart, a woman with short-cropped, spikey, chestnut-colored hair and light-blue eyes, sat forward on a tall stool behind the counter, and asked, "What can I do for you?"

"Galen Tonlenson said there is a tee time available."

She plucked at the front of her shirt as she scrutinized the schedule. "Looks like you've come at just the right moment between our busiest flight times. Let me take down your information. I don't think we've met."

Jane grew an inch and said, "I'm a new member." She gave her name and identification number.

"Welcome, Jane. I'm one of the pros. If you need anything, ask for Genevieve, but everyone calls me Ginny." She turned to me. "And you are?"

"I'm Katie Wilk, a new hire—beverage cart—and Mr. Byron said I have four free games with my golf lessons."

"That makes my paperwork ultra easy. Nine or eighteen holes?"

"Nine," we answered together and tittered.

"Please play the back nine, and would you like a—"

Jane interrupted her. "May we rent two hand carts?"

"Walkers. Yay." Ginny beamed and raised two fists in a cheer. She unlocked the bar securing the carts. "You are free to tee off, but if you should get a load of anxious golfers behind you, you might want to allow them to play through." She quieted. "Some of our golfers can get a little excitable."

We nodded vigorously. She handed us score cards and a miniature pencil and held the door. We shuffled out to hole ten.

Jane teed off and landed on the edge of the green. She waited patiently for me to catch up. Lost in the rough twice, my score compounded. Once I landed on the short-cropped grass, I needed only one more stroke, but when Jane asked for my score, I mumbled disconsolately, "Sixteen."

"Katie, this is your first time golfing. You're doing fine." I appreciated her speaking as if encouraging one of her students. She was very good at that.

"I'm sorry to make you wait so long."

"I'm outside on a beautiful spring day, mildly exercising with my best friend. Don't be sorry."

Each hole played more easily, and I laughed at my mistakes. My next three scores were still two digits, but less than fifteen. Approaching hole fourteen, we walked past a small pond surrounded by flowers and tall grasses. I clutched Jane's arm and hissed "Jane, don't move." I pointed a shaky finger at a furry animal.

Being obstinate, she did the opposite of what she was asked and performed a happy dance, so I gripped her arm tighter. She rolled her eyes and said, "That's a predator decoy to help scare the birds away."

"A what? It looks like an angry coyote."

Jane tugged her arm from my grasp and marched next to the lifelike statue. She rapped on its perfectly sculpted resin head, complete with fine hairs and whiskers, and tickled its chin. My throat opened, and when I could breathe again, she dragged me past the inanimate hunter to the beginner tee box closest to the pin. I checked off my instructions from Byron, corrected my grip and stance, lined up the shot, swung with all my might … and missed. *Strike one.*

"I'll call that practice. Try again," Jane said encouragingly.

My second drive arched high and stayed aloft, looking like

a golf ball should, before plopping into the pond between two iridescent green-headed mallards, who launched into the sky, quacking. I scanned for an audience. Not finding any, I said earnestly, "I'll take the penalty. We've got to keep moving."

Jane removed her driver and trudged up a short rise to the second colored marker. I kept the motionless canid in my sights as I watched Jane and took notes. She sighted her ball and took an actual practice swing when out of the corner of my eye, I saw her cart begin its descent, lurching down the hill.

I stabilized my own clubs and took off running. The hand cart sped up the farther it rolled from me and headed toward the water. Sparkling laughter from Jane and surrounding patrons punctuated the rattling clubs, bouncing and careening down the incline. In my peripheral vision, another person, dressed from head to toe in red, catapulted toward the speeding clubs, and the competitor in me put on a burst of speed to win the foot race. I snared Jane's wonderful tools (and probably expensive too) before they plunged into the pond.

I dug the cleat on the cart into the ground to anchor it, bent over at the waist with my hands on my knees, and panted as if my life depended on it. Not vested in running as a proper form of exercise, it probably did. My cap fell off my head and a snicker burbled from my challenger.

"You won," she said, without gasping for air. "Fair and square."

I took a well-deserved moment before standing upright. "Some race," I said and looked over the glassy surface of the pool, mirroring the cloudless blue sky, the omnipresent trees, the gentle hills, and the perfectly coifed green sod. I breathed deeply and blinked before bending again to scoop up my cap and gasped.

"Are you okay?" the woman in the red sports dress asked. She followed my gaze and let out a blood-curdling scream.

Everything happened at once. I dropped to my knees and reached toward the water. Jane abruptly stopped laughing. She took one unsure step in our direction and another before bounding off the tee. She rammed her driver into my bag and gracefully sailed down the hill, dragging my clubs behind her.

Jane slowed as she closed in on the screamer, saying, "It'll be okay," over and over, every time the girl in red took a breath, and her shrieks gradually turned to whimpers. Jane's inquisitive eyes met mine and tracked my glance to the white leather cleated shoe. She shook her head. "Not again, Katie."

TEN

Together, we tugged and yanked, pulling the heavy form a few inches from the pond's edge. The toned and tanned bare leg attached to the shoe didn't move, and neither did the rest of the body. Jane punched in 911 as I knelt and checked the wrist for a pulse.

She said, "There's been an accident on hole number fourteen at the Shady Oaks Golf Course." I shook my head, and she added. "I think it's a fatality."

When Jane stepped away to continue the conversation with more privacy, the woman in red slid into the grass and appeared to be gearing up for another barrage of screaming. She flinched when I gently touched her shoulder. "Are you okay?"

She spluttered and mewled, "I don't know if I'll ever be

okay again."

"What's your name?"

"Anne. Anne Laura Johansen."

"Anne, I'm Katie." *What could I do to keep her calm?* "Are you a golfer?"

She sniffed and tossed her head of glossy dark brown hair. "I won the club's women's league last year, and I'm leading the board for the women's league this year, so yeah, I guess you could say so." She wiped the tip of her nose and swept a forefinger under each blue eye. "Golf is my life."

A haughty Anne might irritate, but she was way better than the screaming Anne. When I took a good look at her, she evoked a teensy memory, but I didn't know where we could have met before.

"What could've happened to Barclay?" she whined.

I twisted my head so sharply, I nearly gave myself whiplash. The body faced away from me, but at second glance, I might have recognized the hair color and golf clothing, and it did, indeed, have the appearance of Barclay Byron.

Tears trickled down her cheeks again, but she sniffled and said, "What's this club doing here?" She reached for the iron next to his hand.

"Don't," I said much more harshly than I intended. She snatched her hand back and grimaced. I softened my tone. "Anne, it could be evidence."

"Evidence?" Her eyes grew round. "The nine iron's head is caked in red. It looks like … blood." She crab-walked backward, stood, and took three wobbly steps away from the body. She took a quick look around and said, "I'm outta here."

Jane stepped close to her and spoke calmly. "Anne, we have to stay and talk to the police. After all, you were among the first to find the body. They'll be here shortly. Let me call Ginny." She scanned our score card and punched in a number. "Ginny, we have a problem on hole fourteen. Could you join us?" In response to something she heard, Jane hinted forcefully, "Yes, you should be here. There's been an accident, and I think one of the golfers is suffering from shock." She listened and said, "Water would be great."

"Diet tonic with a thin wedge of lime for me," Anne said loud enough to be heard in the next county. Her manic emotions wreaked havoc on my own.

Jane paced, and I knelt by the body. Ginny appeared in no time, the golf cart braking hard. "What happened?"

Anne pointed to the body and began to weep again. Ginny did a double take and scowled. She guided a blubbering Anne to take a seat in the cart and handed her a bottle of tonic water when a gaggle of nosy golfers converged on us.

"Ginny, what happened?"

"What's going on, Anne?"

"Can we play through? You're holding everyone up."

Ginny addressed the busybodies by name, and before they could disappear, she recorded their information on an electronic tablet and asked them to give us space by retiring to the golf club bar. "The first round's on me," she said in response to the petulance.

I heard the undulating high-pitched siren before the lights and police car tore around the drive and disappeared at the front of the clubhouse, followed by an ambulance in a hurry.

I had twenty-four chances out of twenty-five to connect with a friendly policeman, but when Officer Ronnie Christianson marched out the pro shop doors, stomped around the putting green, and strutted onto the fairway with his right hand hooked above the firearm on his belt, I swallowed hard. Ronnie and I didn't always see eye-to-eye. On a few occasions, his misplaced ambition caused him to dismiss my suggestions or patently ignore information I'd discovered which proved necessary to apprehend the perpetrator of a crime, and he didn't like someone upstaging his investigations.

When he saw me, his frown intensified. He probably would've delighted in arresting me on the spot for one infraction or another. He was testy, particularly after being passed over for the position of chief of police. No one on the city council questioned his competence. He constantly sought to make the quickest apprehension, sometimes, however, at the expense of arresting the wrong person. Fortunately for me, this time, he was not alone.

Chief Amanda West trudged next to him, locked in step. Her attentive dark brown eyes scanned every inch of the surrounding area. Amanda had so much going for her. She was intelligent and determined, a dogged investigator, and Ronnie's new boss. Ronnie paled next to her and not only because he was a fair-skinned Minnesotan with Norwegian roots and she was a tall, striking woman of mixed heritage. He couldn't hold a candle to her, but she had her hands full. He wanted her job.

He planted himself in front of me and crossed his arms. "Why am I not surprised? What do you have to say for yourself, Wilk?" he sneered.

Anne primed her lungs to wail again, but Chief West correctly read the possibility. She stood beside Anne and said in a soothing voice, "It must have been very scary. Why don't I meet you in the clubhouse? Jane, can you take …"

"Anne."

"Take Anne to the clubhouse."

Anne nodded, keeping her eyes glued to the EMT team, watching their every move as long as she could while Jane drove her across the fairway.

Ronnie glowered. "It looks like someone moved the body. There are drag marks in the mud. Did you do that?"

"Jane and I pulled him from the water to check for signs of life."

"You tampered with evidence."

The EMTs affirmed nothing more could be done, and Amanda said to Ronnie, "Call Officer Rodgers. I need the two of you to secure the scene." She tossed him a roll of yellow crime scene tape. "After the coroner removes the body, set up a barricade, canvass the area, and pick up any debris within a one-hundred-foot perimeter."

Ronnie loosened the end of the tape. "Why one hundred feet?" His condescending tone grated.

Ignoring his insubordination, she said, "Start with those." Amanda pointed to the golf balls peeking through the weeds. "Then you can join me. I'll begin interviewing the witnesses in the clubhouse." She must have suspended belief I knew how to golf or could afford this course and said, apprehensively, "Talk to me, Katie. What are you doing here?"

Before we took a step, another vehicle made the sweeping curve around the drive, and minutes later, acting as county coroner, my heart-stopping beau stepped onto the course. The smile on my lips lasted all of three seconds before turning down in a grimace when we met. Pete's face was inscrutable, but his warm eyes held me with tenderness.

"Are you okay, Katie?"

I nodded. He opened one arm, and I nestled in, taking the offering of a quick hug. His bag bumped my shoulder, and I backed away. Dr. Pete Erickson had a job to do, and he set to work.

Amanda and I walked toward the path, and she asked

again. "What are you doing here?"

"Jane wanted a golfing buddy and signed me up for lessons with one of the pros. I've had two sessions. Jane and I were trying out the course today when we found the body. The woman in red, the hysterical one, identified the victim as Barclay Byron. She might be correct."

"Do you know Mr. Byron?"

"He's my golf instructor."

Amanda halted in her tracks, and I retraced my last few steps to stand next to her. "*The* Barclay Byron," she said. "Winner of the Five-State Festival Tournament and Minnesota State Open at Rochester, 'Sota Series Match Play champion, Le Sueur Country Club Pro Am champ, and runner-up at who knows how many other golf tournaments across the Midwest."

She began walking again, and I matched her stride for stride. "I guess so. Do you golf?"

Ignoring my question, she went on, "His character, however, has been called into question over the last few years. He has, excuse me, had a reputation for being overbearing, narcissistic, untrustworthy ..." She emphasized each word with a pounding step and curled her lip in distaste. "...lewd, misogynistic, and unfaithful. There have been numerous complaints filed against him." She marched on. "Tell me what happened?"

"Jane's a member of this golf club."

Amanda smirked. "Of course she is."

"And I have free greens fees because I work here now—"

She jerked to a stop again. "You what?" The admonition in her voice struck a minor chord.

"School's out for summer, and I have too much free time on my hands. I can only walk Maverick and bike so far.

Yesterday, when I saw the ad and read the list of benefits, one of which is free golf play, I applied and got the job."

"You need to find something else to do. We're closing the course down until the crime scene is cleared."

We stepped into the large room, and you could've heard an eye blink. The heavy, sculpted wooden bar overlooked the action on hole fourteen, and all eyes that didn't follow the black-covered gurney as it trundled across the fairway and into the parking lot watched its reflection in the mirror behind the bar. Pete led the entourage with his photographer in tow; the EMTs pushed and dragged Barclay's body to the silent, waiting ambulance.

"We'll know what happened. Dr. Erickson will determine manner and cause of Barclay Byron's death soon."

What's a girl to do when she might have lost her job before it began? I asked Ginny for an extra-large Arnold Palmer.

"Barclay taught golf well," she said, garnishing my beverage. "But if you're still interested, I can finish out your lessons."

"I appreciate the offer. I think I might have been getting the hang of it."

When Officer Christianson and Officer Rodgers entered the bar, they separated and briefly spoke to the impatient patrons, taking statements and collecting contact information before releasing anyone. When only Ginny, Anne, Jane, and I remained, Ronnie escorted us one at a time to a table at the far end of the room where Amanda asked the questions. She interviewed me last.

"Tell me again what you were doing here and what happened."

I inhaled and recounted my morning, culminating in finding the body.

"Do you know anyone who would have had a reason to want Barclay Byron dead?"

I carefully observed Amanda's face, looking for a clue. "You act as if this is a murder investigation instead of a tragic accident. I know the club was caked with clay, not blood, but had he been struck with it? Did he hit his head in a fall? Did he have a medical condition which might cause him to black out? Could you tell if he drowned?" I stopped myself before I stepped on her toes and hesitated just long enough for Amanda to read whatever she could into the silence.

"What do you know, Katie?"

"Nothing specific."

"Any little bit of information can help." She waited a beat and drew a disappointed breath after which I spilled my guts.

"I really don't know of anyone who would want him dead, but if he didn't die of natural causes, you need to know, when Jane and I showed up for my introductory lesson yesterday, we heard an angry voice in the pro shop." I added quickly, "But we didn't see anyone."

"Jane recounted the same thing." She scrawled on her notebook. "Male or female voice?"

"Female." I repeated the two phrases we'd heard. "At the end of my lesson, he ranted at the beverage cart girl. I couldn't hear much of what was said, but she ran away, sobbing." I frowned. "When I arrived early this morning, he was arguing with someone again, and before you ask, the door was closed so I don't know who was there or what was said. I guess there were some folks who might not have liked him as well as others."

My knee jerked up and down. Amanda leaned forward and put her hand on it to stem the shaking table. "Katie, there's nothing to worry about. Or is there?"

"No. No," I said then added in a rush. "But a woman

kind of yelled at him from the tee on hole one yesterday, and I couldn't tell if he hadn't heard her or just ignored her." I let Amanda finish writing. "And Byron hinted his wife was soon to be an ex-wife." Amanda knew I had more to say, but she didn't push, yet. I furrowed my brow, hoping she'd see how hard I tried to carefully choose my words, and added, "We met her, Tempest, that is."

"And what's your take on Mrs. Byron?"

"Not to speak unkindly of someone at such a vulnerable time, but as a salesperson, she wasn't very accommodating." The story of Jane's dress took on a life of its own, and Amanda's patience wore thin. She drew in a deep breath, and I added hurriedly, "Byron said her store is a money pit. In fact," I cut myself off before I said anything about the man in her shop and spread rumors about their marital status. "When you see her, please give her my condolences."

"Death notifications are difficult."

"I don't envy you." I added the next words meaningfully. "Byron also gave me a short tour of the grounds today."

Amanda arched one eyebrow. "Why?"

"He thought I might want to explore the inner workings of Shady Oaks to help me better accommodate the guests. I learned that landscape management has a shed filled with lawn chemicals and lethal tools." Amanda crossed her arms. "And he gave me a tour of a strange garden."

A short flash of surprise sparked through her dark brown eyes. "You've certainly muddied the waters. Anything else?"

I shook my head guiltily and lowered it.

"Give me the short tour," she said with resignation in her tone.

ELEVEN

Ginny taped a handwritten "Closed temporarily" sign to the pane of glass, and meticulously wiped away the smudge of her fingerprints on the pristine surface before locking the heavy double doors and waving us away. As Jane and I headed for my modest ride, a sleek, fire-engine-red sports car sporting a bull logo on its hood caught my eye, and I strolled close, glancing through the window. The lush black leather seat set off a white and green water bottle.

"Do you think this car could belong to Byron?"

Lost in thought, Jane didn't answer but walked toward my itty-bitty car on the far side of the lot.

The only sounds I heard were our footsteps and clanking golf clubs. Ginny had foisted the borrowed bag on me, promising I could finish my lessons with her whenever the course reopened—if they reopened—and we piled the two sets of clubs into my trunk.

Jane stood for a long time at the open car door, a debate raging in her eyes. When she slid onto the seat, I turned the key in the ignition, getting the air moving, but not engaging gears. She stared out the windshield over the glasslike water. "Jane, what's troubling you?"

"I wanted everything to be perfect. There aren't any venues left in the entire county of Monongalia, but do you think having a wedding reception where someone died bodes ill?" When she turned to look at me, tears rimmed her eyes, glistening like beads of glitter before trickling down her cheeks.

"For one thing," I said assuredly, "people can, and do, die everywhere at any time. But no one died *in* this country club today, so it can't bode ill."

"How about a venue where someone has been murdered?" I gaped at her. "I overheard Amanda." She swiped at her damp cheeks and sniffed, trying hard to smile. "She's investigating Byron's death as a homicide."

"You know Amanda. She never leaves a stone unturned. It's her way. I don't know what she's decided, but I mentioned there may be a few people who were unhappy with him."

She clutched the door handle. "That's the thing. We heard those folks just yesterday in the pro shop and then that poor girl he criticized on the course."

"And that doesn't even count the argument I overheard today nor the story of his relationship with his soon-to-be-ex-wife."

"Tempest?" Jane asked. "Did you ask Byron about her?"

"Yup. Byron claimed her business was a financial drain, and he seemed almost giddy at the prospect of Tempest becoming an 'ex'."

The dam holding back Jane's tears blew apart again, and she sobbed. "So even my celebratory dress is tainted. I don't know how much more needs to happen before Drew decides we shouldn't get married."

"Jane, you two are made for each other. Nothing will keep you apart." Another car tooled around the drive and pulled up next to us. "Speak of the devil."

Jane quickly patted her face and adjusted her posture. Drew jumped from his car and rushed to kneel next to her. "Darling, are you okay? I just heard."

The accusatory look he gave me over her nodding head as he wrapped her in his arms made me tear up too. "Sorry," he said, as apologetic as I'd ever heard him. "But how do you get caught up in these predicaments?"

"Lucky?" I tried to tease.

Drew's eyes narrowed to slits, and he crouched to be able to look up into Jane's face. With one hand, he loosened the knot of his iridescent bow tie. "Promise me, no snooping, no interfering, no prying. Stay out of it. Leave everything to Chief West." He eyed us intently. "Both of you."

"Promise," Jane and I said together, but I crossed my fingers behind my back, just in case.

His facial features relaxed a tad, and he leaned back on his haunches.

"Drew," Jane said quietly.

"Yes, honey."

She focused on her engagement ring. "I lost the down payment I made to Promise Pavilion."

"I know." She gave him a curious look. "It's okay. We'll find another place, somewhere even better, or we can postpone our nuptials. I want our wedding to be perfect."

She inhaled deeply and sat up straighter. In a strained voice, she said, "Ida helped me find someplace new."

"There. See. I told you." She drew his gaze to our surroundings—the Shady Oaks Country Club, and as realization dawned, his eyes closed, and he blew out a puff of air. "Oh, boy."

Words streamed from her lips. "Ida and I toured two awful venues this morning. The first was damp and dingy. I wouldn't hold a fire sale there, and the second was so run-down, the mice leave negative reviews. There's no other site available in Columbia to hold our reception. Everything is booked and has been since before we met. We can't even rent a tent." Anxiety contributed to the strident voice coming out of my friend. "This venue is iconic and beautiful. The food we sampled tasted terrific. The hotel rooms available in the addition provide accommodations if people want to stay on the premises. And I plan to check out the spa services."

He picked up her hands, taking a breath as if gearing up to share some unpleasant words.

She charged ahead, cutting off whatever argument he might have had. "The dance floor is huge. And I just want to get married … to you."

Drew's eyes lit up at the mention of a dance floor or maybe her wanting to get married. "Then this is it." She grabbed him and hugged him for a long minute.

He finally untangled himself and said, "Now, can I get you home?" He took her hand and lifted her from the seat. "Your conveyance awaits, my lady," he said and guided her from my vehicle. They rumbled out of the lot.

I relished the serenity, but only for a moment. A vague shadow moved along the side of the clubhouse, and I decided I didn't want to be alone with what could be a ghost.

I chuckled the entire ride home and entered my apartment with a self-satisfied grin, to find Ida and Dad with their heads together bent over the kitchen table. Their chatter ceased and the guilt on their faces spoke volumes.

"What are you up to?"

Ida threw her shoulders back and drew herself up. "Five feet," she announced.

"Very funny."

"What makes you think we're up to anything?" Dad said.

I raised an eyebrow, and Ida sighed. "We heard Shady Oaks will be closed to investigate a suspicious death."

"And we want you to stay out of it." Dad turned his head and closed one eye, setting me in his sights.

"Since your job is on hold, you'll need to keep busy with something else to do." Ida whipped out a pair of knitting needles and a ball of yarn. "I'm going to continue teaching you to knit."

"First, tell me all you know about Shady Oaks."

She scrunched her face into a question. "What do you want to know?"

"The story of the ghost."

Ida eased back and settled into her teaching mode. I dropped into a chair. "The Spanish Mission style clubhouse was built in 1928 in the middle of an oak savannah, and has hosted one Vice-President of the United States, several dignitaries from around the world, various celebrities, some rock and roll royalty, a few pro-am golf tournaments, and events too numerous to count. Its lovely location makes it prime real estate, and although partial ownership has shifted from year to year, fifty-two percent is wrapped up in the Murphy Family Trust, a savvy protection against developers."

I planted my elbows ungracefully on the table and nestled

my chin into my palms, eager for Ida's storytelling. "The ghost?" I prodded.

"Quinn Murphy and Liam O'Neil were madly in love. Their families planned the most lavish wedding Columbia had ever seen. But there was a dark heart at play. Rowan, Liam's older brother, wanted to be married first. He did everything he could to keep the two lovebirds apart, but they were soulmates.

"Quinn loved puzzles. She and Liam had matching cylinders used to encode and decrypt secret messages in the scytale code designed by Plutarch. On the day of their wedding, Rowan provided Quinn a long narrow band filled with letters, claiming it was sent by Liam. The message she deciphered requested she make a regal entrance and arrive by boat in the company of Rowan.

"Halfway across the lake, Rowan tossed the oars, jumped in, and swam to shore. Quinn was stranded. However, rather than be late for her own wedding, she jumped into the water. Liam heard the thrashing and witnessed her struggle. He dove into the lake and swam with all his might. But not only did Quinn's bridal gown weigh her down, she couldn't swim. Liam lost her and, shortly after, died of a broken heart."

"What an absolutely heartbreaking story. What happened to Rowan?"

"Shredded by guilt, Rowan became a priest, and it is said, it is he who haunts the golf club, begging for forgiveness."

After a solemn moment of utter silence, Dad couldn't contain his laughter and let loose a loud guffaw.

TWELVE

The story is fabricated from Ida's glorious imagination."
Dad could barely speak, caught up in the delight of
watching my flabbergasted face. "And you, my darling
daughter, fell for it."

I swatted at his arm, and he curled up in laughter. "How
would you know it's just a story, Father?"

He tilted his head and gave me the dad-eye. "Remember, I
actually read the placards at the history centers I frequent, and
one of the displays highlights Columbia's founding fathers.
The Murphys are among them. I concede the family trust
does maintain controlling interest in the golf club, and Quinn
did adore puzzles, but Quinn and Liam had five children, and
there never was a Rowan."

I shifted my intense glare to Ida.

She shrugged. "Who knows if the ghosts are real, but that's the story the country club confesses to whenever anything is misplaced."

"The human relations director who hired me alluded to the same perpetrator." I grunted. *It seems an awful lot of things must go missing there.*

"I guess you need something to take your mind off Shady Oaks." Ida handed me the pair of knitting needles and a ball of Cougar blue yarn. "Let's see what we can do."

In the teaching world, she had an unsurpassed reputation for unleashing creativity, but I was stuck, using the same dishcloth pattern and materials she'd given me months ago. I'd knit a row or two and she'd rip it out while imparting what she considered kind, constructive criticism. Stitches too loose or too tight. Wrong number of stitches. Forgotten yarn over. Over what? I concentrated on what was in front of me and cast on four stitches, letting the occurrences of the day fade into the knots of color. I knitted more easily every time I started up again, and the repetitive process soothed my unsettled mind, even if I only created a malformed square. We sat in companionable quiet, and I almost forgot about Barclay Byron.

Somehow, in the midst of concentrating on the needle chaos, I nodded off to sleep. The sun set around nine o'clock in June, and the orange ball of fire had dipped precariously toward the horizon when I woke. I untangled my fingers and stretched. My stiff neck made a horrible crackling sound. Behind Dad's closed door rose a sonorous exchange of air, and I had no reason to wake him. I knocked lightly on Ida's door, but all was quiet there as well.

My stomach growled and added to my general discomfort. I searched the fridge for leftovers. A note of instructions was taped to the cover of a CorningWare dish filled with a satisfying helping of tortellini. As per instructions, I microwaved Ida's cheesy Italian sustenance, and after devouring a hearty serving, I donned our reflective flashing vests and snapped on Maverick's leash to make one quick twilight pass through the neighborhood.

The sky had darkened enough for me to trip the motion sensor on our backyard light, joining the lights blinking on in many of my neighbors' homes on Maple Street. Before Maverick completed prancing his mile circuit, I wished I'd grabbed a sweater. I rubbed my bare arms and hustled behind my happy pooch.

When we returned from our evening foray, I stopped in front for a moment to admire Ida's lovely Queen Anne home. How had Dad and I gotten so lucky? I blinked back tears as my myriad blessings bombarded me: wonderful family, terrific friends—including one great looking guy, a job I loved, a great place to live, and so much more. I took a tentative step toward my apartment entrance in the rear but wondered why the motion-activated light was still illuminated.

A ghost.

I laughed at the thought foremost in my mind and stepped through the back gate.

Maverick lunged and barked, and I stopped laughing. I clung to the leash and tried to quiet him as I remembered CJ's words, 'Trust your dog.'

"Who's there?" I whispered. "Come out."

Maverick had no fear, though at our training sessions in search and rescue, CJ tried to impart strategies for me to work with my dog rather than in opposition. My arms quivered, restraining sixty pounds of rippling muscle and worrying we might meet something bigger, more aggressive, and wilder—another dog, a rabid animal, a real live coyote, or an unidentified human. "Heel, Maverick."

He stood next to me but continued barking.

I peered into the gloom and the shadows moved. "Come out of there." I dug into my pocket. "I'm calling the police." My heart leaped. My phone wasn't there. I'd left it on the kitchen table, but hopefully whoever was here wouldn't figure that out.

"Please don't," a small voice said.

"Quiet, Maverick." To my surprise, he stopped barking.

"Galen said I could trust you."

"You know Galen?"

No answer.

"Who are you?"

Nothing. The fence rattled.

"Are you still there?"

Maverick glanced up at me as if saying, 'Gone. Now what?' I shrugged. He panted happily, and we went in for the night, but I'd definitely check with Galen.

My phone pinged from the table. I read a text message from Shady Oaks.

Reopening the course tomorrow. Can you begin at three and stay until seven? Orientation plus one shift.

The text had been sent seconds prior, so I thought I could safely respond without waking someone.

I'll be there. Is there anything I need to know before then?

Nope. Check in at the human relations office. Thanks. Lark

I laid out my uniform, scanned the job description, and wondered if the cause of Byron's death might be among the new frequently asked questions. For me, preparation was the foundation. I was also a little nosy. Byron's death bothered me.

Having napped, I had energy to spare and decided my new employment warranted research. I typed 'Murphy family Columbia' in the search bar on my laptop.

Hundreds of articles popped up, reiterating Dad's references to the Murphy family. I clicked on the sepia-toned vintage wedding photo first. The pressed evening shirt, white bow tie, single button black morning coat with shiny lapels, and top hat worn by the groom, the intricate lace outlining the glossy sheen of Quinn's silky gown, and the wide collection of blossoms surrounding them clearly demonstrated the wealth the Murphys must have had.

Quinn's prodigious inheritance contributed to Liam's spectacular success. She was the first female attorney in Columbia, and one of the first in the entire state of Minnesota, so she was the grantor, the individual who created the trust document. I read from a copy, cited as well-written legal paperwork still used to teach aspiring lawyers at our fine Minnesota law schools. It outlined the terms and conditions for the management and distribution of the family's vast estate. Quinn formed the trust using her father's name, determined what assets would be included, identified her five children as beneficiaries, designed a means of appointing a trustee to manage the assets for future generations, and retained consistent family involvement in the golf course she and Liam built for the community.

Another of the articles detailed the lucrative practices of Liam O'Reilly's botanical business and his quest to grow hardy grasses resilient to the disparate temperatures in Minnesota yet soft to the touch. He conducted his experiments with the knowledgeable assistance and financial support of his wife, Quinn, heiress to the Murphy logging fortune. I wouldn't have noticed Quinn's petite stature except in subsequent photos of her golfing at Shady Oaks, testing the variety of grasses with her father and husband. The club she held rose to her shoulder. As a miniature fireball, she must have been a force to be reckoned with.

One corner of my mouth raised in a crooked smile. *Much like Ida and Jane.*

I clicked on an ancestral link. Dad was correct. Liam and Quinn had five children, and after five or six generations, the descendants numbered near one hundred. I perused the lovely Irish names and vowed to research my own ancestry in the near future.

The day caught up with me, even after the nap, and I dragged my lids open just long enough to glimpse a family photo on the bottom of the page. The adrenaline rush roused me when I recognized one of the figures.

THIRTEEN

It shouldn't have come as a surprise. If the golf course was included in the family legacy, it only made sense for a descendant or two to remain part of the day-to-day operations.

Anne Johansen's endearing grin lit the page, and if we hadn't met over a dead body, I might have noticed the happy-go-lucky air about her. And then I remembered feeling as though I'd recognized her. She looked exactly like one of the Quinn Murphy portraits on the wall in the atrium. No wonder she golfed so well. The sport had been in her blood for over one hundred years.

The hyperlink connected her name to a biographical page. By age twenty-five, the accolades and awards she'd earned seemed to rival Byron's, and she had many more years to compete. I clicked on an arrow to see more photos of her golfing from a young age—smiling, laughing, winning, showcasing her form, accepting trophies—and happened upon an astonishing photo of a younger Anne in the arms of a more mature man. Barclay Byron. My lips puckered as if sucking on a lime.

How long had she known him? Had he been her instructor also? Was I misinterpreting the photo? Was it even real? Had Barclay Byron and Anne Johansen been an item? When did Tempest enter the picture? What had their relationship meant to Tempest or to the ownership of the club, although it might be a moot point as Byron wasn't around any longer?

I didn't know the significance of the photo, and it was too late to bother Amanda, so I saved the link to a file on my laptop. Hitting the back button a few times returned me to the family photo page, where I carefully examined the faces for any more familiarities but didn't find any. I sent a text including the link to Amanda to be delivered in the morning. She could figure it out.

Maverick set his nose on my knee, reminding me dawn would break whether or not I was prepared, and he would require food and a walk. I closed my laptop, and for his last act of the day, he leapt onto the end of my bed and curled up next to my feet. I had neither the heart nor the energy to displace him.

When Maverick woke me, I rapidly scrubbed away my crabby face, pledging to be bright and cheerful by the time we returned from our walk and joined Dad for whatever breakfast he prepared. The romp started off well, but when I had completed half our four-mile trek, it began to drizzle. Within a few blocks, my hair was plastered to my face, and my clothes weighed a ton. Rain pelted the trees, tearing the tender young leaves from the boughs. Oblivious to our plight, Maverick pranced and paraded through the streets looking for four-legged friends. There were none. Their owners had been wise enough to look at the radar before setting out for their morning constitutional. At least the rain lowered the temperature a degree or two. With a rumble of thunder and a crack of lightning, we took off running the last few blocks.

A text pinged on my phone, but I waited until we were back inside and peeled off the top layer of wet clothes before I read the message.

Arrive at 1:00 to complete your orientation. If the rain stops, we may deploy the beverage cart. If the rain continues, there won't be many golfers on the course.

Sure. Can't wait.

I hadn't read a contingency plan for my employment on rainy days, so this would be the first test of my summer position.

Unfortunately, Dad's breakfast feasts from the prior days had been replaced by a box of cold cereal. The note taped to the top read, 'Have a good day,' but his sentiment hadn't been realized, yet. With no response from Amanda regarding the Murphy family photos, I texted.

Any thoughts, Amanda?

After breakfast, I accepted a call as I rinsed the dishes.

"Katie, Tempest called and said there might be a teensy problem with my dress." Jane sounded much less stressed than earlier in the week—a good sign.

"Pick me up. We'll go talk to her in person. Remember, the dress was supposed to be an extra, for fun. You already have your wedding dress. Many brides only wear one."

"But—"

"No buts. I believe you and Drew will have a most

beautiful wedding, and it will be just right for you, with or without a party dress, in Columbia or …"

"Not? I talked to my dad. I'd have no trouble planning the wedding in Atlanta. With his connections, we could pull it off. It's funny. I think about my dream wedding all the time and the only constant is watching you and Pete lead the way, me walking down the aisle with my dad at my side, and then standing in front of Drew holding hands and saying, 'I do.'" I could hear the wistfulness. "I love him, Katie." I could almost hear her effervescent smile, "I really do."

"Then let's see what Tempest wants, shall we?" She didn't respond right away. "Jane?"

"I'll be right there."

A text pinged on my phone.

Thoughts about what?

My brow furrowed. Wouldn't Amanda find a photo of a young Anne in the arms of a slightly older Barclay unusual, maybe even compromising?

Follow the link to the photo of Byron.

My phone jangled. "Hello?"

"Which photo?" Amanda's stern voice made me feel like a kid.

"The link I sent should bring up a page of photos from Anne Johansen's biography. You notice she is a Murphy descendant, so she's part owner of Shady Oaks."

"I'm looking at the photos, but you texted something about Byron," she said impatiently.

I opened my laptop, clicked the link and followed the arrows, paging through the photos and panicked. "It was there last night. Honest, Amanda. I saw the two of them laughing and hugging."

"He's not in any photo now." Her voice held a hint of

skepticism.

I had another thought. "Amanda, what kind of car did Byron own?"

"Why do you ask?"

"There was one car left in the lot last night, and if it belonged to—"

"It did not. If you should think of anything else, let me know right away," she said with more than a suggestion of sarcasm and hung up.

Before I had time to wonder what could have happened to the photo or the red car with the water bottle, I answered a text from Jane.

Coming!

Jane sang a happy song along with Bobby McFerrin on our short jaunt downtown.

Adopting that adage, she hopped out of the car, seemingly ready for anything—anything but a locked door.

FOURTEEN

We stood in the rain outside the First and Last Wedding Shoppe. Jane knocked until a completely different Tempest unlocked the door. Her eyes were red and puffy. Strands of her disheveled hair stuck out all over. The makeup she had worn when we first met mimicked a fine porcelain finish, but on this woman, red splotches covered her washed-out face. She'd aged ten years. Even though she wore stylish jeans rolled up at her ankles, the extra-large emerald-green sweatshirt she wore hung limply from her shoulders and looked like a hideous first attempt at appliqué—a golfer sporting a plaid golf tam topped with a red pom-pom standing on a green next to the hole holding a crooked putter looking down at a disproportionately humongous white ball surrounded by two sand traps. The flag on the nineteenth tee flew in the background.

She squeezed through the narrow opening guarding the doorway.

"I'm contacting all of my customers. Ms. Mackey, I can't get your dress altered, and the money to repay you is tied up. I'm sure you understand," she droned unapologetically in a rehearsed monologue. "The shop is closed. You know what happened, and it may be quite a while before everything is settled. I wanted to give you a heads-up and time to find alternate suppliers. Chief West is investigating my husband's death as suspicious." Her voice rose in anger. "I certainly didn't kill him."

Slack jawed for only a moment, Jane regained her composure and said, "Then I'll take the dress as is."

"But ..."

"I have the receipt for the dress. It's mine. I'm not asking you to return my payment for the dress or alterations."

Tempest blinked rapidly and stammered, "I can't return your dress. The police ..."

Jane took out her phone and punched in a phone number. She waited a beat and said, "Hello, I'd like to speak to Chief West, please. Yes, it's urgent. Tell her it's Jane Mackey."

Tempest squinted and the blotches on her face turned a deeper shade of red. She slammed the door.

I tried my best to whisper without moving my lips. "Are you really calling Amanda? Don't tell her I'm with you. She wasn't very happy with me this morning."

Jane acted like she was patiently waiting, tapping her tiny toes, and the soft words snuck out of the corner of her mouth. "I called my own number, something Tempest doesn't need to know. I think she's trying to scam me. I have the receipt. The dress is mine. If she thinks she can sell my dress twice, she has another *think* coming."

She inhaled deeply and exhaled, her shoulders rising and falling. "And I know I can talk the amazing Ida into altering it."

I swallowed my grin as the door flew open and Tempest angrily tossed a black plastic dress bag into my arms. I shimmied the bag over the feathers peeking out.

"Never mind," Jane said into the phone. "Please tell her I'll catch up soon." Jane pocketed her phone. "Thank you, Tempest, and we are sorry for your loss."

The young man we saw Monday stood behind Tempest, resting his hands on her shoulders. "You should leave," he said, with menace in his tone. "And don't come back." The door closed with a click and the deadbolt shot into place.

"That was enlightening," said Jane as we scurried back to her car. She hung the dress and said, "Do you have to work today?"

"I have orientation at one and then it's a game of wait and see. The rain is predicted to stop within the next two hours, but even if the diehards golf, I'm not sure they'll stop on a drenched course for a beverage to wet their whistles."

"What beverages are available?"

"I'll find out at my orientation."

"I'd better get you home." She wheeled down the street at a lightning pace.

We pulled into the driveway, and after a much-needed gulp of air, I said, "The pieces are falling into place for your wedding plans, but if you think of anything you need me to do, I'd be honored to help."

Jane choked up. "You're the best."

Maverick waited for me, tail wagging, leash dangling from his mouth. I clipped on the lead, and he dragged me around the neighborhood for one last quick romp, dodging the few remaining raindrops, but the unexpected rising temperature and humidity made the air feel like a thick soup. When Maverick's tongue hung out and his head drooped, we returned home and plodded up the steps to the back door.

"Maybe we'll try again tonight after work, my friend, but you'd be miserable continuing our walk now. I'd be overheated and sweaty, and I've got to get ready for my new job."

Maverick didn't understand the words, but he understood the intent. His ears flopped. He sauntered across the kitchen and slumped onto his cushiony bed. With his chin on his paws, blinking his big brown eyes, he sulked, and I nearly caved to his accusatory glances.

"I want to be early today." I sat next to him for a few minutes and massaged his jaw. He closed his eyes, leaning into my fingers, and I heard what sounded like a purr of approval. Heaven forbid.

I changed into my uniform, whipped up a peanut butter and banana sandwich, and nervously nibbled it on my drive to Shady Oaks.

Wavering vapors rose from the silver sheen of water gleaming on the asphalt as I pulled into a parking space. I popped the last of my lunch into my mouth before jogging to the club. Galen burst out the double doors, stepping up to the welcome lectern with authority, the crisp creases on his shirt and pants cutting through the thick air.

"Good to know they allow you to wait inside when the temperature or humidity becomes unbearable."

"Only when we don't have patrons waiting which, glad to say, is rare. What can I do for you today, Ms. Wilk?"

"I'm beginning my new job as a beverage cart attendant."

He whistled as he ran his finger down his list of names to admit and stopped. "There you are. BTO."

I had no idea what he meant, and he knew it.

"Big time operator." His shoulders shook as he laughed.

I took a step toward the doors but stopped in my tracks. So much had happened, I nearly forgot about my late-night visitor. "Galen, someone came by last evening and gave the impression they knew you. They said you told them they could trust me. Whoever it was disappeared before they could introduce themselves. You wouldn't happen to know who called on me, would you?"

I thought I detected a glimmer of recognition in his eyes before he furrowed his brow and said, "Can't say as I do, Ms. Wilk." He looked like he had something else to say. "But I'll sure ask around."

Our successful year in mock trial had given my students an edge—they had learned how to slip into character and act like another person at will. I couldn't be sure if Galen honestly didn't know, or if he was playing a role and making up his answer.

I stared into his innocent looking face, hoping he'd crack, but I didn't have a chance. He merely mirrored my stare until I gave in, and he escorted me through the door.

The comfortable indoor environment quickly wicked away the perspiration beginning to bead on my forehead and down my back. I made my way through the comfortable atrium to the human relations office, where I stood in front of the desk and frowned. Lark was nowhere to be seen. Leaning back in her chair sat a young man with curly blond hair, wearing a blue polo shirt with the badge pinned to his chest. Winslow. He'd planted his size twelve black and tan Wolf and Shepherds, Jane's preferred crossover trainer shoe brand, atop a stack of papers. With his eyes closed, his head bounced and the pencils in his hands played rhythmic air drums on his knees, accompanying music only he heard through his earbuds.

"Excuse me," I said cheerily, and waved my hands in front of his face, hoping the air movement might battle through. I said more loudly, "Excuse me."

Lark strode in from behind one of the partitions. She shoved his feet off the desk, and papers flew in every direction. His green eyes flared. At the same time, he said, "Hey, what's that for?" she said, "Welcome, Katie." She pointed to Winslow's ears. He wiggled the device free with as little motion as possible. "Pick those up." He shuffled the scattered pages into an untidy stack, and as he completed his task, she said, "Katie, meet Winslow."

"Hello, Winslow." He would not ruin my second first day this week.

"Whatever," was his response, avoiding my outstretched hand, and I self-consciously checked under my nails for grime, noticing Winslow casually pull the top sheet off the pile, fold the page of red figures and stuff it into his rear pocket.

"If you two step this way, we can go through orientation. The rain stopped, but the temperature is rising, and we absolutely will deploy the beverage carts today." Lark tented her hands in an appeal and sent up a silent prayer before seating us at a large table in a conference room and began her spiel.

"Our beverage carts serve a variety of alcoholic and non-alcoholic drinks, focusing on refreshment and hydration. Common selections include water, sodas, juice, iced tea, coffee, lemonade, Arnold Palmers, and sports drinks. In addition, we offer canned cocktails and wine, but our best sellers include our domestic and imported beers. We want to keep golfers refreshed throughout the day. We also supply granola bars, pretzels, and packages of nuts, which may or may not lead to more beverage sales. The carts feature spacious coolers and shelving for transporting and storing beverages and provisions. Under the counter, you'll find tablecloths, napkins, and extra cleaning supplies.

"The carts are electric so make sure you plug them in at the end of your shift. They are built with a fully enclosed cab for all-weather use. You'll have a register furnished with minimal ones and fives …" Winslow waved his hand. "Yes?"

"Do we accept cards?"

"All major credit and debit cards are accepted, of course, and the card reader is built into the register. But we are trying to maintain a sense of decorum. Some of our patrons do not want to confirm their whereabouts with a digital trail. As I was saying, you'll need to balance your till when you turn it in to me at the end of your shift. If you're short, you'll make up the difference."

"What if we're long?"

"Put that in your tip jar."

Tips? The gig sounded better and better. Of course, with Byron's death still so fresh, it couldn't have gotten any worse.

Winslow smirked and turned to me. "You want to look good for tips, so you should fix your shirt by sticking on these tabs." He turned up his stiff collar, and the crisp collar points had added to his neatness factor. "However." His eyes traveled from my face to my feet. He pointed his forefinger and conjured a circle. "Some things can't be helped."

Lark drew a deep breath. "The golfers have access to a QR code. They can send a request, call for delivery, or step up to the cart. You are permitted to drive only on the cart paths, and do so in reverse order, eighteen to one, so they can see you coming. Visibility is paramount." She handed us each a key. "Usually, you'll pick up your cart in the storage shed—"

Winslow sneered and said, "Ye old barn."

Lark shook her head and continued, "Today they're parked near the putting green and are ready to roll. Katie, you can take the front nine. Winslow, you can—"

"Nope. I get the front nine or I'm telling Cousin Anne."

He didn't look anything like Cousin Anne but certainly acted like another entitled Murphy.

FIFTEEN

Golfers teed off in rapid succession from all holes on the course at the same time to practice for the weekend open tournament. Lark had called it a shotgun start. The fundraising competition would benefit Columbia's homeless shelter, but the contenders had their sights set on the twenty-four-inch trophy. Everyone seemed to be in good spirits, and the singles in my tip jar inched toward the top.

Hydration was a priority, and I had to refill my water bottle reservoir twice. The humidity had dissipated, and I only really noticed the heat as I balanced my till when the number of golfers decreased. Sadly, my shift wasn't as ready to end as I was.

Lark called. "Katie, you weren't scheduled to work past seven, but could you work for another hour? I won't hold it against you if you aren't able to stay. Winslow initially begged to work the hours, but he's already taken off. I don't know what I'm going to do with him."

"I take it he has connections."

Lark sighed. "Yes. He's related to the Murphys and needs to be trained in all areas of Shady Oaks, beginning with the beverage cart. He's not all bad, but sometimes requires a special touch."

That explained a fair amount of his attitude.

"Sure. My evening plan is to walk my dog, and maybe it will be cooler for our stroll an hour later."

"Galen has nothing but good things to say about your canine. Maverick, isn't it?"

"Maverick, yes." All my students loved Maverick. Although he still jumped up on occasion, could bark obnoxiously, and scarfed food from any unwatched serving platter, he could be incredible when he put his mind to it. Suddenly I missed him and had to tamp down my vexation at having to stay late, but business was winding down, and what could happen in an hour?

"Thanks, Katie."

In the time remaining, I straightened the cans and bottles, noting my depleted resources. What remained of the snacks—one lone bag of peanuts—dangled from the brackets like forbidden fruit. The sales register balanced (I would've been crushed and teased mercilessly had it not.). The antiseptic counter spray left it glossy and smelling slightly of lemon. At eight o'clock on the dot, I drove the cart to the stable as fast as I dared through clouds of winged bugs looking for their evening meal. After plugging the cart into its socket to recharge came the chore of restocking the supplies.

I hefted a cumbersome case of water and grunted, con-centrating so hard I almost didn't notice the air shift when a door opened until something seemed to slide across the counter on the other side of the cart. I heard a clatter and used my knee to shove the case back in place on the stack, then snuck around the cart to check out the source of the noise.

The snack rack rested on the ground, empty. In the corner of my eye, I caught the silhouette of a curly-haired person hastily exiting the rear of the stable, pulling the door closed. *Winslow?* I gazed at my tip jar, and riled up, rushed after the thief, yanking on the door to blinding brightness. The direct sunlight caused me to cover my eyes, and I couldn't see anything.

I returned to the cart, disbelieving, angry, and sad all at once, and found Lark impatiently waiting for my receipts and my take on the day.

"You don't look happy," she said.

"Someone waltzed in and pinched my tip money and my remaining bag of nuts."

"Are you sure?" Lark cocked her head, and her bottom lip protruded. "Maybe our resident ghost visited again." She forced a laugh and extended her hand for my till. "I'm sure with your background, every penny will be accounted for." She wrinkled her brow. "Aside from the last few minutes, did you have a positive experience? Will you be back tomorrow?"

Knowing I needed to up my vigilance, keep my eyes on my cart at all times, and leave nothing unattended, I would be ready should the thief try again. I still earned my hourly wage, and the steep golf fees were included in the benefits. "Yes, I'll be back. But I can't stay late tomorrow," I added. "I have plans." I didn't know what they were yet, but something would come up.

"Not a problem. Winslow's not on the roster, and the

replacement is much more reliable. Please lock up when you leave. And don't worry. The bag of nuts will only cost you $2.00. You can make it up tomorrow."

Having to pay for the stolen nuts stupefied me, but Lark vanished before I could compose a cool-headed retort. There had been no indication I'd be required to reimburse the club for the money lost in the pilfering from our carts. It could have been worse, and I'd be ready next time.

A flashy red car was parked next to mine, and I glanced inside as I passed. The water bottle was gone. Maybe it was never there? Maybe it was a different car? I itched to find out who belonged to the fancy wheels, but I kind of promised not to nose around, so I got into the front seat of my car, one of a dozen or so vehicles remaining at this end of the lot, and drummed my fingers on the steering wheel. I would not allow the cause of Byron's death to be relegated to the unknown, but to be honest, I reminded myself I'd accepted the job so I could golf with Jane. I would do what I had to do. And keep an eagle eye on everyone at Shady Oaks.

I pulled into the driveway, and the two faces glued to my kitchen window made me smile so wide my cheeks hurt. Maverick stood on his hind legs. His paws rested on the sill next to Dad. I read anticipation in Maverick, but frowned at the anxiety I saw in Dad, and hustled inside.

"Dad? Everything okay?"

"I think so. Ida and I had supper at Thai Fyre."

"I love their food." Dad's face scrunched as if searching his memory for an appropriate response. "Dad?" He turned his eyes toward me in surprise. The vacant look, reminiscent of some of the time he'd spent in rehab after the shooting, made my heart race. Worried his medical issues had resurfaced, I formulated the most innocuous question I could come up with, requiring an easy answer. "Do you have any leftovers?"

"What?" He blinked himself awake. "Your pad Thai is in the fridge." He reminded me of a kid caught raiding the cookie jar. He said carefully, controlling his feelings, "Did you know ZaZa has a new friend?"

I confiscated the precious white carton from the third shelf, realizing I had to be gentle. "Yes, I did."

Dad's eyes darkened. "I didn't think I'd ever see him again." He gathered me close, and I buried my head in his chest. His arms held me tightly. "Stay away from him," he said quietly as he rested his chin on the top of my head.

"Always. Don't worry, Dad." I leaned away so I could examine his face. "He could have changed."

Dad snorted his disbelief and rocked me gently from side to side, but before our mood grew more maudlin, the door to Ida's apartment flew open and Jane waltzed in with grace and pizzazz, humming a tune, kicking and tap-dancing.

She finished gliding across the floor and sighed. "It's been too long since I've seen *Carefree*. It's one of my favorite Fred Astaire movies. He incorporated his love of golf in his choreography and, sorry to say, Katie, could kick a ball with more distance and accuracy than you can hit it." Her smile faded as she read our faces. "What's going on?"

Dad pasted on a smile. My chin dropped, and I focused on Jane, taking in the elegant white feather gown we'd picked up from Tempest. Jane was radiant.

She laughed at our gawking faces. "What do you think?"

If I'd worn those feathers, I'd have looked like an ugly duckling, but my friend assumed the graceful lines and proud bearing of a beautiful swan. Enormous soft clips pinched handfuls of fabric at her shoulders, back, and sides, cinching the material skintight. She pirouetted and struck a Marilyn

Monroe pose. Jane drew all my attention, and I hadn't even seen Ida enter and skirt the room. I jumped when I heard the raucous applause next to me and looked down to find my landlady beaming.

Dad and I joined in the clapping. Maverick rose from his sphinx position and barked.

"Isn't she lovely?" said Ida. Her question was met with a loud rap at the back door, which I should have expected after Maverick's vocalization.

"Expecting anyone?" Ida asked, getting shrugs from around the room.

Dad got a nod from me before he opened the door.

SIXTEEN

Officer Ronnie Christianson leaned forward, taking up as much of the landing at the top of the steps as possible. "Mr. Wilk, I hope I'm not imposing. Mind if I come in?"

Dad backed up, allowing Ronnie to enter. As I wove my fingers around Maverick's collar to keep him stationary so he wouldn't put Ronnie on edge, I heard our adjoining door snick closed. Ida and Jane had vanished without so much as a nod.

Dad pasted on a smile and asked, "Officer Christianson, what do you need?"

"Could you give Katie and me some privacy, Mr. Wilk?"

I found it difficult to swallow. "I want my dad to stay. I can do that, can't I?"

Ronnie shrugged and held out a hand to lead us to the

table as if he owned the place. I wouldn't have wanted his job and the headaches that went with it, but he could have been more genial. Dad and I took two chairs next to each other, and Ronnie installed himself in the seat closest to me.

"I'm going to record this interview." It wasn't a request. He set his phone on the table and tapped a key. "Katie and Harry Wilk, 3141 North Maple Street."

When Dad crossed his arms, leaned back in his chair, and said, "Fire away," I almost choked.

"I'm here in an official capacity. We're investigating the suspicious death of Barclay Byron." He tilted his head and watched my reaction. "You don't look surprised, Katie," he sneered. "You were one of the last people to see Barclay Byron alive. How well did you know the vic?"

His tone of voice made me uncomfortable. Ronnie would like nothing better than to find me guilty of something—littering, jaywalking, tampering with evidence, withholding information—anything. I took a deep breath. "Jane's a … Jane Mackey's a golfer and wanted a partner, but I didn't know the first thing about it, so she purchased a lesson package for my birthday. Barclay Byron was one of the golf pros at the club, and he got stuck with me."

Keep it short. Just answer the question asked. Don't provide additional information not specifically asked for. I took the words our attorney friend Dorene Dvorak always offered under advisement.

Ronnie scribbled some notes. "Did he do a good job?"

"That remains to be seen, but I appreciated his effort. I learned enough so I won't entirely embarrass myself or Jane on the course. What happened to Mr. Byron?" I heard Dorene's voice telling me I talked too much.

He ignored my question. "What will you do now?" His writing instrument tapped the notebook.

"There's another golf pro at the club. She offered to complete my instructions."

"Who's that?"

"Her name in Genevieve. I don't know her last name, but she goes by Ginny."

"Did the two pros get along? Large egos can get in the way of a professional working relationship."

I wondered for a moment about the voices Jane and I had overheard. "I really couldn't say."

He noticed my hesitation. "Couldn't or wouldn't?"

"Officer Christianson, Ronnie, what do you want to know?"

"Did you know anyone with a grudge, or know of someone he rubbed the wrong way? Did you see or hear a person making a threat?"

"I didn't pay much attention to what happened outside of my minimal interactions with Mr. Byron, and I only had two lessons." I wouldn't do Ronnie's work for him. "I told Chief West everything I heard. That did not include any threats exactly."

"One of the witnesses indicated you had words."

"What witness?" I asked, but Ronnie ignored my question. Dad said, "What kind of words?"

"You seemed flustered." Ronnie enjoyed my irritation. "Did he make a pass at you?"

"I fluster easily, and no. He didn't make a pass at me." *Although some of Byron's statements could have been taken more than one way.* "At the end of my lesson, I needed to join Jane and Ida in evaluating the tasting menu, so I was in a hurry." Fewer words, I reminded myself. "Did your witness also indicate I was with at least one other person the entire morning?" My lips formed a hard line, and my ears steamed.

"Except during your lesson." He let the statement hang.

"Obviously, but we were in plain sight the entire time." My face warmed uncomfortably.

"Again, except when he gave you a tour of the garden."

"But Mr. Byron met a few people after my lesson. There's that Dennis guy for sure. And you can check with Reneé in catering, or Ida, or Jane." My voice rose. "I didn't have the time or reason to do anything to Barclay Byron." When my breath came fast and furious, I upbraided myself. I hadn't listened to my own advice. I intentionally lowered my shoulders. "So, was Barclay Byron's death accidental, suicide, or homicide? Maybe if you shared how Byron died, I could help you put together a timeline."

I shouldn't have said, *help you*. He wouldn't ask for my help if I held the last bottle of water in the caravan after five days lost in the Sahara Desert. His stoic expression gave nothing away. He blinked twice, closed his notebook, and picked up his phone. "That will be all for now. We'd like you to stay in Columbia in case we have additional questions, but you are not bound to do so. However, should you choose to head out for one reason or another, we'd appreciate a heads-up."

"No problem." I led him to the exit, opened it, and after he passed through, I secured the lock with a satisfying snap. I sagged against the heavy oak door, causing Dad to rush over to me.

"What's wrong, Katie?"

"Nothing, Dad." My chin fell to my chest, and I forced my eyes closed to staunch the tears from falling. "I'm overwhelmed." Boring had never looked so good. I'd never complain about doing nothing again.

A spine-tingling squeak made me search for the source. *Ida.*

She peeked around her door. "Is he gone?"

"Yes, Ida, the police officer is gone. Why did you take off so suddenly?" Dad quipped.

"You remember, a long time ago, he was one of my piano students, and we never got along well after I encouraged him to quit." She gazed at Maverick. "Actually, I don't believe he ever forgave me when I told him he would probably do better in football, which he never played. I didn't want to add to the tension in the room."

"Ida, you can provide an alibi for me, right?"

"From the moment you entered the tasting suite, and Reneé is an excellent record keeper. She needed to confirm the time the food left the heat source, when it was delivered, and indicate the critique of our choices."

Jane bounded in next to Ida. "And we went directly to the pro shop without so much as a pit stop. Galen checked off the time we entered the club, and Ginny gave us a tee time after which we were in plain sight of any number of individuals, including Anne. No worries, Katie."

Ida sighed. "It's only rumor, mind you, but Barclay had the reputation for being somewhat of a rake. There could have been quite a few people who had issues with him if he was indeed the victim of foul play. I suppose Amanda wants to look at all the suspects, but Ronnie definitely tried to rattle your cage."

I gave her the side eye. "How do you know that?"

Ida blushed.

Jane said brightly, "We listened at the keyhole."

After about thirty seconds of complete silence, it was as if we'd turned a page. We all spoke at the same time.

"It's late," Dad said. "I think we call it a night."

Ida crossed her arms. "I made sticky cake, and I think—"

When Dad's comment registered, she glared at him.

Jane spun in her white dancing frock, gossamer feathers encircling her, beads and sequins glistening under the lights. "What do you think?" she asked for a second time.

Maverick stood and barked, and this time I paid attention. Dreading a return visit from Officer Christianson, Dad quickly entered his bedroom and closed the door. Ida and Jane disappeared into Ida's apartment, and soon, I heard piano notes vibrate through the wall.

SEVENTEEN

My fingers turned the knob as delicately as a safecracker, and just before completing the rotation, I lifted the edge of the curtain and peered through the glass. It paid to be careful. However, I saw nothing but the orange and pink glow of the setting sun stretching across the horizon behind the leafy trees. I leaned forward to get a better angle and looked from side to side, examining the lengthening shadows. Still nothing. Maverick gave a solitary woof and nudged my hip. I could almost hear him say, 'Open the door already.'

The lock clicked when I finished turning the knob. Maverick prodded the crack wider with his snout and waggled his backside, wriggling through the opening. Our three-year-old neighbor, Emma, beamed up at me through the face-washing she received. "Oh, Maverick," she squealed with an infectious giggle.

Her mother stood to the side on the lawn watching the exchange, smiling contritely. "I'm sorry it's so late. She said she needed doggie time and then she'd take her bath. I hope it's okay."

"It's always okay." I knelt down to be eye level with Emma. "Tell him to sit."

"Maverick," she said in her high-pitched but most authoritative voice. "Sit." She raised her open hand, palm up, the sign we'd practiced exhaustively. He sat, tongue hanging out, and leaned in to get every one of the small rubs her tiny hands furnished. "Good boy," she added.

After a moment, I led the two of them to the lawn where, for the next ten minutes, Emma threw the lime green tennis ball with all her might, and Maverick retrieved it, laid it at her feet, and held his position until she released him with an imperious *fetch,* something I'd not yet mastered. I watched admiringly and hoped I'd learn her trick.

"Thanks for letting us barge in, Katie. Adam is so good with her, and when he's on the road, she's so out of sorts she rules the roost. I've been trying to get her ready for bed since seven-thirty."

I tried not to look surprised. "You're welcome anytime. She's the first friend Maverick made all by himself."

Tears sprang to Pamela's eyes. "And he saved her life."

I choked up too.

"He has an uncanny ability to make good people better and bad people cringe," she said, wiping her eyes.

Uncharitable thoughts niggled behind my plastic grin.

I should've let him have his way with Ronnie.

"Emma, honey, it's time to say goodnight, and tell Katie thank you."

Emma cupped what little she could of Maverick's black

furry face in her hands and kissed him on the nose. He licked her face in return. "I'll be back tomorrow." Her face squinched in consternation. "If that's okay with you, Katie?"

"Of course it's okay. Have a fun bath and a good night's sleep."

"Thank you." Emma yawned. Her mother swung her up onto her hip. Emma's head drooped, and she waved languidly.

"Nice job, Maverick. I should pay better attention to what you're telling me. Sorry. I will remember to trust my dog." I scratched one of the few places on his backside he couldn't reach, and he squirmed, inching closer. "And by the way, CJ wants to get you out for a practice run with Renegade. Sound good? He seems to believe you have promise as a search and rescue canine." I think Maverick rolled his eyes. He went way beyond the promise of being a good search and rescue canine and had all the attributes necessary for success. He was a natural. "Fine, but *I* really need the practice," I said as we reentered the kitchen. "We'll figure out a time."

Dad had a guilty look on his face. The mere whiff of sweets had drawn him from his chamber. He'd joined Ida and Jane around the table, chowing down on an ooey, gooey treat. The fourth place was set with a large serving of the decadent dessert and a perfect, semi-circular scoop of ice cream. The irresistible masterpiece was topped with a generous sprinkling of freshly grated chocolate curls. Minutes later, when the clink of the utensils slowed, and I stopped to fully enjoy a swallow, there was another rap at the door.

"Now who?" Dad shoved away from the table. He painstakingly identified the visitors, peeking around the blinds, grinned, and said, "I don't know how they do it, but they always turn up for Ida's food." He whisked the door wide.

Drew marched inside and held aloft a bottle of wine. "I

come bearing a gift to enhance your dining experience." He fluttered his left hand beneath his neckwear, and it lit up with hearts.

Pete, on the other hand, smiled cautiously. He'd known Ida his entire life and she treated him like a son with both affirmations and disapprovals as she saw fit. "We all know Ida's desserts are unparalleled, and Jane's text made us drool."

Three pairs of eyes lasered in on Jane, who blushed a becoming shade of pink.

Dad grabbed another two chairs and nodded his approval of the forty-year-old Portuguese tawny port.

Ida scurried about the small space, dishing out two additional substantial servings and relishing the attention her food created. Jane poured six small glasses from the bottle, shaking out the very last drop.

Sated, I recounted the day, voicing my opinion about the death of Byron, and observed the surreptitious glances Drew and Pete gave each other. "What?"

Drew's head moved from side to side. "Barclay Byron did not die of natural causes."

Pete gave Drew a scathing gaze and said, "Byron didn't drown, nor did he die from a blow to his head, but Amanda said you tipped her off to a host of possibilities. I'm still running tests, but it could be an accident, or suicide, or death at the hands of another."

"Unfortunately," Drew said, "I don't believe you'll be able to get definitive results before the tournament this weekend. I hope it won't negatively affect the bottom line."

"Just the opposite. I think it's been a magnet for ghoulish curiosity seekers," Jane said. "As stipulated in the original Murphy family trust, in the pursuit of raising funds for a local need, the course is open to nonmembers. There were only two foursome spots left today, and I'll have you know, I weathered totally inappropriate overtures from an obnoxious man to sign up."

Drew's eyes glinted a fiery blue. "Who was it? Let me at him."

"Calm down. He's an intern or something." Jane waved a dismissive hand. "I put him in his place, and he won't try those words on anyone else. Now I'm recruiting. Somebody here better want to golf with me."

"I'm unavailable," Ida said with a sense of longing. "I've been stationed at the registration desk since Casimer's law firm first sponsored the tourney two decades ago." Her eyes lost focus when she spoke of the love of her life, Casimer Clemashevski. "He thoroughly enjoyed playing every Thursday afternoon, and I loved when I could be with him."

No one spoke for a moment. I could feel the churning thoughts behind the eyes of the men as they considered options, and I couldn't decide if they were ready to join Jane or not. "I would," I said, "but I'm scheduled to work the beverage cart Friday, Saturday, and Sunday."

"Katie, the tournament would've been your first practical exam, proof you can hold a club," Jane wailed.

That was all the spurring everyone needed. "I'm in," said Drew.

"I would love to partner up, Jane, but it's been way too long since the last time I was on a golf course. I'm sure I'll bring down any average," said Pete, laughing. "If you're able to find someone else, I won't be disappointed."

"I'll take you up on the offer, Pete. I don't know who else I can find this late in the game." She batted her beautiful brown eyes at Dad. "Harry, I need a strategist with strength and distance here," Jane pleaded.

Dad's head dropped back as if he contemplated a task so

monumental as to be life altering. When his ceiling-reading ceased, he tipped his head forward and said, "I've waited my entire existence for an offer I can't refuse. Of course, I'll be there. And, Jane, rest assured, I'll take care of the deficit."

I didn't know if that meant he'd increase or decrease the total, but he looked as happy as I'd ever seen him.

"But you need to know, although I'm fairly consistent when I putt into a goblet on the kitchen floor—"

"What?" I stared at this man sharing secrets I should've been aware of.

"It's been a considerably long time. Katie was a baby—"

"That's definitely been a long time. Eons," hooted Drew, who received a gentle swat from his fiancée.

Jane and I cleaned up the dishes, and I grilled her about her unpleasant encounter when she registered. "What did the guy say?"

"I wasn't in the mood for suggestive comments. I told him I'd report him if he continued. I had the impression, he wasn't worried, but he backed off."

"What did he look like?"

"Conceited, blond, stuck on himself, green-eyed—"

"Sounds like Winslow."

"That's the name. He'd better be careful not to get in my face again. I might need to tweak his ear."

Dad took himself off to see the sandman. Ida pulled out five decks of cards, but Pete's preoccupation with the numerous texts pinging his phone cut short our game night. He didn't share what pulled him away, but that didn't stop me from wondering if it had to do with Barclay Byron's death.

EIGHTEEN

In the morning, Maverick knew my head was elsewhere and dropped his leash in my lap. We raced around the wildlife protection area before I packed a sandwich for lunch and headed to Shady Oaks. Ginny ostensibly agreed to assume the role of my golf instructor, but we hadn't finalized a time. I hoped I'd get ahead of the crowd. The temperature already hovered at seventy-two, but Ginny predicted serious golfers would take over the course in order to determine the lay of the landscape and improve their chances at winning the coveted title when the tournament started.

Collecting my clubs, I texted Jane.

Your golf hardware is in my trunk

Thanks, but I won't need it until tomorrow.

Galen bowed when I approached the welcome podium.

"Beeauuutiful day, Ms. Wilk. Genevieve said to send you on down if you arrived before nine-thirty. Her earliest lesson is scheduled an hour later." He took a deep breath. "You'll progress nicely at this rate. Barclay Byron will be missed, but Genevieve has five years of experience and several titles to her name. She'll do right by you."

"Are you rehearsing your lines?"

"Yup, these are the words for today, and I figured you wouldn't be too upset if I got them wrong. How'd I do?"

"I never would have known you had a script. What pointers can you provide a beginning golfer?"

"Keep your eye on the ball."

"Ms. Mackey said the same thing." I hiked the golf bag higher on my shoulder.

"Confirmation great minds think alike, I'd say, wouldn't you? You know the way. Have a fabulous day."

In preparing for the tourney, extra frenetic activity filled the usually quiet vestibule. Lark held her clipboard close to her chest with one hand and directed custodial services with the other. The waitstaff peered through the doorway, at the edge of her peripheral vision, out of her line of sight, easily overlooked, rumbling.

I approached slowly and tapped her shoulder. She spun around and huffed. "Katie. You're early for your shift."

"I came for a golf lesson if Ginny has time, but you're awfully busy this morning. Is there anything I can help with?"

She blew loose strands of hair from her face. "Thank you. I think we're covered now." She calmed as she spoke the words, as if reassuring herself of the truth.

"What happened? More ghosts?" I chided.

Her eyes gleamed, and it seemed she waged a discreet discussion with herself. "Nothing you need to worry about."

My attire—sharply creased khakis and blue polo with

newly attached collar tabs and Shady Oaks emblazoned across the back—allowed me to cut through the throng of workmen, unchecked. On my way to the pro shop, I overheard one of them punctuating his words in sync with his hammering.

"Anytime anything goes missing or is misplaced, the ghost is given credit. But Chef Antoine says he's been taking inventory at the end of each evening, and he swears he's missing a pound of his special gold star blend of ground brisket, chuck, and short rib. Expensive stuff, I'll admit." He held out his hand like a surgeon awaiting a scalpel. "Needle-nose pliers," he barked. When he finished using the tool, he smashed it precisely into the palm of a receiving hand. "Personally, I wouldn't have worried about the burgers, but he's an over-the-top temperamental artiste, and they can't afford to lose another important cog in the ever-revolving wheels of Shady Oaks."

He fanned the ceiling, pointing out his workmanship to an eager-to-learn audience of youthful summer-hires. "This is all preemptive. We've installed three video cameras you should be unable to detect because the president of the club wanted them to go unnoticed in order to catch the culprit responsible for the thefts. I'm also hoping, if they're noticed, they'll serve as a deterrent." He winked.

The staff was busily engaged in preparing the building for the weekend, so I slipped down the hall, wondering about the inordinate focus on a pound of specialty ground meat.

The open pro shop door was a welcoming overture. Ginny looked up from where she knelt in front of the display, straightening sleeves of golf balls. "I was hoping you'd come today." She glanced at her watch. "I have just enough time if you'd like one of your lessons now.

"That would be ideal. Thanks."

"How many lessons were you able to complete before …" She momentarily faltered, and so did I.

"Two. We spent one day on the driving range, but according to Byron, I'm a champion putter." I waited a moment before she allowed a laugh to erupt.

"Let's head out. I'm all yours for an hour. Do you have a specific area of the sport you'd like to pursue?"

"I haven't used the chipping or pitching wedges, but I'll take advantage of any pointers you can give me during practice on the driving range, if that's okay with you. Byron declared I could use the most help there."

"Sure." Ginny strapped my clubs on the back of a cart. She took the driver's seat, and I slid in alongside her. "Katie," she said hesitantly, as we rolled past hole one. "You don't happen to know if the police impounded Barclay's clubs as evidence, do you?"

"You mean the iron near the pond?"

"No, his entire set."

Ginny watched me intently, and I recalled the scene around his body. "I don't remember seeing his bag near the water. I think I would have. He boasted about having them; they were so important."

"He owned one club, but the rest were part of a demonstration bundle. The company encouraged Barclay to use them to show off their wares during the tournament to prospective buyers." The corners of her mouth turned down. "The set belonged to the club. I hoped we'd be able to recover it, and the corporate sponsorship might continue, but I can't find the clubs anywhere."

We came to a jarring halt next to the driving range, and she laughed, but it seemed forced. "The Shady Oaks' ghost has struck again."

"The ghost," I repeated.

Ginny hauled a large bucket of balls to my small patch of sod, and I set up my tees. I let Byron's instructions wash over me, but Ginny's words of wisdom helped me straighten half my drives, and a few swings made satisfying sounds, connecting solidly.

Closing in on the end of my lesson, Ginny said, "There's hope for you. My next client will be ready shortly, but feel free to stay as long as you'd like."

"I'll take a few more swipes at my little white nemesis and finish up before I have to get ready for work. Your instruction has been very productive."

A small smile graced her lips. "The tournament events begin tomorrow at nine, but I never know what to expect. Why don't you check tomorrow morning?"

"I'll be there."

Without Ginny's step-by-step instructions, my next drive flew high to the right and slammed into the same tree for the umpteenth time. I thought I could see the dent from the ground and almost abandoned my practice until I realized Jane said we could fix my repetitive slice. Instead, I concentrated on Ginny's advice and the universal admonition to keep my eye on the ball. I felt the satisfactory wallop for another six drives and didn't want to move from the spot lest I alter my stance and change my luck, but I ran out of little white targets.

Minutes later, Ginny returned to the driving range with a portly red-haired man in a tartan kilt and tam, vociferously explaining why everyone should appreciate his authenticity. Ginny smiled graciously and nodded but avoided looking at me. I don't think we could have kept it together. I stifled a chuckle at the sight and packed up so he wouldn't catch my attitude, and I wouldn't catch a lecture.

With more than an hour to go before my shift, killing time by walking the course wouldn't look odd, and I could better familiarize myself with the surroundings. Dressed in my uniform, I unobtrusively walked the path and blended in. I pulled some weeds and picked up a few pieces of trash, depositing them in the garbage receptacle and intentionally avoiding the pond where we found Byron, but my tour only ate up twenty minutes.

My cart checked out, appropriately outfitted with snacks and beverages, shelves and drawers bulging. I located fresh stores of supplies I'd need to refill my cart later. Lark would issue the till fifteen minutes before my shift began, so I still had nothing to do.

I freely took stock of the lovely surroundings. Thirty feet off the pavement through the rough sat a heavy wooden bench, beckoning from under a willow tree. A bronze plaque attached to the back indicated a dedication of appreciation to the Murphy family.

I sat and stared at my phone, willing it to ring or buzz and absentmindedly swiped through the screens, looking for ideas. I alighted on geocaching, a method of constructively wasting time, executing a technological scavenger hunt I often did with my students. Opening the app, it navigated to the first stage of the nearest multi-cache ranking medium in difficulty, and I wished it hadn't.

NINETEEN

A multi-cache involves at least one stage beyond locating the initial coordinates, requiring the searcher to locate a physical container with a log sheet to sign or completing a task in a virtual quest. The name usually gave a small hint. Naturally, the appellation, Hole In One, had me initially searching for a golf-related cache, but the thick tree cover interfered with my GPS. The first stage provided information to lead to the next, but I came up empty, and I needed to get to work.

"We're not having luck with our beverage cart people. You're on your own today, Katie. Do as well as you can." Lark supplied my till, and after meticulously counting the cash, I signed it out and marched over to the garage to pick up my cart, scarfing down my now dry-as-dust lunch, and concluding even a peanut butter sandwich might be beyond my culinary expertise.

The weighty door slid along the rollers, and the man with his back to me startled at the noise. Otherwise, I felt certain I'd have found him tampering with the contents of my cart—again. The guilty look on his face made my blood boil, especially if he'd been the one to swipe the tips from my jar and the last bag of nuts, but I wouldn't confront him without solid evidence

"Can I help you, Winslow? I didn't think you were scheduled to work today."

"Absolutely not. I'm golfing," he said, adjusting the creases in his chinos. He combed his fingers through his curly hair and shook it like a horse's mane. "But you seemed to do well enough the other day. I thought I could learn something from the way you organized your products."

There are so many ways to hang snack bags, I thought sarcastically.

"Today looks better weather-wise, so it'll be another variable in the test," I said. "I'll let you know how I do. Are you working tomorrow?"

"Yes." He raised his chin, and although he looked like he had some parting words, he kept his remarks to himself and marched from the garage.

As instructed, I began at the eighteenth hole and drove slowly past three holes before encountering my first customers.

"Gin and tonic for me," said a tall, thin man with a furrowed brow. He flopped a hank of black hair away from his face and tossed a club from one hand to the other, juggling.

"It won't make you golf any better, Barta, but it might make the loss easier to swallow. I'll take a Bloody Mary with a chaser," said a man with broad shoulders, plaid pants, a red golf shirt, and tasseled brown loafers.

Bloody Marys sold well, but I nibbled my lip searching the labels for something to go with it.

"That's a can of Coors, missy. Bert's a two-fisted drinker." The third man had a merry twinkle in his eye. "I'll have a bottle of water. Someone has to be able to keep an accurate score."

"That certainly isn't you, Sharkey." The playful banter had a competitive undercurrent. "He tends to lose a few strokes here and there. I'll take a diet cola." The tight hold the man with the shiny bald head had on his cash caught me off guard. I tugged, thinking it was a test. "You're new, little lady. What do we call you?" I felt my face redden.

"You can call her Ms. Wilk, Curly, and put me down for a three." Winslow sauntered up the cart path with a putter over his shoulder. "Your wife's waiting in the clubhouse with the other spouses to play bridge," he said sardonically.

The money slipped easily from Curly's fingers. "I can't play bridge well, but I guess we'd better finish up."

The other three men stuffed my tip jar and loaded onto their carts. As Winslow checked over my stock, I asked, "Why aren't you golfing in the tournament tomorrow?"

He scoffed. "I only play when there's real money on the line." He turned and followed the foursome.

Early afternoon would not be my time to drink a cocktail, but I couldn't complain. The sun and humidity made the players thirsty, and I provided hydration. With the continuous line of partakers, I fortunately had to empty my tip jar—twice—which meant I'd be able to put a down payment on a golf club of my own—maybe—unless I allowed Jane a chance to choose it.

The heat of the mid-afternoon slowed the pace, and

because I parked near the location of the geocache, I took a break and continued my search, rereading the hint, 'Look up.'

I didn't know how I missed it the first time. Nestled below the majestic, full crown of vivid green leaves, in the crook of a young maple tree, I found the hole in one, an Ace of Clubs, encased in a quarter inch of resin. The connection between the title and the cache was a little obscure, but numbers on the back confirmed the find. I snapped a photo, listing the follow-up coordinates for latitude and longitude, and replaced the clue, intending to investigate the cache further when time permitted.

A breeze blew in. The number of participants increased and made the rest of my time fly by. But the crowd dwindled to nothing by five, and at six, Lark called me in. "It appears they're saving their finesse for the important play tomorrow. If we get any more golfers needing a beverage, they can get it from the bar inside." Lark took my till. "It balanced again, Katie, and you've paid for the nuts. You're free to leave. See you tomorrow."

Maverick hadn't anticipated my returning home so early. His head popped up, and caught red-handed or rather black-pawed, he jumped from the kitchen table as I drove onto my parking pad.

Dad hadn't expected me either. If I hadn't known better, I'd have guessed the creases on his face and his hair, flat on one side, indicated he'd been taking a nap. "Sorry, hon, I'm trying a new recipe for a hot dish. I just put it in the oven, and it won't be ready until seven."

"That's okay. It beats the cup of canned soup I'd planned. I can wait," I said, spraying the tabletop and wiping away the paw prints with the lemon-scented cleansing foam. I gave my dog a withering look he may or may not have understood.

"I'll take Maverick for a spin."

Columbia wasn't all that large, and I wanted to get a bead on the location of the cache's second stage. I plugged in the numbers and watched the handheld GPS light the way to the wildlife protection area just down the street.

For a while last fall, I avoided walking the paths through the middle of the park, but Maverick loved the trails. It was a good thing I'd put my personal ghosts to rest. The GPS led us to the edge of the pond in the middle of the park, and it appeared the endgame was at its center. I was not willing to get wet but pushed aside the curtain of reeds and grasses and followed the shoreline to a narrow peninsula jutting out into the silver pool, at the end of which stood a lone spruce tree.

Maverick and I tramped across the shifting strip of sludge and closed in on the cache. I ducked underneath the blue-green branches, fishing for a small container, and was rewarded with a flash of metallic purple before Maverick barked and yanked me out from under the tree.

"Wait, Maverick." Ferreting out the solution to a puzzle fed my endorphins, and my words came out quickly. "I found it. It's a bison tube. Just a minute. Let me reach in farther." Talking logically to my energetic dog when he was on a mission never worked. I didn't know why I tried. Balancing precariously on the unstable ribbon of land connecting us to the shore, I grappled with the leash, but he was the stronger of the two of us. He splashed forward and I stumbled headfirst into the cool sludge.

Rising slowly, soaked from hair to toe, I shook tiny droplets and peeled away the slimy green strands dangling over my face. The muck monster of the deep had his clutches on my shoes, and I stepped purposefully to keep them on my feet, not that I really wanted to wear them ever again.

The product details for the GPS unit I carried advertised waterproofing, and it surely had been put to the test. I flicked the globules away, and the screen stayed lit. Score one.

Maverick barked, and this time he put his entire body into his woof. Hair stood on end from his withers to his forehead. His entire body lunged forward with every utterance.

It could have been worse. There might have been witnesses.

And then I heard the deep, warm chuckling.

"Need help, Ms. Wilk?" Dr. CJ Bluestone called. The grin in his voice carried well across the water.

"No, thank you, Dr. Bluestone."

Standing next to him, his daughter doubled over. Her attempt to stifle her laughter failed, and a high-pitched giggle exploded from the shore. "Ms. Wilk, what are you and Maverick searching for now?" Carlee said, nearly gasping around her giggles. Her rambunctious pup, Renegade, stood at her heel, perfectly still, awaiting a cue. I admired their control.

CJ was our veterinarian and provided excellent training for both dogs to enhance their search and rescue skills. CJ hung his head, and a curtain of long, straight black hair swung from side to side as he tried not to laugh along with his daughter. He composed himself and rose to his full height. As he viewed the scene in front of him—me dripping scummy pond water, slipping and splashing to stay upright, Maverick barking, pulling me deeper—the grin on his face shifted. After a sharp whistle, Maverick immediately stopped moving, stepped onto the sliver of land, and sat. Renegade sat as well.

"Katie." CJ's deep resonant voice immobilized me too. "Don't move." He'd already begun striding the perimeter, gliding next to Maverick. "What did you find, my friend?" CJ dropped to his knees next to my dog and tilted his head at exactly the same angle to see what Maverick saw. He pointed in front of me. "There."

Already drenched, I lumbered four steps forward. "Oh, no."

TWENTY

A cluster of shiny metal barely scraped the surface beneath the water. I climbed next to CJ and held Maverick close. *Good dog, I guess.*

"I can't be positive, but those look like the clubs Barclay Byron used. I think the police should be called."

CJ looked at me with questions brewing in his dark eyes.

"Jane and I found Byron's body on the golf course on Tuesday." CJ waited patiently, exhibiting no sign of surprise or curiosity. "And I brought my GPS unit." I held it up in front of me and confessed, "I don't have my phone."

He blinked hard, once, and made the call. "This is not an emergency, but I believe we have uncovered evidence which should be collected." He recited our location and thanked the dispatcher. "Why do you think these belong to Byron?"

"Notice the unique color and pattern on the heads, and the pro at Shady Oaks, Ginny, has been looking for the set Byron used at my first lesson. She said they were very expensive and belonged to the club, not to Byron, so I don't think either of them would have tossed the clubs here."

"What have you gotten yourself into now?"

I had no response.

"Dad?" Carlee called with a more serious tone from her edge of the pool. "What happened?"

"Please stay where you are, Carlee." She knew the drill. She and Renegade began an intense game of fetch. Maverick gazed longingly over his shoulder, but CJ employed serene synergy between them, and Maverick stayed put.

I stood silently too, transfixed by the blurry image below the surface. After examining my water-wrinkled fingertips, I cringed wondering what my toes looked like. By the time Chief Amanda West and Officer Rodgers pulled into the lot next to the landing, I'd begun to shiver.

"Dr. Bluestone. Katie. We'll take over."

We stepped onto the shore. Neither of them spoke, but set out to efficiently collect what Maverick had found. Officer Rodgers tightened the straps on the waders he wore to keep dry as he plunged into the water to retrieve the unwieldy bag. To lessen its weight, he secured the clubs and poured the water from the bag through the sieve Chief West held over a plastic bucket, holding the clinking clubs in place but catching small tokens, ball markers, and debris, items that might be considered evidence. Officer Rodgers snapped a cover on the bucket, and together they wrapped the clubs in a large tarpaulin, hauling the discovery to the rear of the cruiser to store in the trunk. Even with everything they'd collected, I couldn't help but think something was missing.

Only then did Amanda ask, her voice heavy with seriousness, "What were you doing, Katie?" She and I were friends, and she was doing her job, but I wished we were meeting over a glass of wine.

My teeth chattered, and before I could utter a sound, CJ said, "Could we do this at her apartment?"

"Most definitely." Amanda stepped back, avoiding Maverick wickedly shaking cold droplets, and me, dripping and trembling. "I'll meet you there."

CJ shortened his stride and kept pace with me, walking in silence. Renegade and Carlee followed with a little more lightheartedness, not understanding the ramifications. I wondered myself.

Once inside, Dad cast a curious glance at CJ. His eyes followed me traipsing through the kitchen and up the stairs. I walked directly to my room and seriously thought about jumping in the shower, but I didn't want to keep Chief West waiting. Though the temperatures still hovered in the eighties, I donned dry jeans and a bulky sweatshirt. The comb filled with algae and weeds landed in the trash can. I blow-dried the first few strands of light brown hair and tried to blink away the redness in the sunken blue eyes staring back at me.

I heard voices and trudged back to the kitchen.

The aroma of Dad's wild rice casserole hit my nose, and my mouth watered even though I didn't think I was hungry. I hadn't been gone long, but only one seat remained at the table crowded with seven place settings and Ida's addition of Caesar salad and warm yeasty homemade bread. Ida had performed her magic.

The chair squawked as I drew it out across the floor and sat.

"I'll say grace," said Ida. She bowed her head, leaving

one reprimanding eye open to peek around the table, making certain we followed suit. My head fell forward. "Bless us, O Lord, and these, Thy gifts, which we are about to receive from Thy bounty, through Christ, Our Lord. Amen."

The amen echoed soundly from CJ, Carlee, Amanda, Officer Rodgers, Dad, and me. "Eat," she commanded. Everyone always did what Ida told them or faced dire consequences.

After five minutes of stilted conversation, clattering silverware, and throat clearing, Amanda said, "We'll let the techs determine what the clubs can tell us, but Katie, what do you know?"

I carefully set my fork parallel to my knife across the top of my plate and folded my hands in my lap. "The clubs appear to be the same brand as the set Byron used at my first lesson to demonstrate good form. I've come to learn—"

"Excuse me," said Officer Rodgers, scribbling notes in a small booklet. "How did you come to know?"

"Sorry. I'll back up. Genevieve, the other pro at Shady Oaks, told me she couldn't find the Honma Beres clubs Byron had been using. The clubs you lifted from the water appear to be the same brand. I think they're on the expensive side."

"I'll say," Dad said. "On the low end, a set of six irons can cost four thousand—"

"Dollars?" Officer Rodgers asked for clarification as my mouth dropped open.

"I prefer a TaylorMade myself, but beggars can't be choosers."

"Why were you in the water, Katie?"

Amanda's question cut into my thoughts, and as I composed my answer, Carlee giggled. "Sorry, but Maverick's wrenching you into the pond was totally something Renegade would've done. I'm glad it was you, Ms. Wilk, not me."

Renegade and Maverick had squeezed onto Maverick's bed and their heads popped up in unison at the sound of their names.

"Let's rephrase that. How did you end up at the wildlife protection area?" Amanda asked.

"Geocaching. I was completing the second stage of a multi-cache. I found the container hanging on the branches of the little tree on the patch of ground at the end of the narrow strip jutting out into the water. Maverick decided he didn't want to wait for me to claim the cache because he'd found something out of place and more interesting, and he whisked me away from the tree. CJ and Carlee observed me toppling into the water, but CJ noticed Maverick wasn't merely playing. He was on the hunt. Rest assured, we did not touch the bag. CJ called, and we waited for you to join us. That's all."

CJ nodded once with intensity, and Carlee's head bobbed up and down. "That's what I saw too."

I couldn't help wondering if Ginny felt slighted as a backup pro and how that should somehow factor into our discussion about the Honma Beres. I also realized the heated discussion Jane and I overheard on Monday morning could easily have taken place between Ginny and Byron.

After a few seconds of quiet, Ida said, "Can I get anyone dessert?"

Everyone around the table turned her down, and Amanda and Officer Rodgers excused themselves.

"Will you be alright?" CJ said.

"Yes. I wonder if locating the clubs will help with the investigation of Bryon's death."

"Amanda will get to the bottom of this." CJ knelt next

to Maverick. They touched foreheads, expressing gratitude and sharing a tranquil moment before he rejoined Carlee and Renegade at the door.

Ida and Dad sat at the table, unusually quiet. "What?" I asked.

"You need something safe to do, and I might have an idea." Convincing Ida I already had too much to do at the moment was unsuccessful. "I'm in charge of Columbia's summer festival. You can be my handywoman, do a little bit of this and a little bit of that."

She dominated the conversation and wouldn't have heard anything I said.

Her monologue was halted abruptly by a Maverick howl followed by a knock on the door. I looked out the window, half expecting Amanda to return. Gazing around, I found Pamela on our lawn gesturing to my diminutive neighbor, standing primly.

I opened the door and Maverick whizzed by me to plant himself on the top step. "Hi, Emma, what's up?"

"I came for a Maverick kiss." She giggled as he obliged. "And I want you and Harry and Ida and Maverick to come to my birthday party."

"I do love a good party and so does Maverick."

"Here." She held up a linen envelope with our names penciled across the front in red, orange, blue and green crayon. Maverick licked her face and nudged her hand for a scratch. She responded appropriately, swinging her skirt back and forth. "You can bring Dr. Pete, too, if you want."

"Thank you, Emma." A little louder I said, "And be sure to thank your mommy."

"Mommy," Emma turned and called. "Katie says thank you."

"You're welcome. Let's go, Emma. It's bedtime."

Emma's shoulders drooped, but I think the visit had been used as another bribe for her nighttime ritual. "Good night, Emma. Maybe you can come play with Maverick tomorrow."

She turned and climbed down the steps, skipping across the lawn to her mother, saying, "Katie needs me to train Maverick tomorrow."

I closed the door, slid my finger under the flap, and extracted a hand-drawn coloring of a black four-legged animal with a red collar on the cover of an invitation to Emma's special birthday party on … June 10. My heart fluttered, and I sagged against the door.

TWENTY-ONE

Dad caught my elbow and tugged the invite from my fingers. He read the words and eyed me with worry. "You don't have to go. Emma won't care. It's all about presents at age four."

My head swirled with vivid memories as I slid to the floor. Promising to avoid foreign entanglements, Dad supported my odyssey to London to earn a master's degree in mathematical cryptanalysis, but meeting Charles at the Royal Holloway had been my undoing. We worked well together and planned our future, but seventeen days after our wedding, Dad, Charles, and I biked a trail around my hometown. In one horrifying moment, a bullet struck Dad, and he suffered a traumatic brain injury, but he'd managed to relearn many skills. A second bullet struck Charles, and he died in my arms saying,

"Promise me you'll be happy."

My plans changed. Happiness had been elusive until I decided to use his words as my daily mantra. I still missed his intellect, curiosity, and passion, and we would've celebrated our two-year anniversary on June 10.

They never caught the shooter.

Ida teased the invite from Dad, and by the look of concern on her face, she, too, understood the significance of the date. But I couldn't let June 10 define me. I would pull myself up by my bootstraps and face whatever ache the day would bring. Charles would have wanted that, and I felt his encouraging hand on my heart.

I squeezed a smile onto my lips. "I'll make it work. I have the two of you."

"And more," said Ida. "We're all here for you."

Maverick, Charles's last gift to me, smothered me with tickling kisses, and I chuckled. "But first, we need to decide on an appropriate gift. Any ideas?" As I turned to Ida, my phone buzzed. I read the screen. "Excuse me." I crawled to standing, and just like that, my heart picked up the pace. I heard Charles's words in my head again: 'Promise me you'll be happy.' I moved into the living room and accepted the call, forcing a coy lilt. "Hi, Pete."

"Katie, I just got off the phone with Amanda. I assured her Byron did not meet his demise at the end of a club. I'm awaiting test results to help with our final determination, but what did you find this time?"

"I was looking for a geocache on a slim patch of earth in the pond at the center of the wildlife protection area, and at the same time, Maverick communicated a find in the water. It turned out to be a set of clubs like the set Byron used."

"How do you get yourself into these situations?" he teased.

"It was my dog." I bristled and took a calming breath. "Can you tell me anything more about how Byron did die?"

"Amanda's still investigating. When she wants you to know, she'll tell you." Pete sighed. "But for your information, everything at the course is under careful scrutiny."

He said no more.

"Pete, you're invited to Emma's birthday party Wednesday. I hope you can attend."

"It's on my calendar. I'll be there. You're still working the beverage cart tomorrow, right?"

"Yah sure, you betcha," I said in my most exaggerated fake Minnesota dialect, trying to lighten the mood.

Pete couldn't help but laugh. "I'll see you there, but please be careful."

"Will do. Over and out." I understood Pete's inability to answer my questions because the death was under investigation. If Byron's death wasn't an accident, who might have done him harm and why?

Dad stood in the doorway, holding up a pair of white leather shoes with low-profile spikes and polished to a high shine. A grin filled his face like a toddler at Christmas. "I haven't golfed in twenty-five years. I'm afraid I'm a bit rusty. I don't know what I should wear."

He didn't have much in the way of golf-specific attire, but I helped him choose a sea serpent teal polo shirt, which brought out the bright blue in his eyes, and khaki shorts. He still cut a mean figure for a man of sixty. He turned this way and that as he regarded his reflection in my full-length mirror and yawned loudly, indicating an end to his arduous day.

The sky darkened enough for luminous flecks of firefly light to flash in the yard and cooled the heat of the day for Maverick to engage in another walk. We stepped through the gate at the back of our yard, and Maverick's welcome bark and wagging tail drew a familiar face out of the gloaming.

"Galen. What are you doing here?"

Reminiscent of a death knell, the clearing of his throat sounded ominous. When he finally spoke, he was so quiet, I asked him to repeat himself.

"I was working up the courage to talk to you."

"My door is always open. What do you need?" My mind raced, visiting the myriad difficulties a now-high-school-senior could have. "Do you want to go inside?"

"No," he said sternly and relented. "Sorry. I'm worried. I think my friend, Sherylann, is going to need help, and I don't know who else to ask."

"I can't promise anything but fire away." I worried about my student, not quite an adult, yet no longer a child.

His neck cracked as he rolled his head. The words rushed out. "Sherylann worked the beverage cart until Byron fired her, and now she's afraid she's going to be nailed for the thefts at Shady Oaks."

"Which thefts?" His dark eyes grew round and that said it all. "She's the ghost."

"She's been trying to get her life back together. Lark gave her the job, and she earned almost enough to get by … with a little help."

"She's been stealing from—"

He jumped in, strongly shaking his head, and sounded defensive when he said, "She borrowed a few items but returned everything."

"And the foodstuffs from the kitchen?"

"She'd have paid them back. Who'd have thought the chef would miss a little hamburger?"

"Why did Byron fire her? Did he find out she was the ghost?"

"I don't think so. Lark needed someone to take a shift

and asked if she could sub in. She washed her clothes in the locker room but hadn't found time to finish, so she planned to wear her own outfit just until her uniform was dry. Byron caught her before she had time to change. He claimed he was a stickler for rules and decorum, of course only when it applied to someone else." He spat the words as if they soured in his mouth. "Word got around, and she's been questioned as if she's a suspect in Byron's death, but they haven't even told her how he died. Now she's heard you found some golf clubs. If they belong to Byron, she's seen them and might even have thought about pawning one or two, but they're too identifiable. Besides, that would have been stealing."

"If that's the truth, she needs to get an attorney and talk to Chief West."

Galen focused on his sandals. "She doesn't have money at her disposal." He looked up. "You've figured out things before. Please help her."

"She might not want my help if I find out she's guilty." Galen looked bewildered, and I relented. "Tell me about her."

Galen dropped his head, and I strained to hear him. "My oldest sister graduated from high school six years ago. Sherylann was her best friend forever. They played soccer, basketball, and golf together, but her mom died after her sophomore year. She had a falling out with my sister. Sherylann got mixed up with a bad crowd and dropped out of her extracurriculars. She got caught shoplifting and doing drugs. My sister tried to visit her in juvie, but Sherylann wouldn't see her. She never even graduated from high school."

"What's she been doing for the last six years?"

He shook his head. "When I started working at Shady Oaks, I recognized her right off the bat. It took a while, but when she figured out who I was, we talked. She's clean. She got her GED and a job. I tried to get her to talk to my sister so they could maybe get back together, but she said she wasn't ready. She was ashamed. And now this."

His earnest, distraught face melted my heart. I had to do something. "I'll meet with her, but I'll strongly suggest she see Chief West and tell her everything. It would be better than if Chief West discovered the information herself."

Galen looked over his shoulder, and a slight form emerged from the shadows. "Sherylann, I want you to talk to Ms. Wilk."

Tears pooled in the young woman's eyes. She wasn't much younger than me, but her dark blue eyes reflected a depth of knowledge. I couldn't imagine what she'd been through.

"Let's go in and have a cup of tea. Then we can call Chief West and tell her everything. She'll understand."

Sherylann recoiled as if struck and turned to run, but Galen reached out and grabbed her arm. His strong wrestler's grip could be like a vise, but with the gentleness he exhibited, I think she could've pulled away with ease. He tipped his head and led her into my kitchen.

I've come to know my dog as an astounding judge of character. He didn't flinch but sauntered between Sherylann and Galen as if leading his own pack into a well-loved space. Sherylann sat at the table, and Maverick laid his head in her lap. Galen sat on one side, and I sat on the other.

"You can trust her," Galen said, nodding at me.

"I'm listening."

TWENTY-TWO

Basically, you took what you wanted from patrons and staff at Shady Oaks." Sherylann was old enough to know better, (they both were) and I tried to tamp down the disappointment in my voice.

"I worked there, and I only borrowed items I needed," she said defiantly. "My paycheck was automatically deposited, and the only way to access my account is electronically, but I don't have the resources to afford a laptop or a smartphone like some people, so maybe I borrowed the pro shop notebook to check on it. Things like that. I always put everything back, and because I never kept anything, the club never filed a police report." She lifted her chin. "I'm not the only one *borrowing* things."

"What does that mean?"

"I never took anything from members, but having a ghost was kind of a novelty and contributed to the mystique of the century-old course."

"Some personal items have gone missing. If you didn't take those things, is there another ghost?" I said, trying to make trust go both ways.

"I didn't take things from guests. Sometimes other staff members borrowed …" She used air quotes around the word. "… items to lend credibility to the ghost tale." She shook her head and shrugged. "Everything went sideways when the chef went ballistic. How was I supposed to know he had a special blend of meat he weighed nightly? I only took enough for two burgers. And it didn't taste special at all. That place has all kinds of secrets." Her rebellious streak collapsed. She went quiet, but in her eyes, I could see the weight of the chip on her shoulder.

"Where can Chief West find you?" I asked. "It's imperative she talk to you. You might have information she needs. Where are you staying?"

She stared at me, and when I realized the answer, the truth poured over me like a cold shower. With no place else to go, she squatted on the Shady Oaks property. "You're staying in that old caretaker's stone hut." I gasped. "You must speak to Chief West."

"I'll talk to her, but I have some things I need to take care of first just in case they don't believe me."

I started to protest, but she cut me off.

"I've been on the receiving end of the law for too long, and it hasn't always been easy."

"You need to talk to Chief West." I raised my voice to make my point. "If you don't tell her before the end of the tournament, I will."

Our discussion ended with a promise.

Maverick and I walked them out to the street. His tail waved, and Galen and Sherylann melted into the night.

"You could be wrong, you know." I stared at my dog and scratched a spot he was sure to appreciate. So certain Maverick's assessment of her could be correct, I conceded. "Okay, you've never been wrong … *yet* … but Amanda still needs to be informed."

The mathematical corner of my mind developed a syllogism to describe the fallout from the evening's conversation. I believed in Galen, and Galen believed in Sherylann, therefore I had to believe in Sherylann, and I had to consider someone else was guilty. But who? Of what, exactly? And why?

A short mental chart of suspects, motives for stealing or being angry with Byron, and alibis faded as I drifted off to slumberland and had evaporated completely by the time Maverick's hot breath startled me awake. He peered at me, inches from my face, waiting patiently.

Sunlight streamed in around the window shade. "Am I late?" I sat up and checked the clock. "Thank heavens you like to walk early." I nodded. "But couldn't you wait until six?"

I hauled myself down the stairs and tramped outside with temperatures already sizzling. The dew transformed into steam in front of my eyes.

I replayed the dialog from the prior evening, specifically the promise I'd secured from Sherylann, and tried to recreate the list of culprits I might have imagined making, but the names eluded me. No manner of death had officially been released, and Chief West hadn't ruled anything out. In my short interlude with him, however, it didn't seem likely Barclay Byron would harm himself, neither inadvertently nor on purpose.

Experience made me wonder. The many loose ends all led to questions about who might benefit from Byron's death. I shook my head and chastised myself. "Let it be."

But thoughts came unbidden. Tempest no longer needed to go through divorce proceedings, nor would she and Clive be obliged to hide their relationship. Jane and I overheard an argument about a contract, which might still be valid upon Byron's death. The photo of Anne's past relationship with Byron had vanished. To put a wrench in the works, I couldn't understand how Byron's death would benefit Sherylann.

I stopped and searched the kitchen. The quiet gave me pause—why hadn't Dad made breakfast this morning, of all mornings, when he'd need the energy for a full day of tournament play? I raised my hand to knock on his door, but it flew open.

"Morning, darlin'. What a glorious day," he said, rubbing his hands together with anticipation. "There are Mason jars of overnight oats in the fridge and a bowl of fresh fruit. Once you're ready, we can ride to Shady Oaks together. I'll put my clubs in the car, and we can be off in thirty minutes."

My mouth fell open. "The tournament doesn't begin until ten, and I—"

"I'd like to warm up on the driving range and do a little putting. It's been a very long time for your old man, Katie."

"You are really looking forward to this tournament, aren't you?" My cheeks reflected his huge happy grin. "I'll hurry. Maybe if we're early, I can get in one more lesson."

Ten minutes later, I hopped down my steps under Ida's cynical eye. "Took you long enough." Her blinding attire covered the color spectrum from the emerald-green scarf tied around her freshly colored red hair to the swinging yellow sundress, wedge sandals, and absurdly glowing pink nail polish. "Let's go. I've got work to do. Registration starts at eight."

Dad hefted a weighty canvas tote over each shoulder. I tucked in my uniform shirt and hoisted the two sunflower yellow boxes stacked on the kitchen table. Ida stooped and lifted a small purple cooler.

My eye twitched, observing the jarring sight.

"Complementary colors, in case you didn't know," she said. "Paper products and decorations in the yellow boxes, comestibles in the purple cooler."

Maverick watched from his cushion and seemed to roll his eyes when I said, "We'll be back soon."

I slowed as Shady Oaks came into view and squinted at the arresting glare on the mirrored surface of the water, coming to a stop at the front door. Galen delivered a large bellman cart and helped us unload.

"It's going to be a big day," he said. He searched my face for confirmation.

I nodded. Not only would I operate the beverage cart, but my secondary job would be to prove Sherylann didn't steal from the club, and I expected Sherylann to do her duty as well.

By the time I parked my car, Ida had skillfully set up the welcome table, having performed her very important duty by herself repeatedly over the years. She'd outdone herself.

Sleeves of paper cups rose in the shape of a pyramid on the edge of the linen-covered table next to a stack of cocktail napkins bearing the adages, 'Drive for the show, putt for the dough,' and 'May the course be with you'. Narrow citrus circles floated among the ice cubes in a plexiglass water cooler. A stack of sand-colored plates awaited the candy-coated tee-shaped pretzels scattered on a crystal tray, casually tossed among white chocolate golf ball sized truffles. A veggie tray displayed mozzarella balls, bright red cherry tomatoes, and fragrant basil leaves skewered by long white plastic clubs. Dark green pens emblazoned with the Shady Oaks emblem touting numbered pennants filled a tall glass tabletop golf bag.

A large man in a chef's toque used his immense girth to barrel in front of the registrants. His head swiveled from side to side as he surveyed Ida's fanciful treats. He snickered a derisive "Pfft," and inhaled, but before he could elaborate on his displeasure, an anxious server scurried to his side. "Chef, you're needed in the kitchen," and they swept from the lobby.

I selected a bi-fold flyer and read the schedule of the day's events for the expected one-hundred-fifty players in three flights. Immediately after registration, the competitors could try out their skills at various smaller games. In addition to the round of golf, funds would be raised in contests, taking chances for the longest drive or the closest chip shot to the pin. Mulligans, do-overs, were available to purchase for a nominal fee, but if you chose a Mulligan, you would not be eligible for the grand prize trophy. A silent auction lined one wall, and items ranging from books, food, and crafts to tickets for golf events covered the table. After logging in my credit card, I was asked what my identifier would be, and I answered confidently, seven twenty-four. I bid on a weathered wooden driver with a small, tattered envelope attached to the grip. The relic called to me, 'You can afford this.' The item with the next fewest bids was an insulated tumbler from the Masters Tournament, which looked an awful lot like the one Barclay Byron had been so proud of.

TWENTY-THREE

Ida waved away our help and Dad accompanied me to the pro shop; he thought he needed two or three new sleeves of balls. The shop door stood ajar, and we walked in on Ginny and Dennis, deep in discussion.

"It'll be okay. You'll see. I had my attorney look over the contract. Ownership will revert to me. It's solid," said Dennis.

Perhaps Dennis was a shareholder, lost some shares, and was now a shareholder again? The life of an owner wasn't always sunshine and flowers. He looked worried.

"Where does that leave Tempest?"

Dad's eyebrows reached toward the ceiling as Ginny saw us in the doorway and surreptitiously slid her chair back. I glimpsed apprehension as she stood, but it was fleeting, and the smile on her face was very real.

"Hi, Katie. If you're here about another lesson, can it wait until Monday? I've been swamped with tournament gear sales, questions, paying client lessons, and even marketing, if you can believe it. Our sponsor wants me to use the Honma Beres clubs anytime I'm on the course." She ran her hand up the shaft of a driver from the set next to the cash register.

"Have the police already returned the clubs?"

"No. I'm not sure I'd want to use the clubs Barclay used, nor would they perform as well for me. These are personalized to fit my measurements and will work quite nicely. It's a shame about Barclay, but he always knew best."

"What do you think happened?"

"The police say it could have been an allergic reaction or accidental poisoning."

The more I heard, the less I believed in the police theory, but if it wasn't accidental, and I couldn't imagine him committing suicide, my suspect list took a more solid shape, beginning with Ginny. She had a motive, however flimsy— her job might have been on the line, and she now had the use of very expensive and distinctive clubs. Moreover, she no longer worked in Byron's shadow.

I added Dennis to the list. I'd have to find out more about him. He was a regular at the pro shop, but didn't seem too broken up over Byron's death, and the snippets of conversation he'd had with Byron required further examination.

"Last lesson Monday?" Ginny gave me a curious glance.

"Monday's great. Meanwhile, I'll see if Lark needs help prepping for the day." I gave Dad a salute but, enthralled by the goodies on display, he never noticed me leave.

In the atrium, golfers crowded Ida's hospitality/ registration table, greeting fellow participants and sizing up competitors. Ida's gruff words kept the line moving forward and me moving on. "Hold your horses. They won't commence without everyone registered. I'll get to you when I get to you. If you're here for a spectator ticket, you'll have to wait until ten."

I knocked on the human relations office door and reached for the knob. Inside, every cubicle held a tidy, empty desk and dark screen. "Lark?" I called. "Anyone here?"

"I'm here." Winslow said, stepping from the back hall, lazily licking creamy contents of a yogurt cup from a spoon. "Are you ready for your day, Katie?"

"Yes. I stopped by to see if Lark needed any help, but she has you, so obviously not."

"It seems they might have caught the ghost on a camera. She went to check it out."

"I thought they installed the cameras after the theft from the kitchen."

"Our esteemed chef had installed his own. He and Lark are meeting with one of the police officers now, going through the still shots. So, I'm in charge here."

The hairs on my neck bristled. *How did that happen?*

"You could take your cart out to the driving range for the warm-ups." Lapping his spoon once more, his insouciance made me shudder. With the spoon stuck in his mouth, he handed me my cash drawer. "No one else will be out there until eleven, so you're bound to have takers. And if anyone gets too rowdy, call command central. We have two discreet security details."

"Command central?"

He crossed his arms. "Call Lark. She has extra hands on deck for the day."

I acquiesced, but only because Winslow could be right about early customers. However, in an attempt to assert my independent thought, I stomped to the garage as if it was my idea and mentally added Winslow to the suspect list. So far, his crime was existing as a disagreeable man, possibly stealing a bag of nuts and my tip money, and maybe owning a red sports car.

Rolling back the heavy door released stagnant, stuffy air from the enclosed garage and a slightly unbecoming odor. I trooped through the space and opened the back door, waving my hands to initiate positive airflow, and paused when I realized the air would have to pass over the garden looming in the background and wondered about the effects of plant spores and allergens. I glanced at the caretaker's cottage but saw no sign of Sherylann and hoped she would follow through with our agreement.

I parked the cart where a half dozen golfers, awaiting their turn at the row of tee boxes, bought ice-cold bottles of water and sweet tea. The change in the tip jar started to build.

A few golfers even dropped in singles, but as I completed one order, I noticed a ten drift into the jar. Assuming the giver hadn't noticed and mistakenly threw in too much, I said, "Sir." I turned to face the tipper. "I don't think you meant to leave such a large …"

A smarmy voice said, "Katie? Is that you?"

The plastic bottle I held clattered to the ground. My throat closed up, and my heart raced at the sight of the only man who had ever raised a hand to me.

I stooped to pick up the beverage, and a woman's voice with a heavy French accent said, "Monty, there you are. My ball is in the bunker. What club do you want me to use? And would you please get me a … Katie?" The voice took on an edge. "What are you doing here?" She planted one hand firmly on her curvy waist.

I swallowed hard and plastered on a smile of sorts. "I

work here, ZaZa. What are you doing here?"

ZaZa raised her lovely chin and tossed long brunette tresses, flashing her amber eyes. "I am competing, playing golf." Her partner offered her a bottle of water. She shook her head. "I'd like a Chardonnay."

If her request surprised Monty, he hid it well and nestled the bottle of water in a pale pink golf bag. "You heard the lady. Chardonnay." He fished out another bill. "How are you, Katie?"

The time it took to find the can of wine allowed me to harness the buzzing in my ears and calm my quaking hand. I offered the drink to ZaZa. "Enjoy."

ZaZa looked back and forth between us, narrowed her eyes, and said, "How do you know Montgomery?"

"Get away from Katie," growled an angry voice. Dad barreled across the grass and stomped onto the path. "Leave her alone." His face was beet red, and he was breathless from exertion or from anger. Either way he added, "Or I'll call the police."

Montgomery put up his hands in a gesture of surrender. "I was just being polite." His ingratiating smile sent chills up my spine. "See you around, Katie." I froze, trapped by cold blue eyes and horrible memories.

"Over my dead body," said my dad, loud enough to momentarily halt other conversations on the range.

Montgomery grinned with the all too familiar telltale white of a clenched jaw. Reading his eyes, I imagined the words bouncing around in his head, 'That can be arranged,' and I put my hand on Dad's chest. "It's okay, Dad. I'm okay."

"Stay away from my daughter. I won't say it again."

Montgomery grabbed ZaZa's elbow and guided her, sputtering, to their handcarts. Her backward stare pierced me like a million daggers as he chose a club for her and led her to the bunker. I heard muffled words about opening the club face, widening stance, and digging into the hazard. She swung, and along with her ball popping out of the trap, sand splashed into Montgomery's face. Her left hand smothered a gasp.

I flinched and held my breath. After a moment of silence, Montgomery shook his head and dusted his cheek. He smiled, and ZaZa tittered.

Dad's hand rested on my shoulder, and I let out the breath I'd held. "Have you warned her? Have you told ZaZa what he can do? She's your friend. You can't let her become a victim too."

"I know, Dad, but it's complicated. I'm not sure she'd believe me anyway."

"What do you mean? The man can be nasty. You'd never forgive yourself if something happened to her." His head dropped. "I know."

"Dad, you did everything you could." I swallowed hard. "ZaZa believes I stole Charles from her. She won't trust I'm not out to steal Montgomery from her as well. We occupy space in the same town and at the same school, but she does not consider me a friend. In her eyes, I'm a rival."

"You have to tell her before it's too late."

"I know." My hair fell forward, covering my face and the turmoil Dad was sure to see there. "No matter what."

TWENTY-FOUR

I promise I'll find a way to tell her." I tucked my hair behind my ear. "It's been five years. Maybe it was just me, and he's not the same."

"Five years, eleven months, and some-odd days. Can a leopard change its spots?" Dad's warm brown eyes filled with concern, and his mouth formed a razor-thin line. "I'll take an iced tea, please." He looked up, stood tall, and called over my shoulder, "Good morning, Doc. Are you ready to hit the big ones?"

I spun around, and just like that, my anxiety vanished. "Coffee? Tea? Or me?" I said with some sass.

Drew appeared next to Pete. "I'll have a cranberry juice, fair lady."

Pete grinned and raised two fingers. "It's a great day to

be outside."

"How's it going?" Drew said, and not waiting for a reply, leaned in, combed the area quickly right and left, and said softly. "I didn't realize Jane was in it to win this thing. She's in for a rude awakening from at least two members of this foursome, but don't tell her."

She always wants to win. I chuckled to myself.

Pete said, "Harry, we're hoping you can carry us."

"I've got your back," Dad replied with ease.

A queue formed behind Pete. "Catch you later." He stuffed a bill in my tip jar, grabbed the three cans, and hustled Drew and Dad out of the way.

Columbia wasn't a metropolis. I recognized a few faces: parents of my students, parishioners from our church, business owners from some of the retail establishments, even some fellow teachers, but as I was returning change for a purchase of water, my surprise came out as an, "Oh my," when Tempest Byron turned up with her boy toy latched onto her arm.

She looked the part of a wealthy widow, just not a newly minted wealthy widow—a dramatic change from a few days ago. Her black hair hung so straight it appeared pressed, and her makeup, applied to perfection, colored her porcelain face like an ingenue, an unbelievable feat in light of how distressed and out of sorts she'd looked the last time I saw her. They wore matching canary-yellow polo shirts. Tempest's khaki skorts covered the barest of essentials, but her partner didn't seem to mind, steering her through the gathering with one hand on her lower back. He'd tied back his dishwater blond hair, and sunglasses hung from a lanyard around his neck. However, the shoes completed the boldness of the ensemble. Both wore red patent leather golf shoes, solidifying the term arm candy, but I didn't know who the candy was and who provided the arm.

Dennis Chappell rushed down the incline from the pro shop. Clive raised a hand to intercept Dennis's deliberate stride toward Tempest. He rubbernecked around the younger man. "What are you doing here with this gigolo, Tempest?"

"My husband played this tournament for the last five years. I now own his shares, and I want to know what goes on here. I know he registered. Clive and I are playing in his stead."

"Clive, playing? That's a laugh," Dennis said. Clive's hand against his chest held him in place, and Dennis sputtered, "I thought we had an agreement."

"Do you have a signed contract?" asked Clive flippantly. Dennis merely stared at the two of them. "I thought not. The lady is with me, and I'm playing today. If you'd like to discuss a possible buyback of the shares, you can make an appointment. After we win the tournament."

"Buyback? You can't be serious. Tempest, you're not listening to this charlatan."

Tempest stuck her nose up in the air. "Do not forget, I'm a successful businesswoman in my own right. I don't need to listen to anyone."

Dennis reared back and his eyes flashed disbelief. Ginny appeared at his elbow. "Let's go." She tugged repeatedly. "We'll figure this out."

Chappell continued to stare at Tempest and tripped as Ginny dragged him away.

"Show's over," Anne said, tramping among the participants, smiling broadly. "Remember, one small practice bucket per person, then move on to the short game area or the putting green, or one of the other fantastic fundraising games we've come up with preceding the tournament proper.

You'll find the Marshmallow Drive contest happening on hole four. Chances are ten dollars each. Longest shot wins a free six-course gourmet dinner, tailored to your taste by our fabulous new chef, slated for tomorrow evening." As if on cue, the man who'd scoffed at Ida's creative culinary delights appeared and bowed his head. "The winner will be posted near the registration table. The silent auction will conclude right before the banquet on Sunday, so make your bids early and often."

"Even though we've lost an important part of our golf family to a horrible accident, we're doing our best." Like a cheerleader for a losing team, she added with forced gaiety, "You'll notice the golf carts have magnetic panels indicating sponsors. Please thank them for their generosity and patronize the local businesses. We're raising funds for Columbia's homeless today, and we want to make a difference, so get out your wallets and give, give, give." She emphasized the giving with three punches in the air and drove many of the contenders onto their next tournament port-of-call.

"From the little I knew of Byron, he wasn't someone to accidentally do anything. Someone or something contributed to his death," I whispered to Drew.

Drew raised a finger to quiet me. "From your lips to my ears, but there's no proof, so you need to keep your opinions to yourself."

The audience shrank to just Dad, Drew and Pete. "Where's your intrepid leader?" I asked, gathering my goodies to move on to a fresh location and new takers.

"Behind you," Dad said with a welcome grin.

Ultra-stylish in her hot pink golfing togs, Jane sauntered onto one of the now empty tee boxes with a driver perched on her shoulder. She gracefully crouched and pressed a tee into the ground topped with a baby blue ball and made a show of wriggling into position. After flexing her fingers, she lined up her shot, rotated the driver back, and like a spring bound too tight, her weight shifted slightly and she uncoiled, striking the ball with a brutal thwack, following through and freezing in a pose like the topper on the women's league first-place trophy.

I have no idea how far her ball flew over the one-hundred-eighty-yard marker, but Pete whistled, Dad clapped, and Drew feigned falling to the ground awestruck.

"We could really be in this thing," Dad said, lending Drew a hand.

Jane joined us, slowly sashaying from side to side with the driver resting on her shoulder, as if her prowess on the course was no biggie. "I'll take a bottle of water, Katie dearest, and thanks for delivering my clubs." She laid her southern accent on as thickly as I'd ever heard it. I couldn't contain my laugh when she said, "Ready, boys? Catch you later, girlfriend."

Before I followed the trail to another of the pre-tournament game sites, I added names to the notepaper in my till drawer. At the top I'd written Ginny, Dennis, and Winslow. Tiny letters spelled out Sherylann at the bottom. In between, I scribbled Tempest, Clive, and Anne. I hadn't determined solid motives, but they were all part of Byron's sphere, and if he died at the hands of another, I'd have a slate to offer Amanda. I only wished I could add Montgomery's name to the list.

I joined the throng at the Circle Hole game, driving up to a familiar face to get the skinny on the event. "What's happening here?"

Winslow said, "This area was part of the original course, but at the seventy-five-year mark, they redid the landscape and cut some new paths. When Shady Oaks Beginners Golf School opened, this became one of the practice fields. Behind the copse of trees is a private runway for visiting members, and this hole is used for games. The big yellow circle painted on the green is the target for a two-hundred-yard drive, simulating a hole-in-one. However, the likelihood of hitting a target twenty feet rather than four inches in diameter is much greater, and Circle Hole has always garnered a winner. Sometimes more than one. It's ten dollars a drive." He turned his head, eyeing my nearly full tip jar. "Beginning your shift early worked for you, I see."

"Yes, thanks. When will you start?"

He turned back and surveyed the players. "I'll begin when they start tournament play at eleven. I have some work to do." He eyed Clive taking his place to tee-off. "Watch this one."

Clive's ball landed five feet from the center of the painted circle. "He usually gets even closer. He must be off his game this morning."

Jane stepped up to the tee. She repeated her ritual, and her baby blue ball landed halfway between Clive's ball and the hole. She bowed in response to the approval from her three partners, and I whooped. "That's my girl." I rotated to ask Winslow if the only requirement was to land within the circle, or would the closest ball win more, but he'd disappeared.

After Winslow left, I served several beverages, watched a few more attempts, and returned to the garage to refill my supplies before the tee-off for the tournament. I carefully restacked the cartons, but as I finished up, I saw the flashing lights on a silent police car parked on the delivery road next to the garden.

TWENTY-FIVE

Ronnie Christianson held a large clear plastic bag in one hand. With the other, he led Sherylann from the caretaker's hut, her hands cuffed behind her back. Tears streamed down her face. I didn't hear her words, but the plaintive look in her eyes caught mine, and clear as a bell, I understood her.

Please help me.

Sherylann should have trusted Amanda and told her everything before it was too late. I'd let her down, but I had no idea what I could do to fix what happened. She had to suffer the consequences. Ronnie zoomed down the drive, past the clubhouse, and I gawked at his departure. I glanced at my watch and at the stone hut. Technically, my shift hadn't begun, so I eased out of the garage, up the walk, and into the enticing garden.

Botany was out of my wheelhouse, so I used my phone to identify the varied plant life. Was there anything to find in the flawlessly manicured flora, nestled among the small blossoms amid the multi shades of green in the perfectly rectangular plots with sharply defined edges?

Beyond the fenced plot containing a host of perennial flowers like bachelor buttons, peonies, and lilies, beyond the sprouting cucumbers, carrots, peas, and lettuce, strange names popped up, including sumac, wild parsnip, jimsonweed, foxglove, yew, and hogweed. My lips puckered and I inched out of the garden, past empty patches, signs of digging throughout the garden since my first visit. I hoped it had been done by Amanda's team.

Overcome by a strange feeling of being watched, I crept out of the garden and back into the barn. I secured the door and checked the latch before completing the last-minute preparations of my cart for the tournament.

Lost in thought, schlepping the ice-cold cans, Winslow's voice startled me. "They arrested the big scary ghost. It was the cart girl Byron fired. She got caught on camera stealing an expensive, proprietary meat mixture, and the club has finally tired of her antics." He glanced over his shoulder. "We'd better get going. The tournament starts in ten minutes. You line up on hole eighteen, and I'll take nine." He searched my face. "Are you ready?"

"I will be." As I refilled the rest of the depleted provisions and drove onto the course, I rehearsed my discussion with Amanda. I believed Sherylann when she said she'd only borrowed tech items from the club except for the burger mix.

For a while, either the golfers were too nervous or too sated. Fifteen minutes passed, and no one needed anything, so—most unprofessionally—I pulled out my phone and found a string of texts from Galen.

You have to help her. PLEASE.

And,

What can we do? Where are you?

Finally,

They've taken her away.

I texted back.

I'll look into it. They must have caught her in a photo stealing from the kitchen.

He replied instantly.

She already admitted to taking the meat.

I'm not the one who counts. She didn't talk to Chief West yet, did she?

They didn't give her time.

A boisterous foursome finished putting and started toward my cart, looking parched. Before I tucked my phone away, I heard another text ping.

Sherylann has no one.

We'll talk when the day's finished.

If you don't do something, I will.

DON'T DO ANYTHING! I'll think of something.

I pocketed my phone just in time. Business picked up, and I barely had three seconds to make change between customers.

By eleven thirty, the spectators outnumbered the competitors three to one, and they were a rowdy bunch— quiet when the golfer prepared to hit the ball through the actual stroke but noisy and rude in between—not at all what I expected. Their beverage consumption leaned more toward Bloody Marys, Mango Mimosas, and beer than tea and soda. I monitored the questionable early consumption, ready to call in Lark's reinforcements as my supplies dwindled.

On a par three hole, one of the balls landed on the green, twenty feet from the flag, and the crowd oohed in response to the achievable birdie. I spotted a smug Clive lingering behind Tempest and two other golfers, who after repeated attempts, finally landed on the green as well. Clive approached his possible one-under ball and made a show of taking his time. The onlookers murmured. He circled the green, checked the position of the sun, lined up the putt, stepped away, knelt and held the putter parallel to the pin, then resettled into his stance. The crowd hushed. But Clive continued to take practice swings. A voice broke the silence as one of the hecklers pelted him with grief.

"Anyone can make that shot. C'mon. It's easy."

The words roused others to rumble, and Clive lost their undivided attention. He frowned and held out his club to the offensive character. "If it's so easy, you do it."

The voice called back, "What's in it for me?"

Clive laid an open palm out to Tempest, who reached into her hip pocket and removed two bills from a wallet. The partners in their foursome urged her to comply, and under their watchful eyes, she reluctantly passed the cash to Clive, who tossed it on the grass and crossed his arms over his thick chest. "A hundred dollars," he said, boldly. "What do I get when you don't make it?"

"Satisfaction." The throng parted and a very pregnant, muscular blond with blue eyes waddled toward Clive. He couldn't contain a smug look as he passed her the club. "You'd better mark the ball," she said. "I don't want to improve your overall score." She meticulously took in her surroundings as Clive set his marker as close as he could. She leaned over the ball, and Clive inclined toward her. "Back off," she said, raising her head and lifting the club, ready to make a chest-height thrust.

Clive put his hands up in surrender and retreated three steps.

She peeled a leather strap off her shoulder, and a tiny tan handbag dropped to the ground at her feet. She batted a few times at the loose gray shirt getting in her way. When it continued to slip around her middle and obscure her view of the ball, she reached into her hair, untied a scrunchie, gathered the excess fabric, and wrapped it in a stylish knot. She set her jaw and furrowed her brow, wiggled as she drew the club back, and followed through. Only after the ball dropped into the cup and the spectators applauded did she break her concentration, never glancing at her success.

But she didn't move toward the cash either. At first, Clive seemed disinclined to acknowledge her shot, then he pointed at the winnings.

"You can win it back," she said, "Your turn."

Clive accepted the club and slapped on a smirk, but after his first misdirected putt, a spectator in pink plaid pants and a blue polo cupped her hands around her mouth and hollered, "Take the money, honey. He can't hit a watermelon."

Clive pounded the head of the putter against the grass. When he lifted the club, the head dangled precariously and dropped to the ground. "Worthless," he said, chucking the pieces into the tall grasses and nabbing a putter from Tempest's bag.

His second shot curled around the rim of the hole, and though one member of his foursome stared wide-eyed, no one countermanded Clive's, "It's a gimme." As he retrieved his still-rolling ball, he stared longingly at the lost prize money on the carpet of green.

She shook her head. "I don't take money from amateurs,

but I do need information."

At first, Clive bristled but soon pivoted on one straight leg and nabbed the bills off the ground, jamming them into his rear pocket. "What do you need to know?"

"Can you tell me why you're playing on my husband's team?" the woman asked.

The surrounding crowd hushed.

"I'm curious," Tempest said. "Which of these …" Her words drifted away as if she couldn't quite bring herself to adequately describe the partners in her foursome. "… gentlemen is your husband?"

The woman scoffed. "None of them." Her hair blew free and gently circled her angular face. "He's on the roster for this group, and I have a credit card receipt linking payment for the registration. Where is he?" Her voice rose. "What did you do to him?"

"Who are you looking for?" Tempest asked, stepping up to my cart and relaxing against the counter. "I'd like a Tom Collins," she said in a blasé tone.

"His name is John Clay," the woman said and lifted her chin like a queen.

Tempest shrugged and shook her head. "Never heard of him." Clive's eyes narrowed to slits, and a question popped from Tempest. "Do you have a photo? Maybe he's on another team, and we can direct you there."

The woman grunted as she bent to pick up her small bag. She fished out her phone and swiped across the screen, displaying the contents to Tempest. I couldn't see Tempest's reaction, but the woman scrunched her face, words erupting. "You do know him. Where is he? I have to talk to him."

"Don't know him." Clive latched onto Tempest's arm. She moved robotically, barely aware of her actions. Clive led her to the cart and the foursome zipped to the next hole.

In panic mode, the woman held her phone out in front of her, sweeping the crowd with the photo, but everyone ignored her, focusing instead on the new contenders making their approach. She rushed me. "Have you seen him?"

My jaw dropped.

TWENTY-SIX

The poor quality of the photo did not disguise the face of a much younger Barclay Byron. Tempest had to recognize him, and I didn't hide my shock well. The man had secrets.

"You do recognize him. Where is he? I need to know. Please."

She clutched my hand with such ferocity I had to gently peel her fingers away. "Let me make a call."

Amanda answered after the first ring. "What now, Katie?"

"I'm working the golf tournament at Shady Oaks. There's a woman here looking for her husband. She says he's registered to play, but she can't find him."

"If her husband should have been out on the course today, he's not a missing person even if she can't find him.

Why call me?"

The only sound I heard was a pen scratching with unimpeded fury. I lowered my voice. "His name is John Clay." The scraping sound stopped. "You knew?"

"Dr. Erickson sent positive identification of your latest victim."

My eyes went wide. *My victim?*

"He's never hidden his name, but his professional appellation is Barclay Byron." I heard a chair slide across the floor and a door open. "I'll be right there. Katie, can you keep her with you?"

The woman had trudged off the beaten track and sagged onto a wide wooden bench.

"I think she's here for the duration. I'll stay with her. We're on hole sixteen."

I grabbed a bottle of water and took one step away from the cart. Then, remembering I needed to balance the till, I returned and counted out money from my tip jar and, not trusting anyone, relocated the rest of the gratuities and locked the drawer.

The woman looked up at me with sad eyes and accepted the offering. "Thanks. He did it again, didn't he?" She sucked in a few quick, tiny breaths.

"Did what again?"

"He has a bad habit of wooing young, impressionable, beautiful women." She tucked a few loose strands of hair behind her ear. "That's how I met him ten years ago, but he's mine now and has been for the last seven years."

I sat next to her, surveying the calm and relative quiet of the playing field, pondering which part of her description fit Tempest. "I'm Katie Wilk."

"Barbara. Barbara Clay." My discomfort grew. I had no

doubt the photo was of Byron, and it seemed he'd kept her in mind when assuming his new name. She cracked open the bottle and guzzled half the contents. "He's never been true blue, definitely not perfect—neither of us have been, but he stays with me through the winter months. Every summer, he takes off for his seasonal work and checks in all the time. But he hasn't checked in for three weeks, and as you can see—" She fanned the back of her fingers over her protruding belly. "He has some responsibilities." She winced.

"Are you alright?"

She nodded curtly and waved my concern away. "Until this season, my profession kept me busy." Her face contorted.

"You work at a golf course?"

"I golf on the pro circuit, but my schedule has become too difficult." She grimaced. "I need John."

I recognized the foursome approaching the hole, but at first, my hailing went unnoticed. Pete had a nice chip shot onto the green, and he waited for Jane, Dad, and Drew. He looked for me at the cart, and when he found me sitting on the sideline, he and his wonderful smile jogged my way. "Resting already? Who's your friend?"

"This is Barbara Clay."

Recognition of the name rippled over his handsome features and his dimple disappeared. She clutched her tummy. He knelt in front of her. "When are you due?"

"Not for another two weeks," she hissed and breathed heavily.

"And how long have you been having contractions."

"The obstetrician said they're Braxton Hicks." She inhaled sharply. "Fake pain." She puffed out her cheeks.

"You need to be checked out."

"What are you? Some kind of doctor?"

Unbeknownst to me, I'd held my breath but let it out in a whoosh and said, "The best kind."

Drew hollered from the green. "You're up, Erickson."

"Go on without me," Pete called, not breaking eye contact with Barbara.

Barbara bit her lip. "Don't stop on my account. Finish up. I wouldn't leave them hanging if I were you. I'm not going anywhere."

Pete searched her face and saw resolution.

"Anyone can make that shot," she repeated, showing teeth this time, but it wasn't much of a smile.

He grabbed Drew's putter, strode across the green, whacked the ball, and hurried back, not noticing he'd completed the hole. Dad, Drew, and Jane similarly dropped their putts. Jane sidled next to me. Dad and Drew followed closely.

Barbara moaned. "I think my water broke."

Jane clutched my arm.

Pete took Barbara's hand. "Katie, call for an ambulance."

After fumbling with my phone, Susie Teasdale answered, and without missing a beat, she said, "He isn't here, Katie." I could almost hear her eye roll. After Susie married the love of her life, she relinquished her watchful hold on Pete, and we'd formed an alliance. No matter what else I thought, she was a great nurse.

"I know, Susie. He's with me. We need an ambulance."

All business, she asked, "What's happening? Where are you?"

Barbara shouted, "I'm not having my baby on a golf course." She blinked rapidly. "Even if that's where he *was* conceived."

Pete spoke calmly. "You might not have much choice.

Now, please, Susie," he added urgently.

Susie shouted, "Shady Oaks? Got it. Ambulance on its way, ready for delivery. Sending info to the police too."

As the onlookers applauded the continued play on the course, Barbara groaned and rocked from side-to-side. Pete used low, easy words to direct the mother-to-be to breathe. We waited for instructions. And waited.

Amanda pushed through the circle of spectators, parting like them like the waters of the Red Sea, oblivious to the action behind the scenes. She marched next to Pete and dropped her black emergency bag. "I was on my way, and Susie said you might need this?"

Pete opened the bag and said, as if crooning a lullaby, "How are you holding up, Barbara?"

Her arms squeezed around her girth, and she murmured through gritted teeth, "How do you think I'm holding up?"

Becoming aware of Amanda's uniform, she said, "I want to report—" She cried out as if sliced through with a machete. "A missing person."

Pete said, "Barbara, the ambulance is on its way. Can I help you to the front of the club?"

She rocked forward as if to rise and growled at the suggestion she stand. "I can't. My legs are all wobbly."

Pete's brow furrowed. "And I'm not sure the baby's going to wait."

Amanda stationed Jane, Dad, and Drew at the perimeter of our little space to form a human barricade, not that anyone was paying attention. The large old bench and a copse of trees shielded Pete and Barbara from prying eyes.

"I need a towel or jacket or something," Pete said.

"There's a tablecloth under my counter." I raced to the neglected cart and as soon as I opened the door to the linen shelving, the crowd trapped me, clamoring for goodies. I wrestled the fabric free and retreated behind the mob busy exhausting the snacks dangling from the hooks. Thankfully, there weren't many left, and fortunately, the beverage coolers locked automatically to guard the alcohol.

Pete took the cloth. "Amanda, have you done this before?"

She observed the panic in Barbara's eyes and answered the only way she could. "Many times," her calm voice said, but her temple pulsed, her tell every time she wasn't totally forthcoming.

Over the siren wailing distantly and between bursts of catcalling and cheering from the next foursome, Pete said, "Katie, bring the EMTs out here."

I ran to meet the ambulance at the doors, and answered Galen's pleading eyes with, "We have an emergency." The two EMTs hauled a gurney up and down the slopes following my hasty lead, but we were too late.

TWENTY-SEVEN

"Be still, my heart," I murmured, settling thunderous palpitations. The picture of Pete cradling a squirming bundle made an indelible impression.

The EMTs loaded Barbara onto the gurney. Her face, though blotchy and serious, radiated joy when Pete nestled the baby in her arms. "It's a girl." He gave me a quick one-armed hug and accompanied the clattering transport as it carried Barbara and baby to the waiting ambulance. Amanda was not far behind.

Drew rubbed his hand quickly over his white-blond military-cut hair and straightened his black horn-rimmed glasses on his nose. He exercised his commanding voice, dispersing laggers who'd recognized the EMTs and police chief. "Nothing to see here. Get a move on."

Off to one side, Jane pouted.

"What's wrong, lomel?" Drew asked.

Lomel?

Jane frowned.

"What did you say? I don't know if I'd heard you correctly." I concentrated and listened again.

"Lomel. You know. L. O. M. L."

Jane's chin dropped to her chest, trying to hide her amusement. "Love of my life."

"That's what I said."

"Uh-huh. Thanks." Jane sighed and plastered on a resigned face. "You know we've lost all chance to compete in the tournament. I don't think you can deliver a baby in the middle of play and expect to jump back in."

"We'll see about that. We can certainly prove exigent circumstances. Take me to the leader."

I'd like to be a fly on that wall. Someone was in for an earful.

Jane sniffed. "I suppose we can try." She and Drew tramped toward the clubhouse, and I headed to my portable shop, but was totally disheartened to find the hooks empty, the few remaining snacks confiscated.

Dad stepped up behind me. His steady hand on my shoulder made me feel better. "What's up, Katie?"

"I guess looting is okay, but at least no one broke through the locks for something more."

"Do you know what's missing?"

"Not too much. A few bags of nuts and dried fruit are my estimate. My boss has an inventory, so I'll know for certain." I wouldn't tell him I'd be financially obligated to pay for the missing items. Fortunately, I'd protected my tips by securing them in the cashbox. "I'm going to replenish my stock. I hope your team is allowed to complete the tournament."

"We'll play whether or not the scores count toward team ranking. Until this baby bump, Jane tied for the third best score, and negative fallout would be disadvantageous to the fundraiser's future." He sighed.

"You okay, Dad?"

He winked mischievously. "After all this time, I still have it. I was beating Drew and Pete. I hope the disruption in play won't break my streak."

I winked. "Your unrivaled skills won't leave you now."

"I certainly hope not, or I'll have to pay the piper. Jane sure is a pistol. I'll just wait over there for her." He sauntered down the path and dropped onto the bench.

While I reloaded my stores, the garage provided a quiet place to regroup, take a break, and peruse my suspect list, which I thought increased by at least one in the past half hour. Making lists made me feel accomplished. If nothing else, perhaps one or more of them contributed to the ghost gossip.

When I finished refilling as many of the empty slots as possible, I studied the names and added motives to my list: Ginny and Dennis for their conversation about the disposition of Byron's shares; Winslow because I didn't like him; one wife, in this case Tempest, always counted among the suspects; Clive as Tempest's guy on the side; Anne's genealogy and location when we'd found Byron's body; and Sherylann. Knowing her paramour had flings throughout her marriage and even during her pregnancy gave Barbara plenty of motive to be unhappy with Byron. I hesitantly added her name to the bottom of the page and called Amanda.

"Katie." Amanda's annoyance was palpable.

"How many babies have you delivered?"

"None on a golf course."

A little flattery could go a long way. "I'm sure glad you were here."

Amanda grunted.

"Are you looking at Barbara Clay for Barclay Byron's murder? She says he's her husband and was in the area and also had motive."

"I already checked her alibi. They are legally married. She spent all day Tuesday in the ER. A new colleague of Pete's monitored what could have been contractions, but she diagnosed Braxton Hicks and declared the patient A-ok."

I wondered what that meant for Tempest as I sliced a pencil line through the middle of Barbara's name, and I was pleased her alibi would stick, but I didn't envy her the loss of her baby's father, even if they didn't celebrate their marriage in the traditional way. Then I erased the line. She could have hired someone to remove her bigamist husband from the picture.

"Does Barbara know about Byron, er, Clay?"

"We're going to wait until Pete gives the go-ahead before adding more trauma to her day."

"I have another question."

"What is it, Katie?"

"Was Sherylann arrested for stealing hamburger or for murdering Barclay Byron?"

"Not that it's something you need to know, but I'm allowing Officer Christianson to hold a press conference early this evening." She sighed as if he might have released the information with or without her permission. "Sherylann is being detained for stealing from Shady Oaks. Evidence of murder is circumstantial so far."

Not the direction I wanted the conversation to go.

"The chef has pictures of Sherylann accessing the kitchen

and swiping his specialty meat and a cast-iron pan. He caught the thief red-handed and is gung-ho to let everyone know he unmasked the Shady Oaks' ghost. Although all the test results aren't in, Byron was poisoned. If he died from ingesting toxic food, Sherylann had access to kitchen supplies to prepare whatever she wanted. Finding her fingerprints on the strap of Byron's golf bag is tipping the balance against her."

Sherylann gave me her word she'd only borrowed a few devices. She said nothing about golf clubs. Full disclosure would have been advantageous. I was stunned. "The value of Honma Beres clubs is astronomical."

"The what?" Amanda said.

"Honma Beres is the brand of golf clubs in Byron's bag. Those clubs would have brought Sherylann a tidy sum, and she needs the money. Why would she throw them in the pond?"

"That doesn't rule her out. Maybe she panicked. Someone tossed them in the pond, and it was most likely not Byron."

"Byron was pretty proud of them. Are all the clubs accounted for?" Amanda didn't answer. "I'm sure Ginny would know. Do you want me to ask her?"

"Katie, stop. Do not ask any questions of Ginny. In addition to the clubs, we've located items reported missing by staff and patrons in the caretaker's shed."

I felt as though I'd had the rug pulled out from under me. "Sherylann said she never took anything from the guests."

"And you're going to take her word for it." Amanda's voice changed. "Katie, when did you talk to her? Never mind. I don't want to know. Let it go. Let me do my job."

Duly scolded, how could I further expand Amanda's suspect list if they'd already zeroed in on Sherylann? I sighed. Galen was counting on me, so I took a shot in the dark, but not totally off topic. "Have you decoded the missive written on the sheath that fits over Bryon's personal fairway wood?"

"What are you talking about?"

"Byron found numbers written on the fabric covering for his favorite club. He seemed perturbed and stashed it in one of the side pockets of the golf bag."

"The club?"

"No, the sheath." My lips formed a teasing grin she wouldn't see. "It's like something one might attribute to the World War II spy, Phyllis Latour."

"You're not making any sense."

"Just thinking aloud. I've got to get back to work. Thanks for all you did, Amanda. It was enough for Pete to take care of Barbara. I don't know anyone who could have done what you did."

"You never know what assistance you're capable of providing. Don't sell yourself short … except when it comes to investigating. *Capiche*?" She hung up.

My cart must have known its own way on the course, because rather than concentrating on driving, my thoughts were bombarded by stories Charles had told me of the English female spies from World War II. I smiled, remembering. Almost all my recollections of Charles were good ones.

Charles respected the brilliant codebreakers and codemakers. One of his favorites among them was Phyllis "Pippa" Latour, who encoded and transmitted allied messages to the Special Operations Executive, a secret British organization given the task of conducting espionage, sabotage, and reconnaissance in enemy-occupied territories. The sleeve Byron wrapped around his favorite club and stored in his golf bag was reminiscent of the silk on which Phyllis kept a series of codes, which she concealed by wrapping the fabric around a knitting needle inserted into a shoelace. If Byron's fabric held a code, maybe it would shed new light on his death.

Thinking so hard, I barely noticed the thirsty crowd awaiting me and my newly refilled beverage cart on hole fifteen. Observing the foursome congregating on the green huddled together like a rugby scrum—including Anne Johansen, Dennis Chappell, and Ginny—pulled me from my safeguarded reverie.

<h1 style="text-align:center">TWENTY-EIGHT</h1>

Anne was almost as riveting to watch as Jane when her ball disappeared into the cup. The spectators reacted to a living member of the real Murphy clan with awe and stepped back, giving the royalty an unencumbered path as she made her way to my cart.

"Katie, you look well," said Anne. She moved closer and whispered behind her hand, conspiratorially, "I can't believe it. The police aren't ruling out murder as a manner of Barclay's death. Who would have wanted to kill him?" She cast her eyes skyward. "I guess the better question would be who wouldn't?" Her eyes flew to mine. "I shouldn't have said that. His poisoning had to be a mistake, right?"

When my students had information I needed, rather than openly ask for it and possibly shut them down, I waited silently with my head tilted to actively listen more intently, and they oftentimes spilled the beans.

"I'd understand if his death wasn't an accident." Anne tried to appear nonchalant and examined her nails, but she filled the dead air as hoped. "Barclay's creds appeared impeccable, and most people took him at his word. After I won my first championship, I hired him as my coach and found out almost immediately he'd enhanced his resume. He is … was a satisfactory teacher, but I fell for his rizz."

I shook my head. "What's rizz?"

She looked to the sky for patience. "I suppose my *grandmother* would say he was a Casanova. He could charm a snake. Barclay's ironclad contract had only Barclay's interests at heart. Meanwhile, he used his association with me to get his foot in the door wherever he could." Her fingers drummed the countertop. "He bamboozled me, and I was stuck with him for the year with no recourse. Meanwhile, he made himself indispensable around here, so his presence wasn't a total loss. Every spring, he'd show up and do his job well enough no one would think of releasing him. I even introduced him to Tempest. I think she hates me. She certainly learned to hate Barclay."

Anne tried to backpedal. "Maybe not so much hate as distrust. It's fitting. She married him for money. He married her for money, and neither had any."

She continued to talk about Barclay as I served starstruck fans who groveled for her scribbled autograph on a tournament program while they waited for a beverage or snack.

"If this wasn't a fundraiser sponsored by the family, I'd be so out of here," she hissed quietly while grinning at her adoring fans.

My eyebrows rose in response to the entitled voice of

a prima donna, relegating my promising customers and her admirers to a long wait line and commanding my attention.

"*Wha-at?*" She'd drawn out the word as long as she could. "I'm under the microscope here."

I tried not to react. It sounded as if she had some things she wanted to get off her chest. Maybe she'd refer to whatever was in the photo I'd seen on her bio page, the photo which had since been removed.

"Barclay was charming, and I was young and vulnerable. What did you think of him?"

I should have remained quiet, but words just spewed out. "I knew nothing about golfing until I had my first two lessons. He got me started."

"Don't you love it?" The animated change in Anne's voice made me question my hearing. Even talk of Barclay couldn't dull her fondness for the game.

"I've only played four holes, but I love spending time outside with others. My friend, Jane, is always looking for someone to play golf with, so—"

"Jane Mackey? You mean she's looking for someone she can beat," Anne snorted.

My voice rose defensively. "I'm pretty sure she can beat most of the golfers here today."

"Sorry." Anne wore a fake penitent look. "Right now, she's even beating me. I have to get my head in the game if I want to come away with the title."

Why wasn't Anne's head in the game?

I camouflaged my delight at Jane's success by puckering my lips. Then I really stuck my foot in my mouth. "You have quite an online presence. Were you and Barclay close?"

Her eyes sparked with either anger or indignation. "For a millisecond, but when I found out he just used me to get the job here, I was furious."

I must have looked shocked.

"Not furious enough to kill him. But it's almost impossible to successfully scrub the internet of photos; they're there forever. In fact, I recently found another reminder of my youthful indiscretion and removed it."

The answer to the photo deletion.

She surveyed the course, and her eyes followed two members of her foursome as they approached my cart. "However, he wasn't the only one who used me to get a job here. It seems I'm a real chump," she added sourly.

Ginny and Dennis trudged up the hill.

"I'd like a water, please," said Anne. The imploring look she gave along with her request telegraphed a desire to keep our discussion secret.

"And two more," said Ginny coming up behind her. When neither Anne nor Dennis made a move to pay for their beverages, Ginny fished a card out of her stretchy skorts pocket. "I've got this," she added with deference.

"How's your day?" I asked Ginny, completing the transaction.

She checked to confirm I was talking to her, and relieved, she relaxed her shoulders. "Right now, the tournament is delayed about thirty minutes. The judges heard sirens and stopped play. I don't know what that was about, do you?"

"One of the spectators was taken to the hospital."

"Oh. Is he okay? With Barclay's death, this tourney already has a cloud hanging over it."

"He's a she, and she's in good hands."

"Other than the delay, I think the tournament is going well. We've raised a boatload of money. Right, Dennis?"

He tore his gaze away from some distant sight. "Yeah. Sure."

"And the Honma Beres? Are they generating interest?"

"They have a unique look, so I'm getting questions and comments." She hesitated. "I'm still getting accustomed to their feel. It's difficult to play with a new set of clubs, but I hope to do better tomorrow."

"Your bag looks so heavy. How many clubs do you have in there?"

"I have eleven, but a player can have up to fourteen."

"Barclay enjoyed showing off his set, but his bag looked even more full. I was just wondering if all the sets were the same."

"Not all of them. Barclay always played with the maximum number allowed but he bought his own driver, so he only used thirteen of the promotional clubs. He made me acutely aware of that fact when his club arrived in its own silken sheath."

I hoped Ginny didn't notice my surprised expression. She'd mentioned the sleeve again and I wondered what happened to it.

"Katie? Hello-o." Anne waved her hand in front of my face.

"Sorry. My thoughts were drifting."

"I asked if you'd heard anything else about poor Barclay. You seem to be grand central with knowledge."

"No more than anyone else."

"Uh, uh, uh." Anne's forefinger ticked back and forth in front of her face. "Not everyone else has an in with the police chief *and* the coroner."

Dennis tensed, though his response could have been for any number of reasons ... such as thinking about the next hole, or the tiff he had with Tempest, or mention of the luxurious clubs, or maybe he had something to do with Byron's death.

Their fourth, the woman who Byron had breezed by on our first tour of the course, ignoring her attempt to connect with him, joined them and said irreverently, "Poisoning is too good for that jerk." She tipped her sunglasses on top of her head, flipping back mahogany curls, revealing a hint of gray roots. I studied the deep creases outlining her mouth like a set of parentheses on her face and the sun-weathered crinkles around her translucent blue eyes. "He asked for it."

Ginny had tipped the bottle toward her lips and jerked, choking. She sputtered and coughed. The woman rapped Ginny on her back until she was waved away.

"You all know, for insurance purposes and safety, access to the private garden was only allowed at the discretion of the board, but Barclay Byron always snuck in. I have it on good authority he harvested produce and conducted experiments. I don't know what he was looking for, but he found trouble. He might have fixed his own fatal food."

Or someone fixed it for him.

"With his shares, he had a voice and a vote. He threatened to rock our golf community. You know it's true." She glowered at Ginny. "I'll take a Bloody Mary."

"Make that two," Anne added.

The woman glared at Anne. "No adoring fans to watch Little Miss Perfect?"

"I can have one Bloody Mary."

I pressed the opened cans into their waiting hands.

"But can you handle one Bloody Mary?"

"Watch it, Nor."

"It's Nora." Nora took a big gulp of her beverage. "It's a good thing Byron's not here to make the announcement he planned. I tried to talk him out of it, but he wouldn't listen to reason. I've never met a more self-centered man in my entire life. This course has always been in a class by itself, but he was going to bring it down, airing all the dirty laundry."

Anne shushed her. "It's not going to happen now."

"You don't know that. Dennis, tell her. Even though you never got paid, your shares haven't been returned, have they? Your goody-two-shoes move might be the death knell of Shady Oaks yet."

TWENTY- NINE

Ginny tripped and splashed water down the front of Nora's shirt.

"You klutz." Nora spat the words.

"Temper. Temper." Anne scoffed, peering over the top of her can. "You wouldn't want anyone to see you get angry and jeopardize your reputation."

"You may have opened the door for me, but I've earned my reputation." Nora swung her head from side to side. "Besides, there's no one around."

"Except …" Anne's eyes made a sweeping motion and ended up on me.

Until that moment, I hadn't realized how invisible beverage suppliers, also known as bartenders, really were. I lifted my hand and fluttered my fingertips.

Nora stiffened. "She wouldn't say anything. I'm on the board. I hire and fire," she said caustically.

The spectators had stopped milling about and lined up facing the tee box again.

"Looks like we're getting back on track. That's our cue to move on. And I have the honors … again," said Anne with a superior air. When it came to the game, Anne was all in. However, I didn't know if that would be enough for her to win this time.

The four moved as a unit but as far apart from one another as possible. Why would they choose to be a foursome if they disliked each other so intensely?

I reluctantly moved toward hole fourteen and shuddered inwardly, remembering Barclay Byron at the water's edge. The fairway curved around a dogleg, and the bystanders I expected observing the drives crowded around Winslow instead. He parked close to the pond and doled out not only beverages but an exaggerated story to go with them.

I skirted the tee and followed the path toward hole thirteen, wondering if it was unlucky, and shivered when I caught a few of Winslow's embellishments.

"Barclay was found on this spot with his favorite golf club clutched in his hand."

The reality contradicted his fantasy, or was there some truth? Was the club found next to him his treasured fairway wood? But I distinctly remembered an iron.

"Was his death an accident or was he murdered? Where is that club, you ask? Can it identify the perpetrator?" For a moment, no one breathed. "Is Shady Oaks now haunted by *two ghosts?*"

I hustled out of listening distance, and the rest of the day passed quickly, swamped by thirsty competitors and watchers purchasing concessions in a constant stream. As day one wound down, Jane found me on hole eighteen for my third time. "How did you do today, Jane?"

"Pete stayed at the hospital to take care of his patients, so our team won't be in the running for the team trophy, not that we were anyway, but the judges said we could all still play the rest of the tournament. The better news is our individual scores will be ranked, and your dad is currently in eighth place overall, first in his age group."

I gasped and grabbed her hands, pressing them between mine. "Thank you so much for including him on your team. After all he's been through, he so deserved this, and he'll be so proud. Where is he?"

"Drew took him home, so I'm going with you."

"And what's the best news?"

She gave a shy smile and said, "I'm tied for second."

I inhaled and let it out slowly. "Whoa. That's great. I'm accompanying a champion."

"Maybe, but not yet." She laughed. "This is a weird tournament, though. Some of the competitors are cutthroat. I maybe could have worked harder, but I didn't want to be in the crosshairs tonight. First place is within reach, and I can wait until tomorrow to really ramp up my playing."

She helped me clean off my cart counter and stepped onto the platform as I began to move. I drove through the open garage door and parked next to Winslow's mobile stand. His cart was refilled and plugged in, but he must've taken off early again to get it all done so quickly.

As Jane helped me affix the goodies to the hooks, she observed one of the groundskeepers parking a mower. When he left, she said, "Okay, out with it. What did you find out today? I know you saw just about everybody on the course.

How can I be your right-hand woman and help you solve the mystery if I don't know all there is to know?"

I waited until the sounds died down around us and knew we were alone before reciting the highlights. "We still don't know the exact circumstances surrounding Byron's death, but something doesn't sit right with me. One of the golfers in Anne's foursome, Nora, said Byron shouldn't have been able to access the garden, but he had a key. She said he'd been harvesting and experimenting. Maybe one of his experiments went wrong."

"Or maybe someone else knew more about poison than he did. That dude had too many people unhappy with him. There's Tempest, Dennis, Ginny, and Clive too. If you had to choose, do you have a favorite … I mean, do you have one you think is more likely than the others to have done in Byron?"

"Barbara Clay had the strongest motive—"

"The new mom? I can see that."

"But so far, she's the only one I know with an iron-clad alibi."

"What should we do next?"

A tired voice behind us said, "Balance the till and go home." Lark stood in the entryway with her hands on her hips. "This is no place to gossip, and I can't afford to lose you, too. Winslow received too many customer complaints, and he's been dismissed." Everything about her seemed to droop, from her shoulders to her clothes. "I don't know how he succeeded in sweet-talking the board into considering him for the course manager, even if he is a Murphy. He can't even run a mobile snack bar." She grabbed my balanced cash drawer and spun on her heels, vanishing with as little fanfare as when she appeared.

Jane's phone buzzed. She answered it and smiled, turning away.

I finished prepping and stooped to pick up a wad of paper littering the ground. In case it might have some significance as a receipt, a bill, or an invoice, before I tossed it in the garbage, I flattened it against the top of one of the crates. I read it, and my insides flipped. The series of numbers and dashes looked similar to the inscription on Byron's silken sleeve. I inserted it into my pocket for safekeeping, hoping to see if it made any sense later.

Jane tucked her phone in her pocket and, with stars in her eyes, linked her arm through mine. "Drew's taking us to dinner."

We stepped in sync toward the exit when we heard voices yelling. Briefly locking eyes, we bolted through the rear door which opened onto the pathway to the garden. Nora held the arm of an individual struggling to break free.

She shouted, "What do you think you're doing? You can't be wandering around back here." She shook her captive, spinning him to face Jane and me.

"Galen?" I marched up to her, demanding his release. "Nora, let him go. He works the welcome podium." He stumbled from her claw-like grip and rubbed his arm.

"I caught him back here, and I have a right to know what he's doing. No one is allowed." Her nose rose into the air. "I'm on the board."

I turned to my student and questioned, "Galen? Can you please explain what's going on?"

He stood straighter. "Ms. Johansen gave me orders to check the grounds. Two golfing foursomes saw what they thought were raccoons tearing up the course. They're usually night-time prowlers and seeing them during the day raised some concerns. She told me to search for tracks or scat and hire someone to keep them at bay. I found the garden behind the open fence by accident. The whole area needs to be patrolled, and I was thinking …"

An idea lit behind his pleading eyes, and I knew what he wanted.

"No, can't do it. I know he's great, but totally unpredictable."

Nora looked right and left, confirming she was not surrounded by furry creatures, and stepped forward, crossing her arms in front of her. "What are you two talking about?" she huffed.

Galen took three long steps back and rose to his full height. It became patently obvious from the girth of his chest and forearms that, had he wished to escape from Nora, my nearly state-bound wrestling student could easily have wriggled free. Her eyes grew to the size of half dollars. His gentle nature kept him from doing any harm, and now she knew it too.

"But Ms. Wilk, you and I both know when it comes to protection, he's the top dog."

"Who is?" Nora said in a smaller voice.

Galen's broad smile filled his face. He relished saying the name at the same time Jane spoke, "Maverick." He turned to me. "You only need to ask. Dr. Bluestone would be with him. They could patrol the grounds and keep everyone safe. Dr. Bluestone would also be the one to determine if the raccoons pose a physical threat."

"You mean if they're rabid? And who's Maverick? A friend of yours?" asked Nora.

Galen chuckled. "You might say that. He's a dog."

"Tut. That's not happening on this—"

A rustling in the trees behind Nora sent her careening between Galen and me, knocking Jane off her feet. Galen righted her before she toppled. "Are you okay, Ms. Mackey?"

"Thanks to you."

"Hire him." Nora screeched from the protection of the garage.

"He can't work alone, and I don't know if—"

"One hundred dollars a day."

Galen said quietly, with the skill of a ventriloquist, "Wait for it."

"Two hundred fifty dollars … each," she added with more conviction. "My final offer. Take it." She glowered. "Or you're fired."

THIRTY

Jane nearly doubled over laughing as I yanked on the garage lock to double check it.

"It isn't funny." We cut across the lawn to the parking lot. "I can't say no to Nora. If I get fired, I can't afford to golf here." Jane interrupted, but I cut her off. "I know you'd cover my fees, but seriously, Jane, I'd like to pay my own way. Plus, Lark will be in a bind. Without Winslow, I don't know what we'll do tomorrow as it is."

"Don't you wonder what Winslow did or said to have someone lodge a complaint?"

I turned to face Jane and gave her my best really-you-have-to-ask look.

"Okay. I get it. He has no filter. But he should have known better than talking about Byron around Tempest."

"Tempest criticized Winslow's storytelling?"

She nodded. "She called him boorish and crude. He made up stories, like the one about you and Byron having words."

"That malarkey came from Winslow?"

She looked sheepish. "Back to Nora. You can't say no. Remember, Maverick is the best dog ever, and two hundred fifty dollars is a nice sum to add to your golfing kitty. C'mon, Galen did you a favor. You know he's a smart kid. And I absolutely don't want any wild, crazy animals with me on the golf course tomorrow, other than my dreamy beau. Maverick will be a deterrent, if nothing else, until they can find those little beasties."

I backed up a step and said, overdramatically, "And who's going to protect my dog from the crazy golfers?"

"Galen arranged for CJ to be with Maverick the entire time. Consider it a training exercise with perks."

"On steroids," I murmured.

I silently agreed, but there was no way I would let Galen know he'd probably offered a reasonable and safe solution if there really were animals causing havoc. I hoped they weren't rabid. Galen would expect repayment—quid pro quo—and rightly so, but I had no idea what I could do for Sherylann. "Galen has to be careful around here if he wants to keep his job. I don't have much faith in Nora. I wonder what gives her the power to dismiss with just a finger snap."

Wheels turned more freely in my head when Jane stopped teasing, and a thought struck me. "Maybe she doesn't. Maybe she just acts like she can fire someone at will. I need a conversation with Lark to find out more about Nora. I wonder why she was hanging around the garden, anyway."

Jane didn't respond. She gaped across the lot and tempered the lightheartedness in her voice. "What's wrong with your car?"

We approached, one cautious step at a time, and circled my ride, painstakingly inspecting the sticky brown syrup with a maple scent dripping from the windshield down the sides and onto the pavement, tsk-tsking the job of how to clean the mess. The fuel door swung from a broken hinge, and blue crystals clung to the rim around a gaping hole where the gas cap should have been.

Jane touched the tip of her finger to the blue ring of unknown origin, but I stopped her from bringing it to her lips. "That could be anything."

"It's gotta be sugar." Her brow furrowed. "Doesn't it?" Her eyes grew wary. "I don't like this, Katie. I'm calling Drew."

Jane and I sat beneath the sturdy oak trees on another wooden bench dedicated to Quinn and Liam Murphy, lost in our own thoughts until two cars pulled into the parking lot. I let out a lungful of air. Drew must've called Amanda. Together, they strode across the lot.

The day's heat and humidity had taken its toll, and I felt wilted in my work attire next to Amanda in her crisp uniform with her neatly braided black hair. Her hands hovered over the implements on her utility belt at her hips. She closed her deep brown eyes and shook her head. "Looks like someone is mighty unhappy with you, Katie. What have you done now?"

Since I'd merely composed a list of suspects … and motives … and alibis of those who might have had reason to murder Byron, I didn't think that constituted doing anything and answered truthfully, "I don't know."

She walked around the car and took photos, capturing a closeup of the residue around the fuel door. "We don't know what this is. I've called a tow truck. We'll test the substance and clean the vehicle and—"

"Do you have to take it? How will I get to work?" I

sounded pathetic, even to me.

She silenced me with one raised eyebrow. "If you run your car and someone pours, let's say, sugar into the gas tank, you can clog the fuel injectors or ruin the fuel filter or worse. And the cost of fixing it could be exorbitant. We'll have the tank emptied." She tried to keep one corner of her mouth from curling up. "I'll order the maple syrup removed too. Meanwhile, you'll have to find other transportation."

The mechanic's cherry red truck noisily bumped along the drive. The man behind the wheel stepping out was new, but the tow truck and I had met before. He had a momentary conversation with Amanda, and I frowned as he hauled my wheels away. "Amanda, how long do you think they'll keep her?"

She looked a little discomfited. "They probably won't work on it over the weekend, but you can call later Monday." She handed me a business card. "Unless we find evidence of criminal intent with more magnitude, and we have to hold onto it until we check all the boxes."

"Meanwhile," I grumbled.

Drew's arm snaked over Jane's shoulder. "Let's go, Katie."

I sullenly followed Jane and Drew to his vehicle when a royal blue Ram truck barreled down the drive, slammed on its brakes, coming to a dead stop ten feet away. Pete slid from the driver's seat, and the door banged behind him. "Life is never boring with you two, is it?"

"What are you doing here? I thought you were taking care of Barbara and her baby."

"I am ... was, but they're doing well enough. After Amanda informed Mrs. Clay about Barclay, or rather John, her anxiety ramped up and her vitals were all over the place. When she settled down, I told her it would be best if they stayed, so I'm keeping them overnight, and she settled in, but right now I'm responding to the sketchy message Drew left." The look he cast Drew would have singed a lesser man. "But, Katie, you appear to be the picture of health."

Drew said, "She could use a ride home, though. Amanda had her car towed."

"Of course."

A short huff escaped from Amanda as she tucked her head and disappeared into her squad car. The vehicle rolled down the path and picked up speed on the drive, then disappeared. Drew and Jane waved and vanished almost as quickly.

Pete didn't speak. He opened the passenger door and waited for me to climb into his truck, then jogged around to the driver's side. He turned the key and put the truck in gear, without saying a word until we were halfway back to town. "Byron was poisoned. I identified hemlock—"

"Hemlock? Isn't that how they executed Socrates?"

"Don't change the subject."

"Where do you find hemlock?"

"Minnesota is loaded with it. It can resemble wild carrot or parsley, and every part of the plant is poisonous, but we haven't determined if the poisoning was accidental or done purposely." He took a few deep breaths. "What trouble are you in now, Katie?

At first, my eyebrows rose to my hairline and then I scowled. "I didn't do anything but work the tournament. I'm not in any trouble."

"Why would someone use your car for sticky target practice?"

"It was probably a student with a grudge, or someone who let their ire out on the wrong car."

"Number one, no student holds a grudge against you. You haven't been in Columbia long enough, and number two, everybody likes you."

"Then it was obviously a mistake."

"Number three, nobody could mistake a car like yours in *that* parking lot among *those* cars. Why do you put yourself in these situations? This isn't the first time you've been targeted by an unsavory individual. The stakes are not just high, they are astronomical," he said, his tone full of reproach.

"You sound like the mess is all my fault."

He didn't deny it.

We stewed and rode in silence. Before he finished parking his truck in my driveway, I dropped from the cab, threw the door back in place, and marched up my back steps, escaping before I said something I'd regret. I didn't turn around but heard the roar of the engine as he sped to the street. I swallowed my tears and entered the dark house.

THIRTY-ONE

My phone buzzed. "Hey girlfriend, what's up?" I tried to be ultra cheerful, flipping on the lights and petting Maverick with a subtle but strong hand to keep him from jumping up to lick my face. The corners of my mouth, however, turned down, and the timbre of my voice gave me away.

"Katie, what's wrong?"

Tears slid down my cheeks, unchecked, and I snuffled. "I think Pete and I had our first major fight. I screwed up."

"How did you screw up?"

"Pete said this isn't the first time—"

"Pete said? It doesn't matter one fig what Dr. Pete Erickson has to say. I was there, and you didn't do anything to warrant having your car targeted by vandals." Jane blew out a lungful of air. "What did he think you did?"

She was nothing if not contradictory. "He thinks I've put myself in the crosshairs of a dangerous person again." I sniffed and dug out a tissue. "All I've done is take on a summer job."

"And find a body."

"You were there too." I sounded petulant, but the vision of Barclay Byron loomed at the forefront of my thoughts.

Jane's voice lost its edge. "Listen, Pete's probably worried sick about you." When I didn't respond, she said with a bit of curiosity, "What are you holding back?"

"I do have a personal list of suspects."

Jane didn't make a sound.

"Jane, are you there?" I asked, fearing she too had taken issue with my conduct.

She answered with a snort, and more chuckling. "You always have a list of suspects." I laughed along with her. "I'm coming to pick you up for dinner. We need to talk."

"What happened to dinner with Drew?"

"I guess *we* happened. He's working tonight, so he can golf tomorrow. You and I can talk wedding."

Maverick nudged my side, and I grunted.

"What's wrong? Don't you want to go? I thought we could go to Thai Fyre."

"Sounds great, but Maverick is demanding attention. Give me twenty minutes."

I swallowed and cleared my throat. "Jane, are you afraid to be with me?"

"That'll be the day. See you."

Maverick and I jogged through the neighborhood, and when we approached the final yard before Ida's, Pamela stuck her head out her screen door and waved us close. "Katie," she said softly but with urgency. "Adam's still on the road, and

Emma's tied up in knots. She hardly slept last night, and she's overly tired, but the only thing that seems to calm her down is a visit with your dog." She braced the door with her hip and waffled, wringing her hands. "Could you and Maverick stop in for a minute?"

In place of Pamela's customary perfectly made-up face, she wore gray circles beneath her eyes and a wan smile. I'd never seen her in stained, frayed blue jeans nor a wrinkled shirt before. Her shoulders drooped. She had *weary* written all over.

"Absolutely." I figured if Jane arrived before I was ready, she'd understand.

We followed Pamela inside and through a house as neat as a pin, as expected from the Pamela I knew. Emma's upstairs room, on the other hand, had suffered a pink confectionary hurricane. I held tight to Maverick's lead.

She sat on the floor amid piles of pale pink stuffed pillows and fluffy blankets in varying shades of cherry blossoms, in front of a fuchsia dollhouse with delicate flamingo-colored gingerbread trim. She clenched two characters in her chubby fingers, dancing them up and down with her words.

"Emma," Emma recited in a rather Pamela-like imitation. "It's time for bed." In her own voice she answered, "Not yet, Mommy. I promised Maverick I'd help him guard the neighborhood. He stopped barking. But I have to be awake if he needs help."

I scrunched my eyes. *What help would Maverick need?*

"Emma, darling," Pamela interrupted. "Look who's here."

With a huge "Oh!" Emma scrambled to her feet and rushed Maverick, almost knocking him off his paws, burying her blond curls in his black fur. He lapped at her face. She squirmed, cooing in joy. Pamela and I watched as she whispered in his ear. When she saw me, she squealed, "Katie!" and rushed me too, wrapping her arms around my knees.

She leaned away and punched her little fists about where her hips should be. "Where have you been? Maverick's been waiting all day," she said in the most accusing high-pitched voice I'd ever heard.

I nodded. "You're so right, Emma, and he and I just got back from a jog."

"Okay." She relaxed her rigid stance an iota. "I'm making a surprise for you and Maverick. You're coming to my party, aren't you?"

I sucked in the tiniest of breaths. "We wouldn't miss it, Emma. Now, you and Maverick need to get some rest, so you'll be ready for your birthday."

After planting one more kiss on Maverick's nose, she jumped onto her satiny blush-colored comforter, causing the gauzy canopy to sway. Pamela tucked her in. "I'll be right back, and if you're still awake, I'll read your lullaby book."

Though Emma seemed to be drifting off to sleep before we left the room, she murmured, "Don't worry, Maverick. I'm watching."

Pamela softly closed the door and mouthed, "Thank you."

We crept down the stairs, and Pamela accompanied us to the door. She sighed. "I can't wait for Adam to come home. Thanks so much for stopping in."

"Pamela, did Maverick bark a lot during the day? Ida, Dad, and I attended the golf tournament today. I didn't think he'd cause a problem."

She squinted as if looking back in time. "I honestly didn't

notice it, but Emma pays much more attention to Maverick than I do. Will you be gone tomorrow too? Do you need us to make a visit?" she said hopefully.

"You can always visit, and Maverick would love it. But he's on duty with CJ tomorrow." I exhaled and wondered aloud. "Why would Emma think she has to watch the neighborhood?"

Pamela smiled. "Adam's evening ritual with her is to say good night to things in and around our house, their own living version of *Goodnight Moon*. I tried to copy the practice, and she threw a little fit." Pamela pouted. "Daddy only, you know." Her eyelids drifted closed.

"You're welcome anytime, but Pamela, you need to get some rest too. Do it while Emma is sleeping."

"It's hard to get to sleep before the sun goes down, but I'll try."

"Goodnight."

"Night, Katie."

Maverick yanked me out the door and across the lawn when he caught the scent of one of his favorite people walking up the sidewalk. CJ Bluestone, veterinarian and trainer extraordinaire, beckoned us close. He chirped and Maverick sat.

"Wish I could do that." He cocked a dubious eyebrow. "I know. Practice and consistency."

"Maverick and I will be walking the course tomorrow on the lookout for unwanted creatures. I want to verify you know this is happening."

"Yes. Do you think he can do it?"

"He can do anything he puts his mind to. We will be fine. Will you take him with you, or will I bring him?"

"I'm biking to work. My car is being cleaned up, so could

he ride with you?"

"Of course." CJ removed a leather tie from his hair, and a blue-black curtain covered his face when he dropped his chin.

"Thanks."

He'd been able to disguise the chuckle in his voice, but when he looked up, he couldn't hide the gleam in his eyes.

"You heard about my car?" My face heated.

"Word is out."

"I'll drop him off before I leave tomorrow."

CJ nodded and returned to his home across the street, lifting a hand to Jane in greeting as she rolled into our driveway.

"I'll be right out," I hollered, rushing inside for last-minute repairs to my overall appearance.

Maverick snarfed his treat and almost took two fingers with it. I gave him a quick scratch and snatched my bag off the hook. A paper fluttered to the floor. I picked it up, noticing the familiar red characters on the page. I tucked the slip of paper inside my bag and rushed out to share my find with Jane.

THIRTY-TWO

And you found this just lying on the floor. Who has access to the garage?"

"During the day, the storage space remains unlocked until the carts are returned and plugged in for the night. Lark could get in, of course, and Winslow. Byron had a key. I have no idea who else had access. Winslow picked up a page in Lark's office with red writing on it. Maybe this is it? It looks like the code similar to one Byron found on a sheath for his prized fairway wood."

"Do you have any notion about what the numbers mean?" Jane said, dipping the fragrant vegetable spring roll in a sesame sauce. "If that cipher uses our alphabet, forties wouldn't figure so prominently, would they?"

Culling my memories brought me to a long-forgotten

cryptography class called *The Art of Secret Writing.* I constructed a five-by-five grid on a paper napkin, and Jane challenged me. "There still aren't enough spots for all the letters."

I acquiesced but continued to write within the grid. Under the first column, I jotted a, b, c, d, and e and entered f, g, and h in the next column. I doubled up i and j, rapidly filled in the rest of the grid, and spun the page so Jane could read my scrawl. Her eyes widened and she tapped the napkin.

"Forty-three could mean row four, column three or …" She cocked her head. "Column four and row three. And not to put a damper on your great idea, but it's entirely feasible you combined the wrong two letters. I know we don't use j often, but neither do we use z, x or v."

"But it could work. It's a substitution cipher. At least there is a finite number of sequences to attempt, and the characters are arranged like the ones on Byron's silk sheath." I made the substitutions using rows first and penciled a nonsensical 'snymynq.' I dropped back in the chair, and my pencil clattered against the serving dish. "Gibberish."

Jane calmly turned the paper carrying her decryption for me to read. "Onehundredthousandorelse. I used the first number for the column."

"One hundred thousand or else." I swallowed hard. "That's it."

"That's what?" a smooth voice from behind me said. "Hey, Katie and charming friend."

I locked eyes with the insolent man and pasted on a big smile as my fingers surreptitiously tugged the napkin atop the page and dragged the pieces together, gathering them in my palm and crumpling them as garbage. "Winslow. Have you met my friend, Jane?"

"I believe I have. Ms. Mackey, I'd really hate for you to consider the word charming to be offensive." He turned his green eyes to me. "I suppose you've heard they released me from the tedium of the mobile snack bar."

"I heard." I nodded. "What could someone complain about?" I thought I'd done a fine job camouflaging my true feelings, but I wasn't sure when his eyes narrowed and the hairs on the back of my neck stood on end.

"Honesty can be refreshing." He relaxed and shrugged. "They merely moved me from a pedestrian post to upper management. Barclay made a mess of things, and his death has cast a pall over Shady Oaks. Now I'm in charge of cleaning up our public image, something more suited to my skill set." A little softer he said, "And that isn't all."

Jane leaned forward. "Winslow, you'll be the media specialist?" He nodded. "Filtering news? Let me set up a scenario. I'll be a reporter showing up at the awards ceremony Sunday evening." Winslow nodded again, more tentatively. Jane sat back. "How much money has this tournament collected, both historically and for this year alone?"

"According to the records maintained by the current leadership over the last ten years, this fundraiser has garnered inestimable kudos, boundless goodwill, and untold fame." Jane's face registered the words rubbish, and Winslow scoffed. "This year, although the final tally has yet to be determined, we have collected the most yet, sixty-nine thousand dollars, for a ten-year accumulated total of five hundred ninety-seven thousand dollars, give or take a thousand."

Jane applauded lightly and asked, "Next question. Who would have wanted Barclay Byron out of the picture?"

Winslow showed no signs of duress, nor did he hesitate. "Mr. Byron's untimely death is currently under investigation, and I'm not at liberty to divulge information that might jeopardize the case."

Jane pursed her lips. "Not a bad response. I wish you luck."

"But between you and me," Winslow inclined toward Jane and whispered, "they always suspect the spouse, don't they?" Someone across the room caught his eye. "Excuse me."

As he sauntered away, I barely moved my lips and said through gritted teeth locked around a gruesome grin, "But really, which spouse? That's the question, isn't it?"

Jane acknowledged she'd heard with a slight dip of her head. We observed Winslow pull out a chair at a table hosting Ginny and Dennis. They didn't look overjoyed to see him, but he didn't leave.

Jane lightly tapped the back of the hand clamped tightly around the papers with the possible message. "What do we do with this? We don't know who it's from, who it's to, what there is to tell, nor what the hundred thousand refers to."

"It could have been copied off the sheath that came with Byron's club."

"Has Amanda found the club or cover yet?"

"Not that she's telling me. If Byron's death wasn't an accident, and I'm not saying it wasn't, he could've been the victim of blackmail, and if he couldn't come up with the payoff, he might have been the victim of the *or else*." I deliberated, chewing my pad Thai "I guess Byron could have been the extortionist and his attempt backfired." My conviction shriveled. "Everything we have is pure supposition. But we should probably inform the chief."

Meticulously flattening the pages, I snapped a photo of the message and attached the decoding instrument to a text destined for Amanda. I folded the papers and tucked the enigma into my pocket.

I figured it would be much quicker to call and explain

what I found and what Jane had figured out, but Amanda didn't pick up. She knew it was from me, so I waited for her to make a return call.

And waited. And waited.

"Something's going on. She always answers."

Fidgeting, we waited some more.

"Let's see what we know," Jane said.

Silent seconds ticked by. "We really don't *know* anything. The coded message might be a gag or a test or a kid's riddle."

"Or it might be just what it looks like—coercion of some kind. It feels that way, doesn't it?"

I slumped in my seat. "Jane, we've probably destroyed any chance of Amanda finding fingerprints on the page. We'd better come up with a few ideas to steer her wrath away from us."

Neither of us provided any suitable suggestions to redirect Amanda's anger, and Jane changed the subject. "Did you get your gift for Emma?"

"Not yet. Are you and Drew going?"

"Yes, I'm going to ask her to be my flower girl. What about you?"

"Emma's easy—something pink."

Jane rose from her seat and snatched the check before I could get my fingers on it. I volunteered to split it with her, and she brushed me off, saying, "Next time, girlfriend." She looked up. Her smile paled. "Right now, let's get out of here. Too many prying eyes and big ears." I turned around in my chair to figure out what had caught her attention.

THIRTY-THREE

I raised my hand to wave but lost sight of Pete and the leggy blonde clinging to his arm when they were swallowed by a wave of diners.

"I wonder who that is."

Jane peered around the waitstaff seating patrons and shook her head. She tugged at my arm. "Come on. I need to see if Ida has any more worthwhile wedding wisdom for me."

As always, she did.

Although I wanted to be by myself, probably sulking, I ramped up my level of enthusiasm when Jane tried on the finished gown. Ida must have worked every waking moment, and it paid off. The ethereal bedazzled white dress with the feathery skirt floated around Jane as she flounced into my kitchen. It fit like a glove and if her wedding dress didn't rock her groom's world, the party frock would.

"You have attire, a church and officiant, a reception venue and food choices, flowers, a guest list, witnesses, and attendants. You still need a photographer."

"We'll get great candids at our wedding from Dad's plus one; she's an award-winning amateur photographer. And Pamela is hiring out as a photographer and a videographer, so I'm covered."

"Emma's mom?"

"Yup, but I'd hate to miss out on a chance to go shopping, so I might need new dancing shoes." I couldn't help but join in her chuckle.

Ida crossed her arms and rested her chin on the back of one hand, akin to Rodin's The Thinker. "Next up, Katie's attire." Ida and Jane turned their laser-sharp eyes on me.

Maverick woofed. He sat in a perfect pose, as if waiting for his next cue.

"See?" Ida gestured toward my dog. "Even Maverick agrees."

"Traitor." I whispered, "I planned to wear my favorite blue dress." My bottom lip protruded. "I hate shopping."

"You'll still wear blue. It's a good color on you," said Jane and giggled. "I ordered your dress yesterday. It's on the way."

Panic rushed in. "Can I at least see a picture of it?"

Jane's Cheshire-cat grin gave me goosebumps. "It's going to be a surprise."

Like everything else in my life.

When Amanda finally returned my call, she was angry. "Someone's going to get hurt, Katie. Lay off."

"What are you talking about?"

"Officer Christianson's press conference ended in an uproar. When he opened the floor to questions, a certain young man asked why we targeted the homeless. He cited statistics—the total number of homeless in Minnesota, the total number of homeless parolees—and mentioned the work community members were doing in the name of justice. And you know the budding teen attorney personally."

"Galen."

"Any hint of investigating, and I'll be forced to charge you with obstruction of justice."

During her dressing down, I missed a call from Pete, and I wasn't prepared to return his call. Jane had decrypted the coded message, and if she shared the solution with Drew, Pete probably heard all about our find and would only echo Amanda's warning.

I fretted about Sherylann's predicament and worried what else Galen might take upon himself to do, tossing and turning for hours. Every time I closed my eyes, the indistinct vision of Barclay Byron lying on the ground near the edge of the pond came into focus.

I finally succumbed to my fatigue after I decided not to involve myself further. Barclay Byron's death by hemlock had to be an accident.

It rained overnight and continued to drizzle off and on into the early hours. Bleary-eyed and yawning, my mood was as gray and threatening as the morning sky. On the flip side, the temperature had dropped, and heat wouldn't truncate my walk with Maverick. I snapped on his lead, and with every step I took, I felt sure the heavy skies would open up and dump buckets of water. However, though the dawn luminesced a fiery red, the storm held off, and by the end of our walk, the menacing clouds gradually dispersed. Wisps of white hovered in a cerulean sky. It would be another beautiful day.

After a quick coffee and bagel, I headed across the street

and dropped Maverick off early with a backpack of doggie paraphernalia: a leash, toys, treats, a ball, plastic bags, and an admonition to, "Be good." CJ never said a word, just stood off to the side with a patronizing smirk. "See you later then."

Assured Ida would deliver Dad to the course in plenty of time for him to get comfortable and warm up, I jotted the list of small tasks I needed to complete before the tournament tee time, pocketed the reminder, strapped on my helmet, and set off on an invigorating bike ride. So caught up contemplating the message Jane and I had decoded, I didn't notice traffic on the road until a red blur came so close, the turbulence in its wake blew me toward the ditch. I struggled to right the wobbling handlebars, screaming, "Slow down," to the taillights disappearing around the next corner, but my front tire clipped the edge of the pavement. I lost control and slid into the tall grasses.

I laid there, taking inventory. All my parts still moved, but my pride hurt. It could have been worse. I dusted my palms and knees and checked my bike. It might have had a few more gashes, but I got back on and put my daydreaming on the back burner to concentrate for the rest of my ride.

As I was prone to do when I wasn't traveling with Jane or Ida, I arrived with time to spare and locked my bike in the empty rack, scanning the lot for the careless driver. On my tongue were helpful words I thought I might impart, but red cars were a favorite among today's early arrivals, and I'd always been stymied by makes and models.

I made my way to the front of the clubhouse. Galen looked up from the podium with a hopeful expression. I shook my head and said, "What were you thinking last night?"

"You've heard?" He glanced down, shuffling his feet. "The chief wasn't smiling when I finished, but I only recited the facts, no commentary. Did you know there are more than ten thousand homeless in Minnesota, and because of where they are forced to live, they are investigated more closely for every infraction?" He lowered his voice. "Like Sherylann."

"You know how easily numbers can be manipulated. You twisted facts and figures as a witness in our mock trial this year." I gazed at him attentively. "Chief West gave me an order. In no uncertain terms, we are not to investigate. She could cite us for obstruction of justice. That would not look good when filling out a college application."

Galen bowed his head and rubbed the back of his neck. "I'm sorry, Ms. Wilk, but they railroaded Sherylann. She might be guilty of poor judgement and bad choices, but it was one pound of ground meat. She's out on bail, but all she sees is a bleak future. And I'm afraid they've temporarily stopped searching for another guilty person."

I hadn't seen him this dejected since his junior wrestling season ended before it started, when he admitted to taking steroids in the fall. "I promise, I'll watch and stay vigilant, but I can't actively pursue an investigation without consequences. Neither can you."

"Yes, ma'am," he said with a glint in his eye.

In light of our successful crime-solving year, I believe he harbored hope my vigilance might produce results, and I feared I'd created a justice junkie.

"I mean it." I shook my keyring for emphasis.

Galen grinned. "Yes, Ms. Wilk. By the way, you can secure your bike lock key on my board if you'd like."

After clocking in, I breezed by the empty desks in Lark's office, out across the lush, green lawn covered with glittering gems of dew droplets, and through a cacophony of morning birdsong accompanied by my footfalls crunching down the pebble path to the garage. I reached for the door. The padlock hung loose, and the door stood slightly ajar. I knew I'd closed and locked it the night before, but maybe Lark had come in to help with preparation for the day, or better yet, she'd found someone to replace Winslow.

The door squeaked as I pushed it back, revealing the storage space in massive disarray. Tiny pieces of cardboard torn from the beverage cartons littered the floor. The contents of the overturned trash receptacles spilled out. Columns of boxes teetered. Empty bags of nuts and popcorn from my display hooks lay scattered around the open space, and I was glad Lark hadn't taken inventory of my reserves yet. Resigned, I marched into the garage when a crate crashed to the cement behind Winslow's cart.

I took slow, careful steps in the direction of the chittering and hissing. "Who's there?" My voice quavered. "Helloooo."

The sounds stopped. I curled my fingertips around the edge of the counter and dragged myself forward, tentatively peering over the counter of the mobile station into the snarling face of a raccoon. It stood on its hind legs, eyes wide, stretched out its arms, and screeched. I hurtled around the side of the cart in a panic, stumbled back, tripped over a second masked bandit, and jerked to a stop, surrounded by two more.

"Shoo." I stomped my feet, clapped my hands, and shouted absurdities. The little scamps tipped their heads and looked at me as if I was the lunatic as their tiny fingers continued to stuff their faces with treats. And then I heard the most glorious sound. Barking, and it was getting closer.

The raccoons heard it too. At first, they froze, but I could almost see in their beady yellow eyes the moment they recognized the animal making the sounds, and they scampered through the narrow opening in the back on the garden side of the garage. The adrenaline left my body, leaving me slumped forward as my lifesaving dog bounded through the door, wickedly wagging his tail.

My heart rate slowly returned to normal, and I knelt to a messy face washing. "Good boy, Maverick."

CJ limped in after him, his cane raised. "Maverick only takes off like that when you are in trouble. What happened?"

I caught my breath and buried my face in Maverick's neck. I brought my head up. "Those critters were here and made this mess. I counted at least four raccoons."

CJ surveyed the detritus. When he snapped his fingers, Maverick's rump hit the floor, but he jabbed my hand for attention. "When they sense access to food, raccoons are skillful, dexterous, and intelligent problem solvers, but I do not believe they are capable of picking a lock." CJ had noticed the entry.

"Which means that someone else has been here, opened the lock, and either forgot to close the door or purposely allowed the rascals in to do their damage." I watched CJ's eyes travel to the space above. "I guess I should check up there."

Noisily climbing the dilapidated ladder to the loft, I called, "You can come out now." I raised my head slowly and peeked over the edge, scanning three hundred sixty degrees. "The only things up here are tiny claw prints in about a half inch of dust." A sneeze erupted and the tracks disintegrated. "Sorry, only dust."

Once I dropped back to the ground, I navigated through the carts, shimmying around the listing cartons of wine and beer, wedging myself between the refrigerated storage units to the back entrance where the scamps exited, intent on making sure they were long gone.

I expected the rear door to glide easily as it had every other time I'd stepped out but found it blocked. I shoved the boards again. When that didn't work, I rammed my shoulder with too much force and buckled in pain. CJ strode up beside me. He stood his cane against the wall and curled his fingers around the plank at the opening. When I joined him, planting my hands on the rough wood, he said, "One, two …" and on three we drove a space wide enough for me to wriggle through.

My polo shirt caught on a splinter, and I twisted around to carefully disentangle my uniform and saw what had blocked the entry.

"CJ." I blinked. "CJ, you need to get out here."

THIRTY-FOUR

Wedged beneath the door was the toe of a black and tan shoe. And it came with a crumpled body. I backed away, dropped to my knees, and combed my fingers through Maverick's fur. CJ called Amanda.

I thought I'd seen Amanda angry before, but I was wrong. Chief West attended to the victim with fierce precision and detail. When Pete saw me, a look of incredulity passed over his face, replaced almost immediately by a shroud of no-nonsense. He joined Amanda, and neither said a word, but the air around them sizzled. Amanda's eyes blazed. Pete wore a grim expression of resignation. They spoke to CJ in hushed tones, and I attempted to make myself invisible. No one looked at me. No one talked to me. It worked, or so I thought.

Pete meticulously examined the victim, recording the parameters with thoroughness and detachment, the same professional demeanor he employed when we met last August after my first encounter with a dead body in Columbia. He completed supervising the technicians collecting evidence, stepped close to Amanda, said his piece, and headed out after the gurney, accompanying the EMTs as they carefully moved the body.

He never glanced my way. My stomach lurched.

Amanda crooked her finger, beckoning me close. She pinched the bridge of her nose and said, "I don't know what to do with you, Katie."

"I didn't have anything to do with this." I tried to sound cooperative, but I wouldn't let her run roughshod over me either.

"Because of Byron's cause of death, Dr. Erickson is testing the victim for poison at the onset." I reeled back. "The body will undergo careful scrutiny. He's been dead for a few hours. I hate to ask, but did you see anyone when you came down here?"

"Galen works at the welcome podium." I watched Amanda's face for displeasure, but she was a professional and didn't bat an eye. "CJ arrived with Maverick, but I didn't see another ..." I was going to say living soul, but that didn't seem appropriate. "Person. Is it ...?"

She confirmed my suspicion. "It's Winslow Boros."

Even though I was prepared for the pronouncement, I staggered. "Winslow. He was so young. What's happening? Could both deaths be accidental? And why was he at the garage?" He wasn't high on my list of favorite people, but I tried to keep my apprehension at bay. "Yesterday, Lark released him from working the beverage cart and moved him to upper management. He shouldn't even have been here."

"I thought he was a new hire like you. Do you know why he was promoted?"

"Yes. My boss indicated he's a member of the Murphy family."

She muttered, "Nepotism."

Biting my lip gave me time to organize my words.

"Out with it," she said.

"On the course yesterday, Winslow told exaggerated stories about Byron's death, and someone complained. He's supposed to be working his way through all the positions at the club, and Lark moved him to media specialist, kind of a public relations position."

"Who's Lark?"

"She just took over as head of the HR department. She might *be* the HR department. I've never seen anyone else in the office but Winslow."

"Then she knows who criticized him." Her eyes were full of concern as she searched my face. "Katie, please say nothing about Winslow to anybody."

"You know I won't."

Nodding, she continued, "If you hear any comments or questions, refer them to the police department. We need to investigate the circumstances surrounding his death."

"It's too much like Byron's murder, isn't it? There will be speculation."

"A second death in the span of one week, on the same golf course, makes an accident seem highly unlikely. We'll investigate the deaths as suspicious until we know otherwise. I know you feel I haven't listened to you, but I do care, Katie." She laid her hand on my shoulder and lowered me onto a prickly bale of hay. "We've been asked not to disrupt the fundraiser. With no one else available, they'll most likely expect you to work the tourney today, but will you be okay?"

"Yes." I shook involuntarily but affirmed, "I'll be fine."

Her eyes darkened. "I let my righteous indignation get in the way of my judgment, and I'm sorry. We're going to look at Byron's death again. We will do our job."

I worked up my courage and said, "I have a list of suspects and motives."

Amanda sighed. "Of course, you do. I'll let you know if I need it."

It didn't come from me, but word of Winslow's death spread like wildfire. The pall over the players and members of the staff who knew him dampened spirits and subdued conversation, but not as much as the loss of Barclay Byron, who had been a fixture at the club for a number of years. Relatively new to Columbia, Winslow hadn't assembled a large number of associates nor depth of friendships, but the unknown weighed on everyone.

Fifteen minutes before day two should have begun, Nora assembled the competitors around hole one. "In light of this morning's discovery and as representative of the board of directors, rather than delay or cancel our fundraiser, I'm announcing the unanimous decision to continue the tournament." The crowd shifted uneasily, surprised by her statement, and she addressed the murmurs.

"You may think we're callous. To the contrary, we're so tuned in to the homeless problem in our community, we wish to donate another ten thousand dollars to the cause on young Winslow's behalf." The grumbling turned to cautious applause. "But we'd like to take a minute to silently reflect and remember Winslow, the great, great, great ..." She slowed. Her face did a series of calisthenics as she tried to count back the multiple generations. "Progeny of Liam and Quinn Murphy."

After what seemed like merely a ten-second pause, Nora said, "Let the games begin."

Lark hurriedly checked my cash drawer. In spite of his sometimes-abrasive attitude, I think she liked Winslow. I had to admit, he had a good point or two. One just had to look deep.

"I trust you, Katie. I have no need to go to the storage unit." Lark sniffed. "We have permission to enter, but I can't right now. Just let me know the change in inventory you have at the end of the day. I had hoped to reenlist Winslow's assistance, but that's not happening, and I haven't been able to find anyone to take over for him. I'm sorry."

"What about re-hiring Sherylann?"

Lark reared as if stung.

"She's worked the beverage cart and knows the ropes. She'd be perfect." Lark hesitated, and I added, "She's out on bail."

Lark shook her head. "Not anymore. She's back in custody on suspicion of murder."

I stammered, then composed myself. "Why would they think Sherylann killed Byron or Winslow?"

"She admits to stealing from the kitchen, and Doctor Erickson determined hemlock was the poison which killed Byron." Remembering I needed to return Pete's call, I almost missed the rest of her explanation. "Byron could have tested foodstuffs, or mistakenly used it himself, and ingested the hemlock, but he wasn't around to experiment on Winslow. Chief West isn't ignoring a second death.

"If either of the men caught her acting the part of the ghost, taking Antoine's expensive specialty meat or any other valuables around the resort, and threatened to blow the whistle, she had motive, but she'd be arrested even if the poisoning was accidental." Lark blinked a few times before she said, "You can start on hole nine this time. You never know, you may be busy enough you won't have to move from that spot. Today will be different, that's for certain."

The garage was empty but for the minuscule remnant of yellow caution tape Amanda had affixed to cordon off the area where we found Winslow. It dangled from a nail on the frame of the exit. I stacked the boxes to clear a path for my cart to squeeze through to the main door and glanced morosely in the direction of the caretaker's cottage.

An absolutely horrible thought came to me. What if Sherylann had nothing to do with poisoning either man, and we were all at risk?

THIRTY-FIVE

I thought long and hard about texting Amanda again but decided to wait. I needed proof, not conjecture. Research. After my shift.

I drove out to the ninth hole and opened my shop. The golfers moved robotically from one hole to the next with intent. The tournament progressed at a much steadier pace, and the competitors didn't spend much time dawdling. Many spectators found a favorite foursome and stuck with them, following them around the course. Sales were steady, but I sold fewer items overall. I made my way glacially down the path. Tips were nonexistent, but I received an hourly wage, so it wasn't a total loss. I was outside on a beautiful day and banked one of the perks of employment—golfing with Jane for free.

I ran into Maverick and CJ on hole two. They hadn't found the raccoons, but they found more tracks and scat. CJ thought Maverick might have already frightened them away for the day and promised to return for the last day of the tournament just in case our visitors made another appearance. Maverick took a moment, easing under my fingers for scratches, the one bright spot in my day, and it might have been the last. CJ whistled. Maverick dashed down the path and out of sight behind a line of tall oak trees.

When ZaZa stepped to the closest tee, she saw me and froze. Her eyes narrowed, and even from where I stood, I could see her nostrils flare. I swallowed hard, but at the same time, I wanted to cry. Once upon a time, she'd been my friend.

My intention to leave quickly was thwarted by my cart jerking to a stop as it did the first time I attempted its operation. Flustered, I couldn't make the controls do what they were supposed to do, and I heard a deep, derisive chuckle. A chill ran up my spine.

"Need help, Katie?" Montgomery asked.

ZaZa fumed. I couldn't speak, just shook my head and tried again.

"Are you sure?"

"Yes," I said. "I'm sure." I glimpsed Dad, Jane, and Drew through the foliage, putting on an adjacent green. It wouldn't do for Dad to witness this interaction. I concentrated on moving, mentally letting go of everything, inhaled a lungful of air, and expelled it quickly. Ticking off the detailed instructions I'd been using, I tried again. The cart started, and I lurched along to hole one, sucking in air.

Why did Montgomery come here? Had he changed? How would I ever have the wherewithal to tell ZaZa things about her boyfriend she absolutely wouldn't want to hear?

Anne waved the pin on the green to get my attention. I took that as a sign to stop. She tossed the flag onto the ground and marched toward my mini mart. "Mimosa, please."

I opened the refrigerator door. She shoved her hand in and removed a can, but before pulling it out, she lingered, letting the air cool her face as she rolled the can, dripping condensation, over her forehead. "Katie, did you hear about Winslow?" I neither confirmed nor denied hearing anything but kept quiet. "Did you know he alleged he was related to me?"

A rhetorical question nowhere near what I'd been expecting, my conviction to just listen didn't last. "And he wasn't?" The words slipped out before I thought about my promise to leave everything to Amanda.

"I assure you; he was not. I can't believe it. Lark was all teary-eyed and asked me who she should call. When I said I had no idea, she pulled away from me, affronted. How could I *not* know? How *could* I know? Everyone wants to take advantage of me. There's no way I'm playing my best in this tournament. How can anyone expect me to win? Even your friend is beating me today."

I almost fist-bumped her; I was intensely happy for Jane even if Anne was not, but then I thought, if Anne had found out about Winslow yesterday, could she have been angry enough to do him harm? Would her anger prompt her to do something drastic again?

"Everyone is driving me nuts." She grimaced. "Did you know Dennis sold two of his shares in Shady Oaks to Barclay for fifty thousand dollars? Dennis has a soft heart for the homeless in our little town. His mother struggled just out of college but got a break from a group supporting the women's shelter. She pulled herself together and got a job at the library.

That's where she met Dennis's father, and they're still happily married. Dennis wanted to make a substantial donation to this year's fundraising drive, and Barclay thwarted his dream."

"Where did Dennis get his shares? He's not a Murphy too, is he?"

"No, he's not family, but his shares were a bequest from an ancestor, a trusted and esteemed course manager for Quinn and Liam. I hope he gets them back, but Barclay's sneaky contingency clause was a doozy. Dennis knows he made a mistake trusting him. Everyone trusted Barclay Byron the first time they dealt with him. But Dennis didn't read the fine print in their contract. The only way Dennis would collect the money is when the fundraiser earned five hundred thousand dollars."

"Winslow told us that in the last ten years the tournament has already earned quite a bit more than that. What's the problem?"

She looked at me with pity. "You don't understand. The fine print included the words 'in one calendar year.' We're lucky to get anywhere near one hundred thousand, but five is unheard of. Poor guy. With Barclay gone, he hadn't been paid and thought the contract was no longer valid. Tempest, at Clive's insistence, seems to be hanging onto it."

And Barbara Clay hadn't made her claim yet.

Anne's partners made their way toward us. She waved and said under her breath, "But don't say anything."

Ginny dashed next to Anne, scrounging for payment again. "It's on me." As Anne sauntered away, Ginny muttered under her breath. "She needs to be taught a lesson in kindness."

Ginny hadn't noticed me inch out of her peripheral vision, hiding in plain sight—I hoped. She lifted her head, and as she glanced over her shoulder, I sashayed next to her, acting as if I'd been a step or two away, engrossed in the tournament, and hadn't just heard her. "What can I get you, Ginny?"

"Two waters, please." She laid a ten on the counter and sighed.

"I hope you're all taking turns buying the beverages." She'd pulled out a card or cash every time and paid for all three.

"Anne doesn't live in the real world. I'll get it back in good will. Thanks, though."

Many of the other players no longer had the jitters and had settled into the rhythm of solid play. The spectators knew which competitors to watch, and which golfers were out for fun, but Lark's prediction about doing well enough to stay on hole nine didn't come to fruition. My tip jar could have used topping off. Sales were minimal but consistent, though I only had to replenish the cart once, but the single trip took longer than usual. A local delivery truck arrived ahead of me, blocking my entry, and gave my thoughts time to dovetail like tiny pieces of a huge puzzle. While I waited, I tried unsuccessfully to fit the tabs into the blanks.

What might I know? More questions than answers, it seemed. The man who called himself Barclay Byron during golf season bought Dennis's shares in the club. Did Byron's microscopic ownership constitute a threat? Was someone at Shady Oaks hiding a secret? What was the big announcement Nora alluded to? Did Byron's ownership of the shares alter the day-to-day workings of Shady Oaks? He'd wrangled his way into many aspects of club management. He hadn't compensated Dennis, so would the shares be returned? Or was there more to the conversation Byron kept having with Dennis? It could have been Ginny's voice Jane and I heard arguing about a contract being rescinded. What was the relationship between Anne and Byron? That would have made a juicy morsel of gossip. Would it have been a secret Byron wanted to keep? Did it matter? How would his wife benefit from Byron's death? And which wife—Barbara or Tempest?

Who wrote the cryptic message I found and how did it get into the garage? Maybe it was written for someone other than Byron. Maybe it was written *by* Byron. Could Clive have anything to gain, or was he a target? Maybe the note had been written by Nora—she was always around, and her efforts to talk to Byron on Monday had been futile. Did she, like Byron, wield the authority to hire and fire at will? All confounding.

Had it only been five days? So much had happened.

Had Sherylann been the perpetrator all along? Had she duped Galen into believing her? On one hand, Sherylann confessed to being a resident ghost, borrowing items owned by the corporation, but if she was honest, and I tended to believe her, someone else had been appropriating items as well. On the other hand, Amanda found more stolen items in the caretaker's cottage among Sherylann's belongings. She could have lied. Still…

To complicate matters, I found Winslow's body. How did he die? And if he lied about being a Murphy, who was Winslow?

I walked to the rear of the truck and admired the garden from a distance. Its resplendent hallmarks—vivid colors, fresh scents (which I hoped were safe), precise lines, and shades of green across the spectrum—could be deceiving.

The breeze picked up, and the heavy metal doors clanged. My attention was diverted to the empty racks inside the trailer

affixed with labels for liquor, snacks, burgers, beef, poultry, pork, seafood, produce, and bread. Before I completed a mental inventory, the truck tooted its horn, and the meanderings of my mind slid to the back burner. I jumped out of its way. We both had a job to do.

I couldn't wait until I completed my shift and could talk to Jane. Of course, by that time, she could be a Columbia celebrity. I wished I had her enthusiasm for the sport. Maybe after I had a few more lessons and years of practice, I'd feel like it was less of a chore and more fun. Who would have thought such a small ball would be so difficult to control?

"Golf." I shook my head and muttered. At that moment, I tuned in to one of the other adages on Ida's cocktail napkins. "A waste of a good walk."

THIRTY-SIX

The steady stream of spectators kept me busy selling gallons of water on the hottest day of the year so far. At the end of my long shift, I doggedly cleaned up, prepared my cart for the final round of tournament play, and wondered what a normal workday might look like, even if the event calendar boasted at least four more fundraising tournaments. After I plugged in the cart, the urge to peek at the garden overcame my lethargy.

I crept to the door and gazed over the foliage, wondering if such beautiful flora could conceal something deadly. Of course, memories of the gorgeous yet murderous woman who would have buried me under the ice in January, if not for Maverick, made me shiver in spite of the temperature. Basing an opinion solely on outward appearances could be disastrous. I tried to discern what part of the vegetation might have earned a fatalistic reputation and decided you really couldn't judge a book by its cover.

As I slid the door along the track, turned the key, and checked and rechecked the lock, I moaned, remembering I had only my two-wheeled transport to take me home. Heading to the bike rack, I felt my phone vibrate. Seeing the name on the screen, I answered cheerfully. "Jane, how did you do today?"

"And hello to you, too. You haven't answered any of your texts. I worried something might have happened."

"Sorry. Lark prefers we turn off the ringer for a more professional presence, and I complied." I glanced at the screen and noticed five missed calls from Jane, one from Dad, three from Galen, and two from Pete.

"Okay then. And in answer to your question, I finished first in the women's division," she squealed.

"I knew you'd do it." I hummed Kool and the Gang's *Celebration* and danced an uncoordinated jig.

"And fourth overall after today. I'm a little nervous. I think the other players will be gunning for me, but that's okay as long as it's done figuratively and not literally. Granted, I'm not guaranteed a win tomorrow, but I'm not going to roll over and play dead either. Care to get together for supper and talk? I have some news for you."

"I'm still at Shady Oaks and I have to bike home yet. I'm a mess, and it might be too late—"

"I'm in the dining room. You can join me now. When we finish, I can give you and Miss Blue a ride home."

"I'm wearing my work duds."

"Katie, I'm wearing the same clothes I wore playing golf all day, and so are many other diners."

"But—"

"See you in five."

I dashed through the strangely unattended front door. Anne and Nora monitored the silent auction items, so I took one of my five minutes to quickly peruse the offerings. The donations included golf attire, a custom-fitted driver, a basket of wine, greens fees for three rounds of golf at Shady Oaks, and a spa day package. Colossal bids had been placed on four premium tickets to a Twins baseball game, a foursome golf package to two destination courses, and a cooking class with Chef Antoine. Most of the bids were out of my league, but the tally sheet in front of the beat-up wooden club, standing front and center, had only two offers. A touch of gambling fever tingled through my fingertips. The club could be mine and would showcase Dad's favorite sport. I was certain I could talk Ida into creating a one-of-a-kind gift for Father's Day. And it was for a great cause.

As I dashed off a double-digit amount I was willing to lose, I heard Nora's shrill voice. "I'm doing all I can. You may have provided a chance for me to get my foot in the door, but I've made it on my own. This summer's upset never would've happened if I'd had my way. We have no idea who's coming and going, so I ordered maintenance to change every single lock. I'll button down the clubhouse by the end of the evening. Anyone wanting a key will be required to check out a new one from me personally. Then I'll have an updated list of anyone who can get in. The management of the hotel and spa knows it's in my crosshairs, but there are too many ins and outs to change the locks there overnight. They promised to be extra vigilant until I can finish what I set out to do." She rattled a large ring of shiny brass keys and peeled one loose. "They're numbered. Here's yours—number three."

Mockingly, Anne said, "And who has one and two?"

Nora replied as if she should have known, "I have one, obviously, and Antoine has two." Anne tried to accept her key, but Nora held tight. "Don't lose it."

Anne shook her head. "It's like closing the gate after the horse bolted—a little late now."

With seconds to spare, I left them in the silent auction room, rounded the corner, and peered into the dimly lit dining room. Candles flickered at every table with an elegant ambience, twinkling off the exquisite dinnerware, but Jane was correct. Many of the diners wore their golfing togs, although the hostess strategically sat well-dressed couples, perfectly coifed, wearing suits and dresses bedazzled in shimmering jewelry among them.

Jane caught my eye and made a show of checking her watch. She grinned and waved me over, bolstering my courage. I had nothing to lose so I stepped forward with as much indifference as I could muster, as if this was where I was meant to be, and made it the rest of the way across the room.

I recognized some of the servers and caught sight of the back of a large man in a white chef's uniform, who I assumed was Chef Antoine. Reneé caught my eye at the same time I saw her. She swallowed a moment of annoyance, perhaps at my casual attire, but when she saw Jane, she rushed over.

"Good evening, Ms. Mackey. It's great to see you again," she gushed. "You too, Ms. Wilk," she added perfunctorily. "Is there anything we can do to make your evening special, anything I can recommend? The chef is in his element tonight. The winners of the dinner for the Marshmallow Drive are being treated to a fabulous feast at the table overlooking the course. Consequently, we absolutely have the ingredients for everything on the tasting menu."

"Thanks, Reneé. We'll try the regular menu tonight, but I promise I'll bring my fiancé in soon to try some of your wedding delicacies and decide on our reception dinner fare. I'll call for an appointment first."

"As you wish." She snapped her fingers, and three eager servers surrounded our table. They delivered ice-cold water, warm bread, and oversized menus lacking prices. My lips curled over my teeth, and I clamped down to keep my jaw from dropping.

Jane smiled and said, "No worries. I have a running tab, and in case you're wondering, I need to spend a minimum each month. The fees are assessed, whether I use them or not, so please get whatever you'd like. Even if I supped here every night, which can't happen …" I scoffed as she patted her toned abdomen. "I'll never come close to spending the amount I'm charged."

Another server arrived to take our food and beverage order. We dined in style, savoring a robust house red paired with the chef's *prix fixe* special of the evening—a sumptuous meal of *Canard en Croûte, Carottes Vichy,* and *Pommes Dauphinoise.*

We said little. With only my sandwich for lunch, I was hungrier than I thought and thoroughly enjoyed the featured meal. Though the magnitude of Winslow's death made my heart ache, the world, as they cited, continued to turn. One of our waiters delivered a dessert menu, and when asked for his favorite, he recommended the black cherry *clafoutis.* The accompanying mouthwatering photo sold me. Knowing I was too full to truly enjoy the entire treat, I ordered it to go.

"Miss," the waiter said. "The clafoutis is made from scratch. Usually, the order is placed at the beginning of the dinner as it will require an additional thirty minutes to prepare. Is that all right?"

"You're riding home with me, and I have nothing but time. Don't get it to go. We'll share the dessert here," Jane said, and sated, began a running monologue, describing all the boxes she'd checked off or had yet to complete for her perfect wedding.

As she sipped her wine and droned on, repeating everything we'd discussed multiple times before, I set my elbows on the table, dropped my chin on my knuckles, leaned forward, and locked on my interested-face complete with periodic nodding, but my concentration drifted. A symphony of laughter and light music accompanied the low hum of pleasant conversation around the room when my ears picked up a tense exchange behind me. I rotated in my seat until Chef Antoine came into view. With his curling handlebar moustache and towering hat, he looked less like a chef and more like Snidely Whiplash. Dad would've chuckled at the archenemy lookalike of his favorite cartoon hero, Dudley Do-Right of the Mounties. Chef Antoine's starched white jacket instead of the obligatory all-black cape was all that saved him from full villain status.

The chef rubbed his hands together, and I cringed imagining him cackling a 'heh heh heh' while plotting his next nefarious move. In reality, he was probably excitedly describing, in minute detail, the courses to be served, but I couldn't make out too many words through his heavy French accent.

Jane's phone pinged, and her face lit with love. "Excuse me. I'll be right back." She accepted the call and walked into the lobby.

As I sipped the fine beverage, concentrating to detect the tasting notes Jane could always distinguish, the chef stopped to take a breath, and I heard a feminine French answer and spun all the way around. Gilded by the flaming setting sun, ZaZa and Montgomery sat at the premiere table in front of the plate-glass window with a spectacular view of the grounds. If that wasn't a clear enough indicator, then the lighted sign on a stand flashing the word 'winner' clinched it. They should have been set to enjoy the elegant feast befitting the victorious golfer with the longest marshmallow drive.

But ZaZa said something more I didn't understand. Whatever she said flummoxed the chef as well. He sputtered, shook his head, and stomped away.

"What did you say to him?" Montgomery barked.

"I don't think he understood me. I-I-I told him I was looking forward to tasting the-the bouillabaisse." ZaZa's head fell. Her brunette locks covered her face. "I'm sorry."

Montgomery said sternly, "I'm the one who's sorry. It'll be fine."

Maybe Montgomery had changed.

"I'll fix it with the chef. We want to take advantage of him at his very best." Montgomery rose from the table, planted a kiss on her cheek, and disappeared.

Dad's admonition came back to haunt me, and I couldn't forfeit the opportunity to talk to ZaZa alone and make her aware of Montgomery's history with me. I approached slowly, standing adjacent to the table before she acknowledged me. "What do you want?"

"How are you, ZaZa?"

"*Je suis merveilleuse.* What do you really want, Katie?"

I looked down at my feet, hoping for inspiration. "I knew Montgomery five years ago. We dated."

"I know that, and I also know you pursued him indecently, crossing boundaries to the point the courts needed to intervene with a restraining order. You should be staying away even now."

I sputtered. The correct words were all there but jumbled beyond recognition. I took out the restraining order, not the other way around. "That's not exactly true." ZaZa attempted to interrupt, but I ran on. "More importantly, I want to make sure you're doing okay."

"Why would I not be?"

Delicately, I asked, "Do you need any help? There was a time when he frightened me."

"Don't," she said decisively and raised her palm. "Montgomery warned me about you, not that I needed any warning. He said you would probably try to turn me against him. He is a perfect gentleman—kind, handsome, intelligent. He takes good care of me. I do not know why you would want to say untrue things about him."

"I don't. I just …"

"Just what, Katie?" The deep voice echoed behind me. The sneer on Montgomery's face made me want to coil into a tight ball.

"Goodnight, ZaZa." I shambled back to my table, hoping Jane would be ready to leave soon.

In between sips of luscious wine I no longer savored, I answered texts from Dad and Galen, but before I could respond to Pete, my phone rang.

THIRTY-SEVEN

G alen?"

"Ms. Wilk, what are we going to do? Sherylann's in big trouble, but she didn't kill anyone."

"We're not going to do anything. I know you believe her, but she's been in a different world for six years." He grumbled, but I ignored his argument. "I promise I'll talk to Amanda, and I'll ask questions, but you have to be willing to accept she may not be the person you remember."

"Please, Ms. Wilk. She's really trying. That's all I ask."

He hung up, and I stared at the phone in my hands.

"Galen?" Jane said, as she quietly returned to our table and slid into her chair. I nodded. "You look like you have the weight of the world on your shoulders."

I puckered my lips. "And I have no idea what I can do

that Amanda hasn't already done, but I promised Galen …"

A shadow grew over our table. "Eez there something wrong? Eez the food not satisfactory?" Chef Antoine said each word with deliberation as he raised one eyebrow.

Jane smiled broadly. "It was fabulous. Thank you so much."

"Your leetle friend looks troubled."

"My little friend has many irons in the fire, but she's fine."

Chef Antoine's dark eyes drilled into me. If I hadn't noticed the empty tables near us, I would've thought he might be hinting we'd overstayed our welcome. I fought to put a smile on my lips. "I've never had anything quite like this dinner. Our server recommended the clafoutis, and we can't wait."

He nodded and moved toward a table on the far wall, interrupting a strained conversation between Ginny and Dennis. Ginny glowered and the chef's hands went up in surrender. If he was fishing for more compliments, it appeared he failed. Something caught Dennis's eye, and his face hardened. He stood, but Ginny placed her hand on his forearm, and he dropped back into his seat, barely acknowledging the chef awkwardly backing away. I followed Dennis's penetrating gaze. At a table near the entry, Tempest scooted forward on the chair Clive held for her. He locked eyes with Dennis and smirked.

"There's something brewing," Jane said. "Maybe Dennis is still trying to get back his shares, but from the arrogant look on her face, it doesn't seem like Tempest is bothered in the least."

"I wonder what will happen if and when Byron's real wife, Barbara Clay, lays claim. I don't think Clive will be happy."

"I think you need to talk to someone who knows."

I texted our mock trial attorney coach, Dorene Dvorak;

she was not only the smartest attorney I knew in Columbia, but she also could inform without making someone feel foolish for asking and then explain in terms even my students understood.

Who inherits from a bigamist who dies without a will in Minnesota?

The three dots wavered on my screen.

And hello to you, stranger. That came out of thin air. Any more specificity?

Sorry. Hello. But imagine, Guy owns shares in a company. He has a Wife A and Child B, and, without securing a divorce, marries again to Wife C. What would Spouse C get?

Under Minnesota law, bigamy is a crime. Therefore, a bigamous marriage is not legally valid. In such a situation, Spouse C would likely be out of luck for the purposes of inheriting anything, and the estate of the deceased bigamist would be distributed according to Minnesota's intestate (without a will) succession laws, that is to wife A and child B.

Wife C is out?

Unless there's a will specifically naming Wife C as a beneficiary, she would need a lawyer with my superior skill and fortuitous intercessions.

What about getting out of a signed contract?

Same or different folks?

In general.

Could be tricky. Contracts can be cancelled by mutual agreement, if the conditions are not fulfilled, if there is a breach of contract, if it's impossible to fulfill the terms of the contract, or cancellation due to fraud or misrepresentation. Get an attorney.

Thanks.

You realize none of this advice is legally binding, and I'll want a debriefing on these questions ... soon.

I chuckled and waited for Jane. Dennis might get his shares back, but I wouldn't get in the middle, though technically, that was exactly where I sat.

Clive roared with laughter, drawing notice from everyone in the room. My eyes ping-ponged from one table to the next, and I tensed, preparing for the fireworks sure to ignite. Dennis crumpled his linen napkin and stood, but Ginny strategically blocked his advance and hustled him from the dining room, almost knocking into Reneé.

Jane wriggled in her chair, giddy with stars in her eyes, bursting at the seams.

"What did Drew have to say?"

"He apologized for bugging out on us, but, Katie, Pete isn't angry. In fact …" She moved my hand out of the server's path and leaned back, inhaling, as he placed the steaming dish in the middle of our table. The delicious aroma of the simmering cherries upended our conversation.

We picked up our forks and tapped tines. "Cheers." And we finished the meal with probably the most expensive cup of black coffee I'd ever had.

On our drive home, in good humor enhanced by the terrific repast, Jane belted out lyrics to Wagner's *Bridal Chorus* I'd never heard.

"Did you just make that up?"

"What, the song?" She chuckled. "I don't think so. I'm not that creative. I must've heard the words somewhere."

Even though I held tightly to the chest restraint as Jane barreled around the lake and accelerated with abandon, it felt good to laugh. The week had taken its toll, but the amusement subsided when I spotted Dad and Galen sitting on the Adirondack chairs in our yard.

"Do you want support personnel?" Jane offered.

"No. You have a tournament to win tomorrow, but thanks.

Go home. Sleep well, and thanks for the terrific evening."

"We'll do it again and often." Jane saluted and tapped her horn as she blasted back out the way she'd come. Dad excused himself, and I took the vacated chair. Maverick joined us when Dad went inside.

After a few minutes of repeated canine tail attacks on his shins, Galen responded with gentle strokes around Maverick's collar. He kept his eyes on my dog while he extracted a short cardboard tube from his backpack and held it out for me to take. I tried to remember where I'd seen one before.

"What is this?"

"I found it just before that Birdwhistle woman nabbed me—"

"Her name is Nora Birdwhistle?"

He nodded. "I thought this was trash. I found it when I was looking for signs of raccoons." His sad eyes met mine. "There's something inside. I thought it might be important, but I don't understand it. Have you seen anything like it?"

I inserted my first two fingers into the tube and gently tugged out a long, narrow strip of paper covered with letters. I unrolled and examined it. "There was nothing else?"

He shook his head.

"Can I keep this for a while?"

"I can't make heads or tails of it. I was hoping it would help, but I guess not, huh?"

"We'll see." A distant memory niggled in my brain.

Galen unsuccessfully attempted to stifle his yawn. "Sorry. It's been a long weekend."

"Yes, it has. I'll see what I can come up with, but Galen, don't rile Chief West again. She's doing what she needs to do, and she's on your side."

He scoffed. "Maybe." He never looked up when he said sadly, "I hope you are."

THIRTY-EIGHT

The final day of the tournament dawned with a gentle breeze and clouds drifting through a clear blue sky, but the weatherman predicted thunderstorms during the evening hours. After a quick romp around the neighborhood, complete with an early morning quick nuzzle with Emma, I delivered Maverick into CJ's competent hands. His eyebrow arched when I snuggled my dog and said in an exaggerated high-pitched voice, "I'll miss you, but I'll check in, so don't worry." Obviously, Maverick and CJ had a more professional working relationship.

I returned home and the corners of my down-turned mouth reversed direction when Dad removed a warm, eggy *pannenkoeken* from the oven. He spilled a mound of juicy strawberries drizzled with maple syrup inside, spooned on a dollop of whipped cream, and sifted powdered sugar over the top before slicing it in two and joining me at the table, already set with matching cups of his finest brew.

I brightened after the first delicious bite and said, "You look ready for the day, Dad."

"I'm going to win my age group, darlin'. I have to. I'm the only one in it."

I laughed. It wasn't true. On the big screen in the club's lobby, the judges posted each day's top scores and overall standings in addition to the top ten in each age group. I'd watched his competition, and although they were not to be trifled with, he was by far the better golfer, and he'd have been a rockstar if he'd continued playing when I was a kid. After day two, he was three strokes ahead. "And I'll be there to record your acceptance speech for posterity."

"You don't have to bike today. Jane's going to pick me up. You can take my car." He said the words with such gravity, I had no doubt his decision was made after much deliberation. Dad's precious vintage automobile rarely left its protected spot in the garage, and only on special occasions. He recited his often-repeated rhyme, "Get a little gas, and a little bit of oil. Get a little spark from a little bitty coil." I joined in with the last few words. "Get a piece of tin and a two-inch board. Put it all together and you've got a little—"

I completed the itty-bitty ditty as I'd heard it for decades. "Ford," but Dad diverged and finished his recitation with the actual name of his beloved car. "Crown Victoria."

A chortle exploded, and although I loved pushing and pulling all the shiny chrome bells and whistles, I said, "Thanks, Dad, but it's a beautiful day. I'll bike. However, plan on my riding home with the two of you. It could be a long day, and it might rain."

Dad's chair screeched when he stood and carried his dishes to the sink. "I've got KP duty. You." He pointed to the door. "Get to work."

Wrapped in a huge embrace, I whispered in his ear, "You can do it," and ambled out to my bicycle. Riding to Shady Oaks, wary of another close call or inattentive driver, I watched and listened for approaching traffic, concentrating on my rhythmic cadence until I rounded the last turn in the drive and came to an abrupt stop.

A scrum of staff hovered in front of the doors with a rumble of complaints.

I rolled through the air of annoyance and aggravation and chained my bike to the rack. After I fastened the shackle and snapped the padlock, I snaked through the throng and made my way next to Galen. "What's going on?"

He said in a rush, "None of the keys work. They've even tried the back doors, and if we don't get in soon, the kitchen won't be able to use the groceries delivered and we'll have to delay the start of play and we're expecting a storm later in the afternoon. With everyone anxious, it'll be a lousy day." Galen took a big breath.

The workman who connected the video cameras to catch or deter the ghost thief stood back with his arms crossed and watched with amusement. He very likely installed the new locks too.

Is this where I blow the Birdwhistle? I almost chuckled.

Fortunately, the mob parted as a red sports car roared into the circle drive. I couldn't identify the driver through the tinted windows, but Anne Johansen slid from the passenger seat, held aloft a shiny key, bowed to raucous applause, and marched to the entry. Her key fit, and she swung the double doors wide. In all the commotion, I lost sight of the upscale red car.

As the disgruntled crowd filtered inside, Anne made a point to connect with Lark and Reneé and pressed a key into each of their hands, yet haphazardly doled out dozens more. "Sorry. Don't know what happened. Let's get a move on. I know we're late."

Nearing the end of the line, Galen approached Anne. She glanced at her watch and said, "Keep the front door secured. Don't open to golfers until nine. Let's give everyone the opportunity to prep well. There'll be plenty of time for the tournament participants to do whatever they need to do. If you can do that, Galen …" She winked. "There'll be a bonus for you at the end of today."

"Yes, ma'am," Galen said emphatically and hustled to his post.

She put on a great show as the golf diva, but when push came to shove, the real Anne came through loud and clear. She loved Shady Oaks, the Murphy legacy, and knew what to do when it counted to create an exceptional golfing experience. Nothing and no one would put a black mark on its reputation if she had anything to say about it.

I briefly wondered if Barclay Byron really had an announcement meant to sabotage her intentions as Nora had hinted, or was there another target?

"Do you have a key for me?" asked Ginny hesitantly, walking up as Galen bounded away. I hovered discreetly as the conversation turned gossipy.

"Certainly, Ginny. I don't know how Nora got it in her head she's in charge. I realize she loves golf and always has the best interests of Shady Oaks at the forefront, but she's overstepped her purview as admin assistant, adding her own opinions and ruffling feathers."

"Then Barclay made a deal with Dennis." Ginny gritted her teeth. "And with those shares, Barclay threatened to stir up some controversy, maybe put Nora in her place or someone else. If the shares are properly returned to their rightful owner, as they should be, Dennis plans on taking a much more active role than in the past."

"What about Tempest?" Anne squinted.

"Haven't you heard? Tempest and Barclay were never legally married. He and his legitimate wife just had a baby girl. Her name is Barbara Clay and—"

"Clay?" Anne's eyes lit in recognition. "She's a great competitor."

"You know her?"

"I've lost to her too many times to count."

"Dennis spoke to her before she and the baby were released from the hospital today. She wants to do the right thing." Ginny pursed her lips. "I'm just not sure what that's going to be. Tempest is probably out, but Clive is claiming Tempest is getting an attorney to demand what is rightfully hers."

"Barbara Clay and Barclay Byron. I never would have made the connection."

"His real name is John Clay."

"That's almost too much to take in." Anne took a breath. "Ginny, I owe you for all my beverages this weekend. Bill me, okay?" Ginny's mouth opened, but no sound emerged. Anne turned to me. "Katie, you'll need a key as well. Get your cart ready. Lark's going to be busy sorting out the mess Nora made." She chortled, wriggling another key from the metal circle. "I'm gearing up for today. I've got my real work cut out for me. Wish me luck."

I nodded with my fingers crossed behind my back. My

money was on Jane, confident she had an excellent chance to win. Galen guarded the door as I squeezed through the opening and retrieved my till from Lark. The frenetic activity whirred everywhere as I made my way across the course. Being entrusted with this key made me uncomfortable. The metal in my hand almost itched, but knowing I'd turn it over to Lark at the end of the day allowed me to breathe more easily.

However, when I got to the garage door, it stood ajar.

THIRTY-NINE

Nudging it wider, the heavy door squawked and raised my goosebumps. I took one deliberate step at a time, swinging my head right and left, checking for signs of ornery, furry masked creatures or scary two-legged troublemakers, but nothing seemed amiss in the orderly space.

Apparently, there'd been a recent delivery. Neat, tall columns of unopened cardboard boxes and untouched cartons and cases stood against the wall, including a few containers with a hazard label and 'dry ice' printed on the outside.

I headed out to the eighteenth hole.

The competition was so intense, neither spectators nor entrants even glanced at my offerings, let alone made a purchase. No one would miss me, so I drifted to the edge of the crowd to watch and cheer Dad and Jane as they both birdied the sixteenth hole. Drew, on the other hand, swung and missed, looking more like me than anyone else.

A sparsity of clouds drifted through the azure sky. I let the sun warm my face. Scattered, probing thoughts came unbidden. Did I honestly believe Sherylann poisoned Byron and Winslow? Galen was positive she wouldn't kill anyone, and deep down, so was I, but if not her, who else would have had motive and opportunity, or were the poisonings accidental, and were we all still at risk? And what was Winslow doing here if he wasn't related to the Murphys? Would Dennis get his shares returned? How were Barbara and the new baby Clay?

For a brief moment, I let my guard down, and my thoughts rushed to more personal pursuits. Dreaming of Pete's warm chocolate eyes made me blush. I missed him and decided that after the weekend, I'd at least apologize for my laxity in returning his calls and texts. I couldn't be afraid of what he had to say forever.

Ginny, Anne, and Dennis strolled up, interrupting my reverie, and they played in a delighted mood. Anne and Ginny parred, and Dennis claimed a bogie. I even cheered, but deep-down I was rooting for Jane.

I didn't know many of the other players, and my meager salary and possible dismissal were the only things keeping me from admitting retail defeat and turning in the till. My day dragged on. The players focused on completing the round of golf, anxious to turn in and tally the final results, and also fearful the weather might turn against them, but the crowd still took time to unload its curmudgeonly comments on Clive and Tempest when they appeared.

Some of the gossipy words floated to my ears on the

breeze. "That guy tried to swindle Dennis."

"You mean our Dennis? What happened?"

"Dennis wanted to donate in honor of his mom this year and sold his shares to Byron who forged some rinky-dink conditions in the contract before Dennis could collect any money," said a voice very sure of itself. "After Byron died, Clive encouraged Tempest to hold Dennis to the unfair agreement. Turns out, Byron wasn't married to Tempest anyway. I hope Clive gets his comeuppance."

The crowd had listened warily to the disquieting news. Clive drove down the fairway amid an undercurrent of boos and hisses, though the onlookers allowed the golfer absolute quiet during his actual swing. Unfortunately for him, the ball had a mind of its own and plopped into the pond to calculated applause.

"He got what was coming to him," whispered the same stalwart enthusiast I spotted on the course all three days. She approached my cart wearing the identical frayed plaid pants, a scruffy navy-blue collared shirt, scuffed sneakers, and pushing a walker with neon tennis balls on the legs. The name tag hanging on a lanyard around her neck read 'Special Shelter House Guest, Myra,' and I cautiously scanned for Maverick, who might chew the tennis balls off the legs of her walker without provocation. "That boy's got a mean streak. Gots to be careful 'round the likes of him, I seen him sneakin' around," she warned and tossed a bill on my counter. "Water, please, and keep the change."

"On the house," I said, sliding the bottle covered in icy droplets, wondering about her financial circumstances.

"Thanks for the offer but not this time." I mirrored her gap-toothed grin. "It don't embarrass me. I'm flush today."

I smiled appreciatively and inserted the two cents change

in my tip jar as Myra ambled after the group.

Watching and waiting patiently for the occasional buyer, I finally observed CJ and Maverick scouting the rough, and inwardly gloated over my handsome canine, chasing one pocket of scent after another. My dog high-stepped around the edge of the taller grasses and returned to CJ's heel, seeming to be aware he'd been hired to do an important job keeping the pesky wild animals at bay. Too bad he wasn't allowed to perform the same task with people.

When ZaZa approached the closest tee box, I hustled down the cart path to avoid another encounter, sadly realizing she'd never listen to anything I might have to say.

I stuck out the entire tournament, circling around and finishing when the final group bought a round of beverages for the few remaining diehard fans. After balancing the money box, I filled the empty display hooks and restocked the beverages on the cart, keenly aware the carton and box stacks had shrunk, and not through sales made by me.

My footfalls reverberated in the empty halls of the club. Lark sat at her desk, and she barely counted the money in the register, glossing over the totals. "How was your first week?" she said, forcing a grin.

"It had its moments, but thanks for taking me on. I hope I did well enough."

"I'll keep you on the schedule, but it won't be this intense again. It simply can't." She hemmed and hawed. "It'll be sporadic. I'll need help for our tournaments, but two of our regulars asked for their jobs back. Barclay was right. Nora overstepped and never should have let them go."

My face gave away my emotions, mixed though they were, and she said, "You look relieved. Can't say I blame you. Just know you've earned *all* the perks of employment. The banquet begins in ten minutes. You're down as one of Jane Mackey's guests. She said she'd meet you at your usual table. I'll see you inside."

If I hustled, I could freshen up, tame my unruly hair, wash my hands, and splash water on my face. Not much improved in my mirror image, but I pulled my collar taut remembering Winslow's helpful advice.

I almost strolled by the silent auction exhibit but stopped mid-stride to check my bid. Nora, the only other person in the room, anxiously picked at the corner of one of the pages on the first table as I entered, so I scurried to the center display containing the battered vintage golf club. The amount topping my last offer was within reach. The auction would close in two minutes, and I scribbled another affordable sum.

The slightly dented, used white and green thermal water bottle, now the item least desired among the donations, begged to be included in my generosity, so I scrawled another amount I could live without. Dad had traded an activity he fancied to be the best father ever, and I owed him more than I could ever repay. If I lost, so be it, but I felt lucky.

I bumped into Lark as I left the room and had an inspiration. "Lark, if I win any of the items I bid on, would you mind pretending to be me? They have my payment information, but I don't want my dad to know. They might be gifts for him."

"What did you bid on?"

"That old wooden driver and water bottle."

Lark sighed. "I probably shouldn't tell you, but the club was a family heirloom, donated by Winslow." My brow furrowed on its own. "I know he could be a pain, but he had a bit of heart."

"Do you know why he called the item Bait?"

"Nope, no idea." After a second's thought, she acquiesced. "I'll collect the club and the tumbler … if you win."

"Thanks. I'm bidder 724. I'd better skedaddle."

The glitz and glam of the banquet décor had taken over the dining room. Yellow candle flames flickered off the shining silver and gleaming crystal. Gold metallic streamers fluttered at the hint of movement nearby. An occasional voice burst through the soft music, telling a story or laughing in revelry.

"Excuse me." I threaded through the sea of jovial bodies. "Pardon me." I slipped past a table laden with trophies in various sizes, and headed toward a wall framed by tall windows, their panes opening onto a stunning view of the grounds. I paused at the head of a semicircular perimeter of the imagined force field encompassing larger-than-life headshots of Winslow and Barclay hanging on the wall. Bright picture lights cast them in a reverent glow. I bowed my head and paid my silent respects among the subdued onlookers. Unwilling to break into the unoccupied ring in front of the portraits of the victims, as if doing so might constitute a sacrilege, I scooted around and bumped into a solid chest. "I'm sorry," I said, looking up.

Ronnie Christianson sneered. "Careful, Wilk. I'm here to make sure you don't foist yourself on Monty and Ms. Lavigne again. She told me what you said. You're lucky they don't file an *ex parte* order of protection. You will not harass them again."

"I didn't …" I would have though. My knees quaked, and I'm sure my heart thudded loud enough to drown out the music. "I won't bother them."

The bodies became impediments, a maze of moving walls to overcome. As I pushed my way through, I thought over my conversation with ZaZa. What had I said to have her sic Ronnie on me? I stumbled, scanning the crowd for my best friend's blond hair, finally shuddering and flopping into the only empty chair at Jane's table, sitting between Ida and Dad.

Jane's joy was palpable, and I wouldn't do anything to bring her down. I bit my lip. I decided, if it wasn't school related, I would never speak to ZaZa again. I'd been warned.

FORTY

The fundraising event's celebration commenced with a welcome by Anne, a short tribute honoring Barclay, a shorter tribute to Winslow, and an invitation to partake of the Sunday ethnic predinner fare—a fabulous Norwegian *koldtbord* with pickled herring, smoked salmon, cheeses, berries, and *lefse*. Arnold Palmers poured freely. In honor of the Murphy Irish heritage and in conjunction with the local Norwegian descendants (the Johansen part of Anne's ancestry), the bar announced its opening of an 18-year Tullamore D. E. W., 18-year Jameson, and Linie Aquavit.

I kept my eyes glued to Jane, following closely through the cold food line, almost running up her back.

Dad lowered his head and spoke softly, "Katie, what's wrong?" He always knew when something bothered me.

I contemplated my answer as we zigzagged through the throng and worried about his reaction. I couldn't bring myself to tell him everything completely, so I pasted an unconcerned smile on my face. "ZaZa asked Officer Christianson to intervene on her behalf. She'd prefer to limit our conversations concerning Montgomery."

"That's too bad." We stopped at our table. He surrendered to gravity and sank into his chair. "I'm sorry, darlin'. You tried."

I read the chef's unique menu and pecked at my dinner consisting of salade nicoise, Côte de Boeuf, ratatouille, and tried not to hear ZaZa's adamant voice declare from a table not far enough away, "There are no hard-boiled eggs, tuna, or anchovies in the salad," and "What is this? My mother's ratatouille always includes eggplant."

Montgomery laughed and teased, "It's the Monongalia County version, my dear."

Dad swooned over the dessert service, which included a warm Norwegian *Rømmegrøt* and Irish bread and butter pudding. Ida took one discriminating bite of Chef Antoine's special éclairs and turned her attention to Lark and Reneé as they announced the winners of the silent auction items. Lark put on quite an exaggerated, enthusiastic show when she claimed her winnings, two of which were mine. She raised her fists, danced a jig, and even feigned grappling with Chef Antoine over the golf club, never relinquishing her hold. Watching the two of them, I couldn't imagine Dad had a clue who had actually won the water bottle and golf club.

At the conclusion of the distribution of treasures, Lark and Reneé flanked Anne and assisted in delivering the countless trophies, and there were interminable ways to qualify. My hands were busy filling my water glass when Anne announced Montgomery's fifth place in the men's division for the longest drive, so I didn't have to acknowledge him at all. Ginny placed third among women in the longest putt category and reluctantly claimed her award, but she clapped wildly when Dennis took second, and she and Dennis won the tandem trophy.

After the endless list of recipients came the top prizes, and my grin grew so big, I could barely see past my cheeks when Dad received first place in his age group. In the overall tournament standings, Jane placed second, and she incandesced. Anne was the pro, after all, and had taken first, but only by one stroke. She raised the humongous trophy over her head in triumph. Then Anne wrapped one arm over Jane's shoulders and the other around the waist of the third-place winner, a relatively tall, slim man with an astonished look on his face, and together, they took a well-deserved triple bow.

"We're still adding up the generous donations," Anne said. "But the total as of the beginning of dinner was—"

A loud crash disrupted her announcement. Harsh words echoed from the entryway. Stunned, no one moved.

"Get out of my way. You're not worth the effort," Clive's voice carried over the uncomfortable quiet. "I should've won the tandem trophy and the Shady Oaks shares, but no way was that happening saddled with you as a partner. I'm so out of here. You won't see me again."

A door slammed.

Rhythmic heels clacked across the lobby. Tempest stomped into the silent dining room and froze like a deer in the headlights of the banquet attendees until a small but spirited Myra clapped, gradually joined by the rest of the onlookers. Tempest bowed. Myra caught my eye, pursed her lips, and her head bobbed an I-told-you-so. I returned the nod. We agreed, at least at the moment, Tempest had grown a backbone.

She'd proved her mettle. She complained about Winslow and had him removed from cart duty. Was it possible she removed Barclay from her sham of a marriage too?

After dinner, Anne tapped her champagne flute, commanding the attention of everyone in the room, and at that moment, she looked very much like the portrait of her regal, yet formidable, ancestor, Quinn Murphy. The microphone howled, and she laughed as she experimented, adjusting the mic's physical position, holding it closer and farther away until she severed the feedback loop.

"We've had a great turnout again this year and don't want to wait for these rare opportunities to allow non-members a chance to play our gorgeous, historic course. There are too many days when the challenging experience and exquisitely maintained grounds appear deserted. Our esteemed colleague, Dennis Chappell, and Barclay Byron's widow, pro-golfer Barbara Clay, have proposed an amendment. The board…" She gestured for members to stand and impatiently urged the slow movers. "…voted to open playtimes on Fridays, Saturdays, and Sundays. We're adding two at-large representatives to our executive committee to help develop an equitable strategy with reasonable fees as Shady Oaks continues to accommodate our partner members."

The board scanned the crowd with pursed lips and wrinkled brows of concern, but the proposal was met with enthusiastic applause, and the tense frowns of trepidation dissolved into smiles.

Anne continued, "Nora Birdwhistle has decided to step down from her role as administrative assistant. She's done so much to maintain the mystique and allure of Shady Oaks.

Please, give her a round of applause."

Nora rose haltingly to a smattering of approbation, blinked back surprise, and wiped shiny perspiration from her forehead with the back of her hand before sinking back into her chair with a dazed look.

Ida leaned close. "Nora's narrow focus was driving the Oaks into the ground. To top it off, and to keep the legend alive, she acted as one of the resident ghosts. Anne finally fired her."

The air in the room seemed to lift.

"I have one more announcement." Everyone returned their attention to Anne. "This was my final tournament." She staunched the hum of discontent by raising her hand. "I've decided to concentrate my energy on managing Shady Oaks and bringing it back to its illustrious roots. Thank you all." After a minute of applause, including a standing ovation, Anne hollered, "Now, let's par-tee."

Servers bustled, removing the few remaining dishes and moving tables to clear the dance floor. When all extraneous lights dimmed, the prisms on the fiery chandelier cast an eerie oscillating rainbow around the room, lighting up faces and glinting off the hardware of the victors.

A voice resounded overhead, "Let's dance."

The DJ sat at a table in front of a marquee displaying a black and white photo montage of Bing Crosby while playing a recording of *Straight Down the Middle*, and no one but Jane and Drew had the courage to take to the dance floor with their jaunty swing moves. When they finished tripping the light fantastic, the music fast-forwarded forty years, and Ginny and Dennis joined them, followed by an undulating throng.

I slipped into the entry, intending to head home, and

grasped the handle of the heavy door, but a bolt of lightning, flashing through the window, stalled my hand. I plotted a short, dry escape route, but my shoulders fell when I remembered I'd biked to work. I turned back to the dining room and came face to face with Montgomery.

"Excuse me, please."

He mirrored my attempt to pass him, blocking my path, and echoed my words. "Excuse me, please."

I tried to sidestep around him, but he moved in perfect synchronization.

Deep in conversation, Chef Antoine and Lark barely noticed us as they marched through the atrium. Attempting to look the part of a perfect gentleman, Montgomery's unrelenting reflection of my movements eased enough for me to feint one way and successfully bolt toward the HR office, chased by his mocking sneer.

FORTY-ONE

The thudding in my ears slowed. I fumbled with my phone and stumbled down the shadowy hall, aiming for the protection of Lark's office, when excited voices inside brought me up short.

"I'll buy eet from you. Name your price."

"Step back, Chef." Lark said firmly. "It's not for sale. Besides, Anne locked it in the display case with the other vintage items until I get back, and it's not even mine."

"Who does eet belong to? Surely you can tell me."

"I'll share your request with the true owner. That's all I can do."

"Tell them I will create a one-of-a-kind menu in gratitude."

Footsteps closed in on the door, and I darted deeper into the shadows, curious about the item in question. Chef

Antoine bustled back toward the dining room, and I crept into the safety of Lark's office. Her eyes flashed angrily until she recognized me. She sighed with relief.

"Lark, are you okay?"

"Did you hear him? The audacity of the man trying to intimidate me. Katie, he wants your club in the worst way. You might be able to make a killing." She gulped. "Sorry. Poor choice of words. You could probably make good money, though I can't figure out why."

She swiped everything into the top desk drawer and slammed it, then withdrew a key from her pocket and locked it. "Both of the items you won are old and used." She shoved the rolling chair into place at the desk and strode out from behind the counter. "I told Anne I was exhausted and leaving for my three-day vacay beginning …" She whipped her wrist up to eye level. "… immediately. She locked all the winnings I came away with in the display case in the lobby, including yours. The case is armed, so your club and tumbler will be secure until I get them out, but I just can't right now." She held up her hand in a halting gesture. "I have to get out of here."

Far off thunder rumbled, and we both turned to the window. "Great. It always rains when I take time off." Lark grunted and continued, "I won't be back until Wednesday. I'll text you." I glimpsed a fleeting look of concern. "Will that give you enough time to do whatever you plan to do with your prizes?"

"No problem. I'm just so grateful for your help. I don't think my dad suspects a thing. I'd like to give him the club and souvenir tumbler for Father's Day, and after that, Ida can take her time creating a masterpiece."

Rain pattered the windows. She closed her eyes, inhaled and exhaled, and said, "It seems like I've been punished for every good turn I've made." She sighed. "You'll find out soon enough. Barclay knew. My first hire was Sherylann. I set her up in the caretaker's cottage, but …" Lark's whole body sagged. "She's my niece. I was gobsmacked when Byron fired her. We already needed additional help because she wasn't the first employee fired recently. Nora swung her weight around and fired two servers, our long-standing chef, and restructured catering. Then you dropped in my lap like a gift—a teacher Galen knew and couldn't recommend highly enough. When Winslow claimed to be a Murphy-in-training, I hired him without thoroughly checking his credentials, and we know how that turned out."

"What can I do to help?"

She seemed to consider my offer but shook her head. "Nothing, thanks. Just don't make me regret claiming your items." She flipped off the light, and I accompanied her through the atrium. "I'll be back on Wednesday, if only to clean out my desk, but I hope it doesn't come to that."

Thunder boomed as we neared the front door, and Galen swung it wide. He stood outside under an enormous umbrella, partially shielding him from the drenching rain, and grinning from ear to ear. "Ms. Wilk, I moved your bike to the locker room. It's late, and you can't ride home in this downpour. Do you have another ride, or do you have someone to call?"

"I'm good, thanks. I'm sure I have transportation." The deluge drummed against his umbrella.

Lark bowed her head. "Just my luck. When it rains, it pours." She pointed her chin across the glistening asphalt to a red car under the streetlight and used Galen's protective canopy to get there as rain-free as possible.

I watched her back out of the parking space. She revved the engine and rocketed down the drive, bringing back the helpless feeling I had when a similar red car took up more than its share of the road and blew my bike and me into the ditch. Could I depend on her to return? Or did she have reason to disappear? I held the door, intending to ask Galen what he knew about Lark until he rushed in, dripping and laughing, looking over my shoulder.

"Hey, Mr. Wilk. Congrats on your first place. That took some finesse."

I spun around and smiled at my handsome dad.

"Do you golf?" Galen's head bobbed. "I'll take you out sometime, young man." Dad held his crystal award up in triumph, and his grin lit the room. "Are you ready to go home, darlin'? Jane and Drew are testing the dance floor for durability, but your pup awaits." I stared at the keys dangling from his forefinger. "Ida will be out shortly and is passing off driving rights ... to you. She's imbibed a drop too much." He winked as our landlady twitched and jiggled from the dining room in time with the music.

"Love this song, but I'm beat," she said. "Let's go home. I'm hungry. The *lefse* was satisfying, but something was off for the banquet fare. I'll have to monitor food preparation for Jane's wedding reception."

"This from someone who makes soufflés in her sleep," Dad said.

She pulled up the hood on a rain slicker when an electric bolt arched across the sky and crackled. The lights went out, and I grabbed Dad's hand. He squeezed my fingers.

No sooner had Galen said, "Hold on. This happens, but we've got a generator," than the lights flickered back on with a little less intensity. "Works every time. Ready?"

"I'm ready. Galen, if you get me out to Ida's Barracuda as dry as possible, I'll drive us back to pick up Dad and Ida."

Dad thought I had a brilliant idea, though the slow drive back to Columbia through an unparalleled thunder and lightning show took forever. The sounds and sights kept me awake well after our arrival and thinking (always dangerous) through the early hours, but the torrent didn't let up for days.

* * *

Nonstop rainfall kept me indoors except for Maverick's miniature zippy jogs around the neighborhood. Galen called as we trudged the same mind-numbing steps for the fourth time.

"Ms. Wilk, have you thought of anything we can do to help Sherylann? Nothing at Shady Oaks had screamed toxicity until Dr. Erickson identified the hemlock plants in the garden near the caretaker's cottage. Now she's in real trouble."

"I'm sorry, Galen. Chief West has been unable to find exonerating evidence. Sherylann has motive, albeit flimsy, opportunity, and means. But the garden isn't difficult to access, so she isn't the only suspect. We'll keep trying. If you think of anything, let me know, but promise you won't go off half-cocked again."

I heard a small chuckle. "Promise."

I felt powerless. No one but Sherylann fit the parameters surrounding Byron's murder quite so perfectly, and if she committed one murder, it's been said the second is easier. But maybe the pieces fit like the infinite chocolate magic trick, a little geometric deception—the edges didn't actually align.

Barclay Byron had sensitive knowledge about some individuals at Shady Oaks. According to Nora, he intended to make an announcement damaging to the club. He could've revealed the connection between Lark and Sherylann or

Winslow's dubious heritage. I still had no idea whose contract was in jeopardy. Byron might've been ready to come clean about Barbara and cut Tempest loose, or he'd realized Nora had overstepped her authority and would have demanded her termination earlier. He might've been ready to disclose private information regarding the relationship he'd had with Anne or return the shares he'd purchased from Dennis. Was there yet another Shady Oaks ghost?

Barclay Byron took the secrets with him, but he would forever be my first golf instructor, and his loss saddened me.

Winslow took away secrets as well. What prompted him to claim to be a Murphy? Why was he in Columbia? Did he perform some ghostly duties?

I checked in with Amanda.

"Chief, do you know how the poison was administered to Byron and Boros?"

"Both had food and drink laced with hemlock in their systems. It's doubtful there's another perpetrator. Sherylann's fingerprints are all over Byron's clubs. She admitted to finding them in the caretaker's cottage and claimed it was an attempt to frame her, but the clubs are too unique to pawn or sell so she tossed them. Ronnie convinced anyone who will listen that she's guilty of murder too. I'm not finding proof to the contrary. If you do, let me know."

"But—"

"I've got to run. Bye."

To assuage my frustration over the railroad job Ronnie seemed to be intent on manufacturing, I let myself be caught up in Ida's plans for the summer festival, sampling desserts, stuffing envelopes, and cleaning decorations. Dad and I solicited other volunteers, verified repeat vendors, and solidified the entertainment schedule.

Poor Maverick was almost as anxious having the three of us around constantly as he was noting our absence. Only when he wound between my legs and tripped me, thrashing his excited backside, did I wonder about his intentions. I opened Ida's front door to let him out in the yard. He ran to the gate and barked with his entire being. The object of my curious glance around the neighborhood caught me off guard.

"Dad?"

"Yes, darlin'?"

"Do you see that red sports car in front of the stop sign?"

He smiled indulgently and took my place at the window. "You mean that fire-engine red Lamborghini Temerario?" His excited eyes met mine, and he immediately furrowed his brow. "Katie, you've turned white as a sheet."

"That car's been following me." I donned a slicker and bulldozed outside. The door crashed against the frame behind me and drowned out Dad's words of caution. I stomped down the walk, but even before I opened the gate, the engine thundered, and the car disappeared around the corner.

After the non-encounter, Dad wouldn't allow Maverick and me to walk without an escort, and the remainder of our jaunts in the spring showers were short.

But the car never returned.

FORTY-TWO

The day of Emma's party, I stood a gold-framed wedding photo of Charles and me on the mantel and picked up the oversized silver-papered gift, clutching it in front of me like a suit of armor.

"You don't have to go to the party. I can deliver your present."

"Thanks, Dad, but I do need to make today something extraordinary. I was euphoric on this day two years ago, and I want to make it that way again."

"Then are you ready?"

I inhaled and exhaled. "As I'll ever be." I slipped Maverick's leash around my wrist, and we stepped out into a beautiful evening. I threaded my arm through Dad's, listening to happy party sounds. Children's squeals, tinkling music, and peals of laughter wafted from the Farleys' backyard.

The three of us walked among the pink lights, pink balloons, and pink streamers adorning every inch of space. Emma, dressed in ruffles the color of bubblegum, wriggled from her daddy's arms and rushed me with a bear hug. "You came. And you brought a present. Thank you, Katie."

The strength I gained from my four-year-old friend's embrace assured me I'd made the right decision in attending her party. Emma released me, but before she turned her attention to Maverick, she said, "I think you should pick a pink car."

Maverick stood stock still, seeming to grin as she cuddled him. She removed a homemade treat larger than her hand from her pocket and checked with me before passing it along to my dog. Who could refuse those big, beautiful eyes belonging to both the big black dog and the little pink princess? I made my appearance, and positive party vibes filled the hole in my heart.

I sidled next to Pamela. "She's so grown up."

Pamela sniffed. "She even let me help her bake Maverick's special dog treats. Thanks for coming. And thanks for all your help when Adam was away. You must know how much this means to Emma."

I cocked my head. "Why did Emma say I need a pink car?"

"She's noticed a red car cruising the neighborhood, but you know she prefers a lighter shade." Pamela took proud, joy-filled eyes from her daughter and gasped, noticing me shift the weight of the box from one hip to the other. "Oh, my. I'm sorry. Here, let me help you."

Together we carried my gift to the table heavily laden with boxes and cylinders and spheres and nestled it among the towers of pink. I sighed. "She scarcely resembles the tiny tot I met at the beginning of the school year."

Pamela nodded. "We've had some profound conversations this week. I didn't realize how much she picks up from adult talk. She wanted to know where Maverick worked. I explained the concept of fundraising for the homeless, and she asked me to drive by the shelter. One of her classmates was on the playground. It was a difficult discussion, explaining why she was playing alone behind a locked wrought-iron fence. I would have forewarned everyone, but I didn't find out until I overheard her telling Adam she's planning to give all her birthday gifts to the children at the shelter."

"Kids. Always looking out for someone else. We can learn so much from them." I swallowed hard, thinking how much Galen believed in Sherylann and how he'd tried to help. "That is the most selfless act by a four-year-old I've ever heard. Had I known, I would have made my gift even bigger or purchased a second one. If it's okay, I may do that anyway."

Pamela smiled. "Have some food and cake, *please*. Ida made enough—"

"To feed an army," we said in unison and broke into giggles. Pamela hugged me as Pete sauntered up the walk, steering a miniature bicycle dwarfed by an enormous fuchsia ribbon. My smile faded when the tall blonde followed in his wake.

"Dr. Pete," Emma squealed. "You're here." She turned to Pete's guest and curtsied. "Hello, I'm Emma, and I'm four years old. What's your name?"

The corners of my mouth lifted in a casual smile. Inching across the lawn, I tried to listen as the woman replied, "I'm Oralia, and this is my husband, Blaine."

Oralia turned and dragged forward a tall, attractive

man. He combed his fingers through long black curly hair and knelt down to Emma's level. Flashing a warm smile, he said, "Thanks for letting us crash your party, Emma. It's our very first celebration in our new hometown, and we are most pleased to make your acquaintance."

Emma replied in a voice belonging to a mature twenty-year-old. "And I am pleased to make your … to meet you too. Welcome to my party."

"Happy birthday."

A presence next to me made me jump.

"Hello," said the familiar baritone.

"Hi." I turned and was immediately drawn into the depth of Pete's steady, chocolate-brown eyes. "I'm sorry I haven't returned your calls."

"And I'm sorry I got so bossy. I want you to be safe and not do anything that …" He shook his head. "And there I go again. Forgiven?" He reached out his hand.

Too filled with emotion to answer, I took it and squeezed.

The leggy blonde and her husband joined us. "So, you're the intrepid Katie Wilk," she said. "I've heard so much about you. I'm Oralia Golding, and this is my husband, Blaine."

Dumbfounded, I struggled to repeat Emma's words. "I'm pleased to meet you."

"Oralia's my new partner. We're still one practitioner short, but at least the wait lines in the ER are more manageable. Susie will be taking time off soon, with the baby, so we needed someone in place." Something caught Pete's eye. "Excuse me. A horse named Adam has an endless line of tiny-tot jockeys anxious for a trot. I think he needs help."

Pete cantered across the yard and whinnied before he swooped in and knelt on the lawn. A giggling little boy jumped on Pete's back and put a strangle hold around his neck before they galloped after Adam.

"Welcome, Doctor." I knew how to be cordial if I could get my foot out of my mouth.

"Oralia, please."

"Oralia, where were you before coming to Columbia?"

Blaine put his hand on her shoulder and gave her a peck on the cheek. "I'll get you some lemonade. I'll make sure it's your favorite flavor—*pink*. Katie, would you like something?"

"No, thanks."

He laughed and headed toward the punch bowl.

"We came here from Montana. Blaine has family in Minneapolis, and it's nice to be closer. Columbia's been fabulous. We've been here two weeks, and already it feels like home. Pete's been a dream, too."

Always.

"He's helped us make connections and see some of the highlights. He really loves this town." She turned to look at me. "And you, too. He never stops talking about you."

I felt the warm blush rise up my neck as we quietly watched Emma remove a flamingo-colored wand from a long, narrow box. "Isn't she the cutest? I hope we have kids one day," Oralia said wistfully.

My phone pinged with a text from Lark.

I'm back. Let me know when you want to get together. I have your items.

Oralia sounded concerned. "Is everything alright? You look anxious."

"It's just work." I liked Oralia. She noticed things.

A child's giggle drew my attention to an orchid streamer unfurling at the end of a wand, highlighted by a bright pink bulb, and a distant memory of a specific section of Quinn's portrait on the wall at Shady Oaks became clear. Its significance had bothered me throughout the tournament. Pulling up the photos I'd taken, I realized the message on Galen's narrow scroll might yet be revealed.

"It really has been a pleasure to meet you, Oralia, but I've got to go back to work. Could you tell Pete I'll talk to him later? He's having too much fun to trouble him now."

FORTY-THREE

Maverick and I receded into the landscape of Farley's yard and withdrew across Ida's as I punched in a return call to Lark. It zinged to voicemail, and I almost kicked off the message with who was calling, but Jane already informed me, in no uncertain terms, how utterly annoying redundant identification could be. "I'm coming by to pick up my silent auction winnings. I hope you're there. If not, I'll be out again early tomorrow. Lark, it's very important." And just in case her phone didn't have caller ID, I added, with a hint of defiance, "It's Katie."

I disconnected the call and scrounged through the key basket, nabbing Dad's spare ring. I stared at the keys in my hand, wondering if I had time to tell him what I planned to do, but he loved Emma, and I wouldn't want to take him away from the party. I wanted them both to have fun, and I had no idea whether or not my solution had any validity. With the date forever etched in our memories, he might believe I needed time to myself and wouldn't immediately worry, so I jotted a note instead, and left it on the table where he wouldn't miss it.

Maverick rocked from one paw to the other. Although we'd crowded his space this week, he'd been left behind for too many days during the tournament. Anxiety rolled off him in waves. "No worries, you're coming with me, boy." I snapped on his lead. He pranced to Dad's Crown Victoria and hopped onto the back seat. I rolled down the windows and he excitedly hung his head out even before the movement of the car generated enough wind to flap his ears and bubble his cheeks.

I pulled out of the driveway, hoping my intuition paid off.

The mesmerizing sun dipped toward the horizon with an intense yellow and orange radiance. I barreled through Columbia and around Lake Monongalia amid deepening shades of pink, red, navy, indigo, violet, and Viking purple. Billowy clouds filled the sky and reflected off the mirrored surface of the water. We pulled into the spot in the lot between two red streamlined cars.

"Popular color." I said, and Maverick yelped in corroboration. "I don't imagine they need nor want you roaming the grounds today, but I'll see, and if your presence will be acceptable, I'll come back for you." He barked again and threw his head over the seat, digging into my cheek. I scratched his forehead, and he leaned into my hand. "I'll be back as soon as possible." The disappointed look he gave melted my heart. "Promise."

I glanced back. The tip of Maverick's black nose poked

through the window opening and slid back and forth, scenting. The gap would provide ventilation but not an easy exit from the car for my sixty-pound companion.

I put all my weight into opening the heavy door to the club. It closed behind me with a whoosh as if the building had a vacuum seal. My footsteps reverberated in the absence of other sounds. The hubbub from the last few days had taken a hiatus. Before I made my way to Lark's office, I stopped in front of Quinn's portrait, admiring the artistry of the painter and the elegance of the century-old work, quietly observing the narrow scroll encircling the handle of her club. Because of Ida's interpretation, I translated the first few words—*mo stór*, my dear.

Though I couldn't decipher the rest of the message, the letters on the spool in the painting surely formed additional words in Quinn's mother tongue. I dug in my bag and ran my fingers around the lip of the tube containing Galen's parchment discovery, itching to wrap it around the shaft of my winning driver to determine if it, too, displayed a secret message.

A bright clink of kitchenware cut cleanly through the heavy quiet.

"Hello? Anybody here?" Thinking the kitchen staff must be closing down for the night, I headed to Lark's office and knocked on the door.

"Come in," said Lark in a cheery voice.

I leaned on the knob, and it carried me forward to meet a smiling, refreshed HR director. "You look great."

"Time to recharge does wonders, and when I collected all our goodies, Anne assured me my job was safe." The old driver lay on the counter next to the tumbler among a handful of winnings: a gift card, a fruit basket, a pristine gray golf bag, and a box filled with golf balls, tees, a pair of gloves, and a cap. "I love this fundraiser," she cooed and poured iced tea from a pitcher into my new old tumbler and a mug on her desk. She lifted hers and urged me to do the same. "Cheers."

"I didn't know you golfed." I sipped the refreshing Arnold Palmer and reached for the club, but Lark grabbed it first.

"I've golfed since I was a kid. Katie, I've researched this driver. Do you know what you have here?" I shrugged. "It belonged to Julius Boros."

"That's Winslow's surname, isn't it?"

"Indeed, it is."

"And the name obviously means something to you."

"This might be the Wilson staff driver used by Julius Boros in his 1968 PGA win, but even better." She donned a pair of white cotton gloves and extracted a card encased in plastic from an envelope attached to the club. "There is a PSA/DNA certification sticker on the top. If authentic, a signed Jack Nicklaus rookie card from 1971 could be worth thousands."

Stunned, I blurted, "Do you want to split—"

"You misunderstand. I'm in the presence of the finest golf artifact I've ever seen, and you let me be a part of its discovery. It belongs to you. Could I just hold it for a few seconds?"

"Of course." For an authentic rookie card of one of his favorite golfers, Dad might even get over my leaving Emma's party without telling him. "Meanwhile, could I take a look at the club?"

She passed it over the counter without a glance. I removed the cardboard tube from my bag and gingerly eased out the narrow scroll. I lined up the end of the parchment with the tape on the grip and began wrapping, covering the entire length of the skinny shaft. "May I?" I pointed to the roll of tape on Lark's desk.

"Hmmm," she hummed, gazing at the card in her hand.

After affixing a piece of tape to secure the paper, I rolled the club in my hands, hoping the circumference of the shaft would provide an answer. The tiny letters lined up in neat rows and translated into words as I'd rotated the club and read aloud, "Fake. Counterfeit. Stealing." My voice drifted off as my eyes traveled the length of the strip of paper reading, 'Tony.' A compilation of secrets Byron might've divulged lined the shaft.

"What did you say?" said Lark, still admiring the find in her hand.

"What do you know about Chef Antoine?"

Lark dragged her twinkling eyes away from the signature. "Just a minute." She reverently lined up the rookie card with the edges of her desk and flipped open the desktop computer. As her fingers flew over the keys, the power went out.

FORTY-FOUR

A strong flashlight beam danced in the hall. "Madame Lark, have you returned?" Chef Antoine's bulk filled the doorway. He stepped in and maneuvered a circular tray onto Lark's desk. With flair befitting a magician, he lifted the domed lid and shined the light on a beautifully plated steaming tenderloin and vegetable puree smothered in a mushroom gravy. "Voilà."

"Merci, Chef. You didn't have to go through all that trouble. You already delivered the Arnold Palmer." Lark hummed in satisfaction. "I thought you let everyone go for the evening."

"Everyone eez gone."

At the same time, I heard the distant beep of a car horn, the lights blinked back on, albeit a bit dimmer. "Eez thees lovely woman the owner of the antique golf club?" Lark reached for one of the forks provided on the tray. Her hand hovered over the comestibles, waiting for me to answer.

"Yes. I am, but I'm afraid the golf club is not for sale," I answered quickly. As Lark's utensil pierced the tender meat, I said with a fierceness, "Don't, Lark."

Momentarily transfixed by the seriousness in my tone, the fork clattered to the tray. An understanding clouded her features. Her fingers sprang to the desktop and assiduously jabbed at the keys. She scanned the screen and relayed her abbreviated findings. "Hired March 15 by Nora Birdwhistle. Full name, Tony Rossi. Not very French." She nibbled on her bottom lip. "Forty-two, but, Antoine." Lark looked up, confused. "There's nothing listed under your work history, nor does it appear any references have been contacted."

"Someone's finally doing due diligence." Antoine's accent had vaporized.

Lark's chair rolled back at his vehemence.

"You aren't any more French than I am, Tony, and neither is your food. ZaZa almost uncovered your fraud, didn't she?" He never understood her French, and his recipes weren't authentic. I couldn't quite control my actions and spoke my next thought aloud. "You're a fake. Ida couldn't eat your éclairs and went home hungry after a supposed first-class French dinner. When Sherylann cooked up the prize blend of meat she stole from your kitchen, she said it tasted just like hamburger, nothing special, because that's what it was. Right?" I remembered the labels in the delivery truck. No brisket, no chuck, no short ribs. "But why kill Barclay?"

"I hoped to cash in on what I'd uncovered concerning his two wives, but blackmail backfired. The vindictive con man had other plans." He cast his eyes on the rookie card and golf club. "He caught me on camera and said we belonged to a mutual disdain society and he'd ferreted out my deceptive culinary practices." He shrugged. "I used a few shortcuts."

"The cartons in the garage. Your food comes frozen."

"He was blackmailing me."

"But Barclay never would have trusted you. How did you poison him?"

Tony shrugged. "I ate when he ate."

"But not *what* he ate."

He turned his burning black eyes on me. "I had too much to lose." One eyebrow rose in menace. "You shouldn't have continued with your questions. I heard you initially say Barclay's death couldn't be an accident. I thought you might have second thoughts about working here when I trashed your car or when I ran you off the road. I followed you home in case I needed to make a house call." He huffed. "You're not even smart enough to quit when I loaded the storage area with raccoons."

Heat and anger crawled up my spine. "Winslow?"

A snort escaped, and he blinked unhurriedly. "I hardly recognized the kid. I ran a scam on his family five years ago, and he finally caught up with me. I thought he'd agree to a cut of the proceeds, but he wanted his righteous family honor restored. He tried to lure a confession out of me by showing up with—"

Lark tossed the trading card onto her desk. "A counterfeit card."

"I supplemented my income." Tony scoffed. "Being a chef is hard work," he whined. "But I know a thing or two about botany too." The tip of a malicious-looking carving knife glinted in his hand. "Eat. Now."

"Antoine?" Lark's forehead creased.

He rotated his head, and his neck cricked. "I brought

perfect fixings for a private party."

"The food is poisoned." I glared at him. He shrugged, gesticulating with the weapon, and Lark picked up the fork with trembling fingers. I wasn't so accommodating. "You'll have to kill me, Tony."

"That can be arranged, one way or another." He tossed items around the room. "It will look like you two walked in on a thief, and he retaliated, leaving you dead." He shattered the red glass bulb at the top of the status indicator on Lark's desk.

At the same time I heard Lark gasp, I also picked up a distant but familiar clicking. With more volume, a lot of anger, and uncharacteristic difficulty, I slurred. "You don't want to do that. Chief West won't fall for it." I hoped I sounded more confident than I felt. Tony swatted me with the back of his hand. I grunted and sagged to the floor.

"By the time she looks at me, I'll be long gone. I know how to disappear." He jeered and pointed the knife at the plate. "Mangez!"

I forced the words past my lips. "The chief will figure it out. You're nothing but a two-bit …" The words halted on my lips as it dawned on me. "The Arnold Palmers."

"They are difficult to resist, aren't they?" Tony sneered.

I wiped blood from the corner of my mouth and worked up a pain-filled smirk but couldn't quite control my appendages. "Tough guy. Can't cook. Can't hit." He wound up to kick me. Curling in a ball, I wrapped my arms around my head. He landed a bone-crunching blow to the small of my back. I stifled a groan.

"Stop," Lark pleaded in a small voice.

As he turned on her and shouted, "Shut up, or you're next," I crawled toward the doorway. He spun and poised to stomp again, but a growl halted his leg in midair.

Maverick's ears laid flat and the hairs on his back stood at attention. His lips quivered around a terrifying snarl.

Tony brandished the knife to swipe at my dog, but before he finished smirking, the antique club crashed down on his head and the weapon flew from his hand. He swayed, and as Lark prepared to land another blow to incapacitate him, a faraway voice stayed her hand.

"Katie."

"Pete," I croaked, as my dog burrowed into my side.

The last thing I heard before my world went black was running footsteps.

FORTY-FIVE

Days later, sunbeams speared the kitchen. Austin and Sandi, my step-siblings, called and wished Dad a great Father's Day, and he basked in a sentimental afterglow. Pete and his dad, Lance, joined us for brunch. We'd eaten our fill of a fabulous baked sausage and egg dish smothered with cheddar cheese, dotted with red peppers, onions, and mushrooms over hashbrowns, delivered by Ida. The sugary residue from her delicious caramel rolls proved difficult to remove without licking my fingers, as I listened to Pete retell our story.

"How did Maverick get out of the car?" Lance used the voice of interrogation he'd honed over his long law enforcement career.

"Katie told Oralia she was going to work." Pete's head dropped. "I assumed Katie had gone to Shady Oaks, and my tremendous apology couldn't wait. I found Maverick barking obnoxiously from the front seat of Harry's Crown Victoria." Pete gave Maverick an admiring look. "I'd heard it often enough. 'Trust the dog.' When I let him out, he took off like a shot. By the time I found him, the hard work was done. Lark and Katie had already figured out Tony had killed Barclay Byron and Winslow Boros. Lark stood over Tony swinging a wicked golf club. Maverick guarded Katie, and Amanda was on her way."

"But Katie blacked out," said Lance.

If I moved in just the right way, my bruises didn't cause too much pain. I knew I could safely move my lips. "And woke in Pete's iron arms."

"Tony doctored the Arnold Palmer as added insurance against Byron the first time. He used it against Lark, too, and, advantageously for him, the only other obstacle in his plan, Katie, just happened to be there. Fortunately, I know how to take care of an injured Katie." He rubbed the back of his neck, and a lock of dark curly hair fell forward. "It's the everyday woman I can't keep up with."

"What happened to Barbara Clay and her baby girl?" Lance continued.

"Barbara returned Dennis's shares with an apology." Dad slurped his beverage. "Although she loved him, Barclay had a tough time with second place, and that's exactly where he was when it came to the two of them, so he was always trying to one-up her. In atonement, she's offered to join forces with Anne to revamp the Shady Oaks charter. We'll see what happens next."

"Casimer's law firm is drafting the paperwork with

Dorene at the helm. She'll clean up the legal issues."

Maverick kicked up a ruckus, barked, did a full body shake, and lunged at the door. Dad laughed. "I guess I'll have to wait to open my present."

I pouted. I'd hidden his gift in the front closet behind the long winter coats, but he'd been known to search high and low for presents at Christmas, on his birthday, and on any other special day of the year. However, it was a safe bet the dimensions of this box would never give away its contents.

As expected, shortly after Maverick barked, the doorbell rang, and Dad looked at me hopefully, his soulful eyes imploring me to get up from my terribly uncomfortable spot on the rigid wooden chair, while he sipped his creamy coffee confection. It was an easy decision.

I pulled open the door and came face to face with my half-sister, Ellen. She grabbed me in a fierce embrace, and I cringed. She held me at arm's length. "What on earth happened to you?"

"Later. Come in. Come in. What are you doing here?"

She hemmed and hawed, looking down at her feet as she slipped off her strappy sandals. "Well, I never knew my dad, and Harry…" She looked at him adoringly. "You've been more than a father to me. It's your day, and I brought you this." She tugged a wrinkled envelope from her pocket and handed it to him. Dad always said she was the epitome of everything good about our mother, and in that moment, I could see my mother's best traits wrapped up in Ellen. I was grateful she was in our lives.

Dad peeked inside the envelope and brushed at the corner of his eye.

"Oh, Harry, don't cry." Ellen's voice broke.

"Allergies," he sniffed. He carefully extracted a stack

of worn photos of a much younger Ellen and our mother. "Would you like breakfast?" he asked, clearly wanting to change the subject.

Ellen gave me the side-eye. "As long as Katie didn't make it."

Ida breezed in carrying a crystal serving platter, the perfect way to display her two-tiered cake. "No chance of that." She slid the beautifully decorated dessert into the center of the table. "La voilà." Covered in a navy-blue fondant and baby-blue butter cream, it looked too good to eat, until Ida dug a black plastic scabbard from her denim apron pocket and whipped out a long silver blade. My heart thudded, but only until Pete squeezed my hand and gave me a reassuring smile. Wielding it with finesse, she cleaved the sweet and held out her hand for a cake server. She lifted a chunk of chocolate cake oozing a dark red center and placed it on a dish. With a fancy flourish, she positioned it in front of Dad. "My take on *gâteau mousse à la cerise noire*. Happy Father's Day, Harry." My mouth watered as she proceeded to cut additional generous portions.

"It's black cherry filling, right?" Pete said. "You've outdone yourself, Ida."

I mumbled an agreement, wiping every crumb off my fork. If it wouldn't have been embarrassing, I might've licked the plate clean. We finished, and Ida nodded. "It's gift time."

Like a kid at Christmas, my shoulders rose to my ears, and I dug the no-longer-a-surprise box out of the coat closet. Ida had hand-painted the avantgarde, one-of-a-kind wrapping paper with multi-sized clubs, pins, golf balls, and hearts. Dad picked apart the taped ends and removed the paper, rolling it to reuse. He carefully lifted the top off the box and gingerly reached into the tissue paper, patting the box innards uncertainly. I don't know what he expected, but it certainly wasn't the slender, well-worn shaft of an antique wooden club. He ran his hand from the head to the grip. He examined the worn engraving and opened the pale blue envelope anchored around the end. His mouth dropped open. I seldom found him at a loss for words, but Ellen snapped photos to forever memorialize the moment in time.

"Katie, this is a 1960s Wilson staff driver!"

I laughed. The rest of the story would come later. A smile inched across my face as I watched some of my favorite people relishing time together.

"Ida, I thought Jane would be more upset losing the chef for her reception," Pete said as he collected the dirty dishes and handed them to me.

"It was a good thing. Reneé Forge has always been the brains behind the catering service and is a bona fide chef. She promised no hitches in Jane's plans. She even has a few better ideas for the reception and is looking to expand services," my spirited landlady said. "Lark made Sherylann promise to ask before using onsite devices, so the club is not pressing charges, and she rehired Sherylann as a Girl Friday to help wherever needed."

"Sounds like you won't be too busy, Katie. What are you going to do now?" Pete asked.

"Absolutely nothing."

His eyes gleamed.

"I can do nothing, if I put my mind to it."

One corner of his mouth turned up in a delicious smile.

Well, almost nothing.

ACKNOWLEDGMENTS

Thank you, dear readers, for buying my books, listening, checking them out at the library, and sharing with friends, making writing so much fun. I wouldn't do it without you.

I'm so fortunate to work with a fantastic group of people who put the finishing touches on my words. To make sure I deliver what I promise, Stephanie Dewey and Lee Ellison keep me on track and help me make my stories so much better. Thank you.

The best beta readers: Paula Webb, Sandra Anderson, Susan Gross, Eve Osborne, Gabi Hoffnecht, Isobel Tamney, and Marcia Koopmann. They catch the little things, the big things, and everything in between.

Much appreciation to great friends Colleen Okland, Dennis Okland, and Mary Gruber, who took time out of their busy lives, holding me accountable, giving honest opinions, and helping me wonder how I might improve my tale. Master Gardener Michael Gehlen provided wisdom and practical plant information.

I had fun recalling the true examples from the golf lessons I endeavored to take and the tournaments I ventured to attend. Visiting gorgeous golf courses is fascinating, but I wish I had an iota of talent, a smidgeon more patience, and a loud inner voice telling me how to carefully hit the little white sphere.

All the mistakes in the story are mine, and since I do not golf enough, I have to thank the wonderful athletes who talked to me. I wish to most sincerely recognize the help I received from Casey Haugen, Taylor Blomquist, Jim Brown, Jim Ellingson, and Mitch Ronning, and the conversations with Eve Blomquist, Joan Christianson, and Maria Hughes. A special thanks to second-to-none golfer Anne Laura Bruckner who indulged me and let me use her name.

I am fortunate to have wonderful author friends who often provide terrific advice and stalwart support: Kate Michaelson, Judy Jones, and Sylissa Franklin. Kudos to Cozy Mystery Party, and Cozies, Conversations and More for bringing the cozy world together. I want to recognize Bell Cow Productions and Rendezvous with a Writer for providing venues to share my stories.

I also have the most supportive spouse with a fount of knowledge, the patience of Job, and the skill of a top chef. Thank you, Mr. Right.

ARNOLD PALMER

Mix your favorite tea and lemonade in equal proportions and pour over ice. Garnish with a lemon wheel.

JOHN DALY (SPIKED ARNOLD PALMER)

1 ½ ounces vodka
2 ounces lemonade
2 ounces iced tea
Mix well. Serve over ice and garnish with a lemon wheel.

IDA'S NORWEGIAN RØMMEGRØT

1 (22-ounce carton) small curd cottage cheese
5 eggs
1-pint heavy whipping cream
1 C sugar
3 T flour
½ tsp salt
1 tsp vanilla
Mix cottage cheese and flour. Add eggs and beat well by hand. Add sugar, salt, cream, and vanilla. Bake at 350 degrees for 1 to 1 ½ hours in a deep casserole dish sprayed with Pam, until golden brown on top. You can test it with a toothpick in the center for doneness. It will be dark brown around the edges, but watch not to burn.

HARRY WILK'S PANNENKOEKEN

¼ C butter
½ C milk
½ C flour
¼ C sugar
2 eggs
1 tsp cinnamon
½ tsp nutmeg

Preheat oven to 425°. Put four tablespoons of butter in a pie pan. Mix the rest of the ingredients well. Melt the butter in the preheated oven. Pour the batter into the hot melted butter. Bake for fifteen minutes. Reduce the temperature to 350° and bake for another five minutes. Fill with fruit, lemon curd, dust with powdered sugar, or drizzle with syrup, and if you've a sweet tooth like Harry, you use a combination in addition to a dollop of whipped cream.

Thank you for taking the time to read *Golfing, Gardens &* *Ghosts*. If you enjoyed it please tell your friends, and I would be so grateful if you would consider posting a review. Word of mouth is an author's best friend, and very much appreciated.
Thank you,
Mary Seifert

What's Next for Katie and Maverick?
Ida solicits more of Katie's help in organizing the summer festival so she won't get into trouble, but at this stage of the game, it's almost a lost cause. Katie and her loyal crew try every way to keep her past from haunting her, and just when they think they've solved their problems, a body crops up, and Katie needs to do some fast talking to direct the investigation. This time it might not be enough.

Get all the books in the Katie & Maverick Series!

Maverick, Movies, & Murder
Rescues, Rogues, & Renegade
Tinsel, Trials, & Traitors
Santa, Snowflakes, & Strychnine
Fishing, Festivities, & Fatalities
Diamonds, Diesel, & Doom
Creeps, Cache, & Corpses
Pranks, Payback, & Poison
Juleps, Jockeys & Justice
Airplanes, Atlanta & an Assassin
Golfing, Gardens & Ghosts

Get a free short story from Mary—click here to find out how!

Visit Mary's website: MarySeifertAuthor.com/
Facebook: facebook.com/MarySeifertAuthor
Twitter: twitter.com/mary_seifert
Instagram: instagram.com/maryseifert/
Follow Mary on BookBub and Goodreads too!